For David xxx

the Café in Fir Tree Park

KATEY LOVELL

A division of HarperCollins*Publishers*
www.harpercollins.co.uk

Harper*Impulse* an imprint of
HarperCollins*Publishers*
1 London Bridge Street
London SE1 9GF

www.harpercollins.co.uk

This Paperback Edition 2017

First published in Great Britain in ebook format by
Harper*Impulse* 2017

A catalogue record for this book
is available from the British Library

ISBN: 9780008240882

Set in Birka by Palimpsest Book Production Limited,
Falkirk, Stirlingshire

Printed and bound in Great Britain

PROLOGUE

August 1977

Pearl

Poor Alf.

The song was a bad choice for a first dance, but he wasn't to know. Why should he? There was no reason for my new husband to be aware of the feelings this song was stirring inside me. He hadn't been there two years previously, when I'd first slow-danced to this song with another man.

But I'm aware.

Aware of the nausea; the bilious liquid rising in my throat until I fear for the future of the off-white satin court shoes that are pinching my toes.

Aware of the solid knot in the pit of my stomach.

Aware of the pain in my heart on what should be the happiest day of my life.

The joy of the day has been washed over – no, flooded out – by the actions of my past, as though everything that's gone before is weighing me down and now I'm sinking, sinking, sinking.

I paint on a smile and force myself to sway along to the music. A ripple of applause fills the room as Alf and I move, and the flashing of a hundred cameras keen to capture our first dance pierces through the darkness of the church hall.

Relief rushes through me as the song comes to an end, replaced by an upbeat disco tune that gets even my sister Vivienne on to the dance floor, toddler balanced on her hip as she spins. The baby responds by releasing a full-on belly laugh of undeniable happiness, and I pull my husband just a fraction closer.

"Mmm, that's nice." Alf smiles, squeezing me back tightly. He follows my gaze, to where I'm still watching my elder sister, now twisting and twirling like a ballerina on a music box as the little one clings on to her hand for dear life. "What're you thinking?"

"Nothing."

I can't tell him the truth. Not now, not ever.

"It looks like fun, doesn't it? Having a little one." The unsteady toddler excitedly claps along as my brother-in-law Glenn struts his stuff as though he's cock of the town. "Maybe we should start thinking about having one of our own...we are married now, after all."

I blink. "A baby?"

"No, a giraffe," he teases. "Yes, a baby! That's not such a crazy idea, is it? You'd make a wonderful mother." He beams, and I know he's imagining me with a sleeping child cradled in my arms, a perfect Madonna and child scenario. "We could be a proper little family. Just think, if we hit the jackpot right away we could be parents by summertime!"

My knees quiver beneath the lacy layers of my dress, and I tighten my grip on my husband's arm.

"It might not happen right away." My voice wavers. "Some couples try for years before getting caught."

"It won't take us years," Alf says, his voice brimming with macho confidence. "I'd put money on it happening fast."

It had happened fast last time. Too fast.

"Don't get your hopes up, that's all. We've got plenty of time, we're only twenty-one!" I strain to keep my voice jovial and light, but Alf's face looks pained. I feel awful for raining on his parade, especially when none of my reluctance to rush into starting a family is his fault.

"You do want children though, don't you? I know we've not spoken about it much, but that's what most women want...a husband, a baby or two..."

"I do, I really do. In the future I want us to have a family of our own, and maybe a puppy too. I just think I'd like to enjoy being married for a while first though." Alf's face falls, so I hastily add, "But we can always get some baby-making practice in?"

That obviously raises his spirits as he visibly brightens.

"Promises, promises," he replies with a cheeky wink. "If you want to wait a few months, that's fine by me. Whatever my beautiful bride wants." He leans in, placing the softest of kisses on the tip of my nose, and I'm reminded of what a sweet, lovely man he is. "You'll be a wonderful mother, one of these days," he repeats.

"Thank you," I whisper, burying my head into his chest. His heartbeat reverberates against my cheek. "And you'll be a brilliant father."

"I'll do my best, for them and for you. I promise you, Pearl, I'll never let you down."

The words are so beautiful that I want to make the same promise back, but I can't bring myself to speak. I'm not the person Alf thinks I am. By keeping the secrets of two summers ago from him I've already let him down.

But I did it to protect him, because it would break his heart if he knew. That's why he must never find out. He must never know that I am already a mother.

May 2017

Maggie

Fir Tree Park's one of those delightful places that exudes beauty whatever the season, and I know how lucky I am to work here. I'm blessed with the opportunity to appreciate its magnificence all year round; when the muted blanket of fallen leaves coats the weaving paths and walkways in autumn (well worthy of the admiration they get from welly-wearing dog walkers and exuberant toddlers alike) and when the icy layer atop the lake sparkles with winter wonder, pretty enough to adorn any Christmas card. And spring's pale pink buds of cherry blossom are a welcome vision, cheery and uplifting in the extreme.

But during the summer months there's something extra special about the park. It's abuzz with life, more so than at any other point in the year. Once the days become longer crowds come out of hibernation, everyone keen to capitalize on the extra hours of sunlight. The armies of new mums pushing the latest must-have buggies walk with increased purpose and drive, office workers bring their sandwiches and cans of Coke on to the flat plain of grass in front of the café at lunchtime instead of wolfing their food down at their desks, and the fair-weather joggers whose trainers haven't seen any action since the clocks went back – they all return to the park as the weather brightens up.

As the owner of The Lake House Café, a popular meeting point in Fir Tree Park, I'm delighted to see the park at its busiest. Busy means business and that can only be a good thing. But there's more to it than that. It gives me a warm glow to see the masses celebrating the great outdoors; the children splashing in the waterpark, the keen-to-please parents puffing away as they exhaust themselves on the pedalos and rickety rowing boats, the dogs chasing their tails on the large, lush lawn. These people are *my* people. There's an affinity between us. Knowing the café is at the heart of both the park and the community makes me so proud I could burst.

Every day starts the same way, with me rustling up cakes in the small yet pristine kitchen at the back of the café.

"Looks like it'll be another busy one," I call out to my eighteen-year-old daughter, Kelly. She's up bright and early especially to help me set up for the day ahead. "I might have to conjure up another lemon drizzle cake."

Even the thought of running out of cakes brings me out in a cold sweat. Heaven forbid it actually happens: there'd be nothing worse than demand outstripping supply. When I opened the café my mission was for every customer to leave happy, satisfied and itching to return. It's still my aim now, nine years on.

Kelly's laugh rings out as she continues to wipe the red and white polka dot oilcloths that cover the tables. I can see her smirking through the serving hatch. "There's no chance you'll sell out of cake. You're a baking machine!"

Deep down I know she's right – once I get started I can't stop myself – but there's a loyal band of customers who come to the café year-round in order to satisfy their sweet tooth. It's all about giving them a varied choice, ensuring people can have the old favourites if they so choose with a few more experimental options thrown in for the more adventurous clientele.

That's why from the moment I arrive at the café each morning and pull my cream chef's apron over my head I'm in the kitchen mixing up batters and doughs like a whirling dervish. By the time the doors open at 8.30am a deliciously sweet smell permeates the air – people say that's what makes it nigh on impossible to resist my wares. The baking continues on and off all day, even if the café's already well-stocked with an array of yummy cakes and biscuits. The waft of sugar lingers so you can taste it with each breath, tempting customers to buy a slice of sponge for the road as well as one to go with their drink-in cappuccino. It's a happy, homely scent. The kind those reed diffusers try (and fail) to mimic.

My over-baking is a source of great amusement to everyone. Staff often end up taking brown paper bags stuffed full of the leftover goodies home with them at the end of the day – chocolate chip cookies that don't snap until they're almost bent double; rich chocolate cupcakes with lavish buttercream frosting and rainbow sprinkles; and of course, generous wedges of my signature lemon drizzle cake. They say it's a perk of the job, taking the unsold goods home. I say it gives me a chance to do more baking the next day, so it's win-win.

"The day we run out of cake is the day hell freezes over," Kelly calls out. She's facing the other way, yet I can almost hear the sarcastic eyeroll that no doubt accompanies her words. "It'll never happen."

"I hope you're right," I answer cheerily, "but I might do something quick, just to be on the safe side. Another Malteser fridge cake, maybe?"

Kelly pops her head into the kitchen and lets out a long, purposeful sigh. Even when frustrated and flustered she looks beautiful – blonde, lean and glowing. Youth wrapped up in a neat daughter-sized package. "I know you'll not listen to a word I say, but there's plenty, and you've got a fridge full of millionaire's shortbread too, remember? You're making work for yourself again, Mum."

"It keeps me busy. Stops me having time to worry about you."

It's a tongue-in-cheek remark, but the truth nonetheless. Being a parent is terrifying at the best of times, and when exams are looming and you can do nothing to help but provide them with tea and cake, parenting is ramped up to a whole new level. If I'd known how much brain-space kids take up, I'd have thought longer and harder before having them. Not that I regret Josh and Kelly, not for a minute, but I had them young – too young probably – and now I'm a forty-year-old single parent on the verge of an empty nest.

I've done my best for the pair of them, but there have been many, many times I've fallen short. The days they had to wear their grubby school sweaters for a third time because I'd not had chance to put a wash on, or when I was forced to serve beans on toast for tea four nights in a row because I couldn't afford anything more substantial. Things have been tight over the years, in terms of both time and money, and I never understood it before, but I realise now that sometimes you can be doing your best and it's still not enough.

"When you get home you can knuckle down to that history revision. There's only three weeks until your exam, remember." I throw a pointed look in my daughter's direction, willing her into action.

"I am aware," Kelly says brusquely, every inch the know-it-all teenager.

It's a funny age, eighteen. She looks like a young woman but still has the capability to act like a petulant child. Her long blonde hair's cascading down her back and her hand's jauntily placed on her hip. Attitude aplenty, although she's a good girl, mostly.

"It's me that's going to be panicking about it, not you," she fires.

'Ha, that's what you think,' I want to say. It might be Kelly revising long into the night and it might be her again, sat at a small, square desk to frantically scribble down everything she remembers about World War I and the Industrial Revolution on exam day, but I'll have as many sleepless nights over these A-levels as she will. They're all-consuming, I remember how it was with Josh.

It had been a different battle three years ago to the one now, but a battle it had been. I'd spent hours reminding him that although he was a natural academic, his aptitude for learning was no excuse for not hitting the books. With Kelly it's something else entirely. She works hard, colour-coding her notes with fluorescent sticky tabs and a multitude of neon highlighter pens. They're as bright as the accessory aisle in Miss Selfridge in the '80s, but for all her organisation and effort, study doesn't come easy to her.

I'm a hard worker myself, never satisfied until the glass

cabinet that runs the length of the old wooden counter is jam-packed full of sweet offerings. Since the day I bought the café, way back when Kelly was in junior school, it has always been the same. But it's been a gruelling slog at times, and I hope beyond all hope that my children will have an easier ride than my own.

"What time's Fern getting in?" Kelly asks, throwing the now-grubby dishcloth she's been using into the hot soapy water that fills the kitchen sink. "Because I've loads of revision planned for today. My head's a mess trying to remember all those dates and laws. I need to put the hours in if I'm going to get the grades for Birmingham," she reminds me, as though I'm likely to forget. It's all she's spoken about for months.

"She'll be in at ten, so you can get off after that. Or you can sit at the corner table all day if you prefer? I'll make sure Fern keeps your cup filled with tea."

I'm a great believer in the power of tea. A warm hug when the world feels cold, rejuvenating when you feel beaten. I pretty much live off the stuff and have passed my love of it on to both Kelly and Josh, who are equally addicted, although they're far more liberal with the sugar than I am.

"It's up to you," I add. "Wherever you think you'll concentrate best. My only worry is you'll go home, turn on your laptop and fall down a YouTube-shaped rabbit hole."

Kelly's hooked on the beauty vloggers' channels, constantly looking for tips on how to perfect her eyeliner flicks and discover which foundation offers best all-day coverage on a shoestring budget. All the important stuff.

Kelly groans. "Mum, really! It's me you're talking to. I'll put in the work, I'm not like Josh."

"I know you'll put the effort in. I do," I answer, ensuring my voice stays soft and reassuring. I don't want to risk it veering off towards fussy fuddy-duddy mode, because Kelly doesn't respond well to being told what to do. Never has, even as a tot. She'd been one of those puce-faced children who kicked and screamed at the supermarket checkout when she wasn't allowed a packet of chocolate buttons, always knowing what she wanted and doing her level best to get it by fair means or foul. Both my children had been like that, and I don't want to dwell on what that says about me. A psychoanalyst would have a field day, I'm sure.

I choose my words carefully, talking slowly. "But I can't help but wonder if you only want to go to university because you think it's expected of you, and that couldn't be further from the truth."

I catch Kelly's gaze. Her turquoise eyes flash, but not with anger, and a tangible rush of love flows between us. For a second I wish I could turn back time. Things were bloody tough when the kids were little, but at least then I'd felt I was making a difference. Back then I'd had some level of control over her life and how she experienced the world. These days I have to trust the mistakes she'll inevitably make will be minor rather than major. Kelly's very much her own person, a glorious muddle of juxtapositions – stubborn and flighty, beautiful and petulant, angry and delicate – but beneath the lipstick and mascara she's still my baby. She always will be.

"You don't have to take the same path as your friends, you know," I continue. "There's more to life than university, other options you could explore. I was already pregnant with Josh when I was your age..."

"Are you saying I should get pregnant?" Kelly jokes. Quick-witted as ever, especially when a conversation takes a serious turn. Just like her dad. He never wanted to talk about anything heavy either. I bat away thoughts of Clint because there's no point ruining a perfectly lovely morning. "I didn't think you'd be up for being a grandma just yet."

"Absolutely not!" I exclaim, flustered. I can feel my cheeks burning up; they've probably already turned an attractive shade of beetroot.

"All I'm trying to say is that what's right for one person isn't always right for another. I was married with a baby on the way when I was eighteen, whereas at the same age Josh got accepted on to his physics degree. Your dad..." I pause, consciously trying to keep the distaste from displaying on my face. I never purposefully badmouth Clint to the kids, as much as I've wanted to at times. It's not their fault that their dad's a waste of space. "...well, he was already in with the wrong crowd by then. But you, my gorgeous baby girl? The world's your oyster! You can do anything you put your mind to. And you don't need a piece of paper from a stuffy university to do most of it, and you *definitely* don't need the debt that goes hand in hand with it. I wouldn't be saying this if I thought history was your passion. But I don't think it really is, sweetheart, do you?"

I wait for an answer, but nothing's forthcoming. Kelly's nibbling on the skin of her thumb, a bad habit she's had since she was small, and I resist the urge to tap her hand away from her mouth.

I smile gently, hoping it can reassure her. "All I'm saying is three years is a long time to be miserable."

Kelly smiles back awkwardly, more grimace than grin. "I don't know, Mum. Everyone'll be going away in September – Tash, Meg, Luke...I don't want to be the only person stuck here when they're all having fun at freshers' nights and drinking bright blue cocktails from plastic fishbowls."

There's a tinge of fear in her voice, which I expect is linked to the thoughts of missing out on the rite of passage that is going to university. The youngsters today all seem to go, leaving in their droves every autumn. Surely they can't all be brainboxes?

Even in my day things were different, and it's not like

I'm from the dark ages. Half my classmates went straight into work from school – poorly paid jobs as receptionists, barmaids, checkout girls – ordinary jobs for the ordinary people we were. There was no shame in that back then, it was the norm. How can the world have changed so much in such a short time?

I'd worked as a waitress before having Josh, serving stone-baked pizzas and rich cannellonis in a little Italian restaurant on the high street, a family-run eatery. Every available surface had been bedecked in the traditional national colours of red, white and green. It hadn't paid that well but had provided a bit of pocket money, enough to get by. Even now I'm hardly Deborah Meaden; I just got lucky, buying the café for a song and slowly but surely building up the business. The Lake House Café's doing well at the moment, with café culture on the rise.

"Who said anything about being stuck here? If you work over the summer, you'll earn a bit of pocket money and maybe have enough to travel. You've said you wanted to see the world. Why not do it now while you have the chance? I always fancied getting one of those train tickets that lets you go all over Europe, packing a backpack and seeing where I ended up. Imagine what an experience that'd be! You could go to Rome…" I say dreamily. In my mind I'm drifting off on a sleeper train heading towards the Eternal City, rather than wondering if I've got enough plain flour in the cupboard to last the rest of the week. As much as I love my job, Rome sounds infinitely more appealing.

Kelly, however, looks doubtful. "I don't know. I'd have to come back sooner or later, and without a degree I'd struggle to get a job."

"For as long as I own this café, there'll be a job here for you. I know it's not much, but it's something." I cup my daughter's hand, giving it a gentle squeeze of reassurance. "Just have a think about things, that's all I'm asking. Why don't you head off home? Fern will be here shortly, and I can manage till then." I nod towards the café door and the sprawling green park beyond. "Go and hit those books."

Kelly reaches for her black leather satchel and slings it across her body. "Thanks, Mum. And I'll think about it, the travelling."

I'm sure she's only saying it to placate me, but I humour her back, leaning down and kissing the baby-soft skin of her cheek. They're growing up fast, her and Josh. If only I could slow it down a touch before they're gone for good, lost to significant others and the daily grind.

"Do. There's more to life than exams. I may not have got here by the most direct route, but I'm happier now than I've ever been before." I can't help but smile with a quiet satisfaction. "It took me the best part of forty years to achieve what I wanted, so don't you go beating yourself up for not having your life mapped out at your age. You'll get there soon enough. I've got everything I want now. It just took a bit longer than I thought it would, that's all."

Kelly makes for the door. "Everything you want except a man," she says cheekily, quickly closing the panelled door behind her whilst I stand agog, wishing I was a bit sharper.

She's right though. It's the sad truth that I *do* wish I had a bit of male company once in a while. I don't need a man in my life, but it'd be nice to have someone special to share the highs and lows with. There's been no one serious since Clint, nothing more than a few paltry dates that didn't lead to anything fulfilling. I'm only forty: surely I've not used up my share of romance already?

I sink into one of the wooden chairs, the plump gingham cushion softening my landing, as I reminisce.

Clint Thornhill had been my childhood sweetheart, a wild bad boy with convincing patter. As a teen, I hadn't noticed his (many) obvious flaws, instead blindly worshipping the ground his bovver boots walked on. I'd fallen hard and deep, smitten by his white-blonde hair and strong features. He'd reminded me of my first major celebrity crush, Matt Goss from Bros. The similarity had set my heart aflutter.

I'd had to pinch myself to believe Clint would be interested in me, but for some reason he'd kept hanging around, turning up at places he knew I'd be. When he finally asked me to the pictures I'd accepted in a flash. We shouldn't have wasted our money because we hadn't watched the film: instead we'd snogged for two hours solid in the back row of the local fleapit. My lips had felt like they were burning, a blissful pain searing through my fifteen-year-old self that was full of both danger and excitement.

Two and a half years later we were married, a small register office do on my eighteenth birthday. Seven months after that came the two blue lines on the white plastic stick that had revealed I was expecting Josh, and I'd been so, so happy. Other people my age seemed so unsure, but I'd got it all – a husband, a council flat, a baby on the way. I'd foolishly thought I'd got it sussed.

But it hadn't taken long for me to realise my mistake in marrying too young, and although I'd never regret Josh and Kelly, I do regret Clint. Mostly I regret the shame he brought on my family, the absolute heartbreak both his mum and mine had suffered when he'd been sent to prison ten years ago. Armed robbery, like one of those bank hold-ups in a cartoon. He'd even been wearing a black balaclava in an attempt to hide his face, just to live up to the stereotype. It was almost laughable. All he needed was a swag bag and a black-and-white-striped jumper to complete the Burglar Bill look.

The balaclava hadn't worked, anyway. The bank teller he'd threatened had recognised him despite his disguise. In court she'd said that she knew it was Clint who'd pointed that gun at her because she'd recognise his eyes anywhere. Funny how the piercing blue eyes I'd lost myself in so many times were the very thing that eventually tore us apart.

After that things changed. Every time I walked into a shop people would stare, gossiping behind their hands about what an idiot I must be to have ended up saddled with two kids and a criminal for a husband; and his poor mum, you'd think she'd given birth to the devil himself from the way people spoke to her. People judge you on how your kids turn out, and Vivienne's parenting skills were well and truly under scrutiny after Clint's escapades. There's no hiding in a small town like this.

Soon after Clint was locked up, I filed for divorce. Unreasonable behaviour, although I could have easily named adultery as the reason for the breakdown of our marriage. Clint might have made me feel like one in a million at the beginning, but a string of affairs throughout our married life left me with zero confidence. He came back grovelling time and time again, plying me with platitudes about how it was me he loved and how he only ever strayed when drunk, but I'd become a laughing stock, one of 'those women'. His prison sentence was a chance for me to break free and reclaim my fragile heart, although I'm still recovering from the damage our toxic relationship caused.

If I'm being completely honest, that's why I threw myself

into The Lake House Café with every ounce of my heart and soul. The café had been a welcome distraction from the romance that was sadly missing in my life. It gave me a purpose, along with a ready-made excuse for turning down the occasional offers of dates I did get – always claiming to be too busy for love when really I hadn't found anyone I was willing to take a chance on. Once bitten, twice shy, as they say.

But today's a Saturday, and Saturdays mean one thing – football coaching in the park. And football coaching means the handsome Italian with the floppy jet-black hair; tall, lean and athletic with rich olive skin and strong, taut thighs. Yes, Saturdays are especially pleasurable. He's exceptionally easy on the eye.

It hardly matters that I've barely said a word to him in all the months he's been running the kiddies' football course. I've seen him, and that's enough. My heart flutters more than I care to admit at the thought that he might pop into the café for an Americano and a slice of gingerbread at the end of the session. He doesn't call in every Saturday, but when he does it brings a spring to my step and a smile to my face. Sadly, it's the highlight of my week, so I hope today will be one of the days he rewards his hard work with some home baking. Please, please, please...

Pushing back the chair, I catch my reflection in the window. I plump up my dark brown curls to give them more volume and smack my lips forcefully together in the hope it'll enhance their colour. Ensuring I look my best, just in case.

The jangle of the bells over the door catches my attention and my heart pounds for all the wrong reasons as I see my assistant Fern. Her face is blotchy, her eyes narrow and red. She sobs loudly and I dash towards her, placing my arm around her shoulder.

"Fern! Whatever's the matter, sweetheart?"

The young woman pulls away, dragging the backs of her index fingers underneath her eyes in a bid to wipe away the tears. It works, but she smears her mascara in the process, leaving prominent dark streaks stretching to the edges of her face. She looks like a bedraggled version of Elizabeth Taylor in *Cleopatra*.

"Oh, Maggie, it's Luke," Fern says, referring to her younger brother. He's a friendly, handsome boy; energetic and confident, the polar opposite of super-shy Fern. He's been in the same class as Kelly since infant school. They dated briefly, and I'd been surprised and quietly disappointed when they'd called time on their relationship. He'd been good for her: far better than Mischa, the moody goth girl she'd dated last year. Mischa had a notebook full of depressing song lyrics from bands like Depeche Mode and The Cure, and the amount of kohl she used on her eyelids would have given Robert Smith a run for his money. It made her look like a raccoon. I'd never understood why Kelly was with her. They had nothing in common. Not once did Mischa's purple-coated lips crack a smile, whereas I can't help but smile at the thought of Luke, all youthful effervescence and enthusiasm. He's a cheerful boy, uplifting and full of zest. "Last night he was screaming in pain and saying he couldn't see. He's been complaining of migraines for weeks, but this was the worst yet. Dad rushed him straight to the hospital and they ran all these tests, dozens of them."

Fern whimpers, helpless, then swallows. When she finally speaks her words hit me like a sledgehammer.

"They found out what it is that's making him feel so awful. It's not a migraine, Maggie. It's a brain tumour."

Fern

If Maggie looks stunned by my revelation, she can't feel as shocked as I do. It's still sinking in that this is actually happening to my brother.

It had been one hell of a night, with all of us sat on uncomfortable plastic seats in a strip-lit hospital corridor while we waited for any scrap of information we could garner from the white-coated medics that hurried past us. Mum had started wailing at one point, a deep and hollow baying cry that echoed horrifically around the clinical grey hallway while I'd stared at a poster about diabetes testing for three hours solid because if I focussed on that I didn't have to think about all the awful tests Luke was so bravely enduring in another room. It had been, without a doubt, the worst night of my life.

"They're going to operate on him as soon as they can, but he's too run down right now. They're not sure he's strong enough to survive a ten-hour operation, so they're treating the infection first." I laugh, but it sounds empty and joyless. "It's funny, isn't it, that he's got a bundle of cells attacking his brain and trying to kill him but they can't try and remove it because he's got a runny nose and a tickly cough."

"The specialists at that hospital are nothing short of amazing. Honestly, they're some of the best in the world. They know what they're doing." Maggie's calm reassurance is exactly what I need. She's the voice of reason. "So when are they hoping to operate?"

I shrug. "It's hard to know. As soon as he's well enough for the anaesthetic to not be a danger, I think. Days rather than weeks, from what they were saying."

Repeating this information to Maggie keeps me centred. It's almost as though when I'm relaying the cold, hard facts of the story it isn't real, as though my baby brother isn't lying on a hospital bed with tubes sticking out of his body and drips pumping him full of medication. I can pretend everything's fine here, away from the stark, cold corridors of the hospital. I'm glad to be at the café and especially glad to be away from my parents, so I don't have to watch them crumble for another minute. I'd never seen my dad cry before, but last night he must have cried every tear he'd stored up inside.

"It's not going to affect my work though, I promise. The customers don't need to know anything's changed. I'll still be here on time every day and I won't be a misery. I won't let you down."

Maggie places her hand on my shoulder and squeezes. "You wouldn't be letting me down by putting your family first, Fern. If you need to be at the hospital, you go. This should be the last place on your mind with Luke so poorly. Pearl can always do a few shifts if we need an extra pair of hands, so cover's not an issue. I think she's lonely, being on her own. She'd be glad to help out."

"I'd rather be here," I admit. "Although it's good to know that Pearl's available. I'd hate to leave you in the lurch if I need to dash off for whatever reason."

I resist the urge to check my phone for the millionth time, just in case. I'd turned the ringer up to the highest volume and made my mum promise to call me if there was any news, no matter how small.

"Pearl's more than happy to come whenever. That's the thing about having family close by, they're always on hand in an emergency."

Pearl's related to Maggie by marriage – she's Maggie's ex-husband's aunt – and is a warm-hearted woman with a friendly smile. She's usually being dragged around the park by her dachshund puppy, and has admitted that she sees the shifts she helps out with at The Lake House Café as some much-needed respite from her livewire canine companion.

"Hopefully there won't be any emergencies," I say grimly. "At the hospital we're sitting around waiting for news and the time goes so slowly. I kept looking at my watch and the hands were moving that slowly I thought it had stopped. At least here I can find things to keep me busy, and it'll do me good to see happy faces rather than wallow in self-pity all day long."

"If you're absolutely sure, then I'm always glad to have you. You know I couldn't run this place without your input. But any time you need to dash off, you go. You don't even need to tell me, just whip off your apron and get out of that door. Family's important, Fern. I'm an only child, but I know that the bond between siblings is strong. Even though Kelly and Josh are tearing each other to shreds half the time, they'd be devastated if anything happened to the other."

My heart sinks, Maggie's words reminding me of my promise. I've got a phone call to make.

"Can I just have five minutes before I start my shift? I told Luke I'd ring someone to let them know what's happening..."

"You take your time," Maggie says soothingly, before switching on the radio. It's playing a rock-and-roll song, the kind that'd normally have me tapping my feet along to the beat. Today I don't feel like dancing. I don't feel like much at all.

"I'll go and clear that table," she adds, humming quietly as she starts stacking the plates left by some of the morning's early-bird customers.

Retrieving my phone from my pocket, relieved not to have any missed calls or messages, I scroll through the list of names. Café. Dad. Dentist. Doctor. They all flash before me before I see the name I'm searching for. I press the call icon, dread eating me up from the inside. I swallow as the phone rings once, twice, three times, and then a familiar voice answers with a sharp, and slightly irritated, hello.

"Kelly? It's me, Fern. Luke asked me to call you..."

Lacey

There's a nagging burning sensation nipping at my waist, the familiar gripe of a stitch building in my muscle. I've tried pinching it between my fingers and blowing out, something my old PE teacher used to insist was an instacure, but it's not helping. I tried massaging it with my fingertips too, but that didn't solve the problem either. There's nothing for it but to slow down to a walk. The aches and pains are obviously my body's way of telling me it's had enough for today.

I've been running for a month now, which is approximately three weeks longer than I expected to stick at it. I made the rookie mistake of telling anyone who'd listen that I was doing a charity run, and because I have kind and generous (and borderline sadistic) friends and family they'd all been thrusting fivers at me and congratulating me on doing something so impressive. Admittedly, there were a few people who laughed in my face – namely my boss, who told me he'd offer sponsorship of a hundred pounds on behalf of Fine Time Events so long as I ran the whole half-marathon, obviously insinuating that he didn't think I'd be capable. Well, I'll bloody show him. There's another nine weeks until the half-marathon. That's plenty of time to up the mileage and my fitness, so long as I can find a way to get rid of this stitch.

"Lacey!" The cheery voice lifts my spirits and brings a smile to my face. The familiar tone wraps me up, warming and reassuring. "Don't you go overdoing it, now."

"Don't worry, Uncle Carrick," I say with a grin. "I know my limits. I managed forty minutes' running today before I had to stop though, so I must be getting fitter."

I'd been delighted with the improvement. My first 'running' session had been almost entirely walking, and whilst I still jog with a lolloping, ungainly gait, at least I'm picking up speed and covering more ground.

My uncle beams back, his wonky grin and twinkly eyes as sunny as the weather. "She'd be so proud of you for getting out there and doing something proactive. She was all about fighting for change, was Marilyn."

"I think of her all the time," I confess. "She inspires me to keep going when my legs are telling me to give up."

I'd loved my aunt so much. Now, when my feet were aching and my thighs burning with pain, I close my eyes and imagine her face. Somehow it makes everything seem just that bit more manageable.

"It's funny how you and her are so different to Dad," I muse. "He's always been so serious and strait-laced. It's hard to believe you all have the same parents."

Uncle Carrick snorts. "Well, Terrence always had ideas above his station. He was never going to be the type to settle for staying around these parts. Me and Marilyn, we were home birds, but your dad was forever talking about getting away. It was no surprise when he joined the army. Your Grandma Braithwaite told anyone who'd listen about how wonderful he was. He was her favourite. Youngest child by a country mile, see. Spoilt rotten."

"I'm the youngest too, but I'm not spoilt."

I know I sound defensive, but my parents have always been more lenient when it comes to my sister, Dina, even though she's wilder than I am. She was the one that school would be making calls home about because she'd pierced her ears with a needle (and that one time she pierced someone else's ears with a needle – it looked like someone had committed murder in their dorm, there was that much blood), or dyed her hair turquoise. The boarding school Dad had chosen for us was strict, and the headmistress a stickler for the rules. I lived for the weekends when I could escape the prison-like confines and stay with Uncle Carrick. It's probably because of those weekends together that we're so close now.

He'd never had children of his own, which was a shame as

he was a natural with kids. He'd listened to me and Dina, valuing our opinions and not just humouring them like Dad did when he made his weekly phone calls from wherever he was stationed at that time. Uncle Carrick had encouraged thought and debate and offered a safe place for us to form our own opinions. Those weekends had been my highlight, when Auntie Marilyn and Uncle Lenny would pop over too with a hearty vegetable pie and we'd stay up late playing board games and laughing at *Carry On* films, even though I didn't understand half the bawdy jokes. Those joy-filled Saturdays and Sundays had almost made boarding school worth it, and were far more fun than the holidays where we'd get shipped back 'home' to wherever Mum and Dad were at the time.

"Your dad wouldn't know how to spoil anyone," Uncle Carrick replies pointedly, pulling out a packet of mints and offering me one, before thinking better of it, taking one for himself then folding the half-empty packet into my hand. "He only ever looks out for number one."

"And Mum," I say defensively, although I don't know why I'm standing up for Dad. "He looks out for her too."

"He does," Uncle Carrick concedes with a nod. "I just wish he was able to show you and Dina how much he loves you both. One of these days he's going to regret missing out on your childhoods."

"He thought he was doing the right thing, sending us to St. Eugenia's. It's an outstanding school."

Everyone knew of my alma mater. There was a reason it was regarded as one of the top all-girls schools in England. The extortionate fees were offset by the fact they were top of the national results tables that were printed in the broadsheets each summer.

What people didn't know was how miserable it was for some of the girls there, especially those like me and Dina. Our family weren't poor by any stretch, but we didn't have the country mansion and the London flat that the wealthiest girls had, or stables full of ponies, or Daddy picking us up in one of the cars from the collection of vintage autos in the family garage. Fellow pupils had teased us for having Uncle Carrick turn up in his sea-green Ford Fiesta, and when Auntie Marilyn showed up for prize giving wearing a gaudy paisley-print sundress and a wide-brimmed sunhat that she'd bought especially for the occasion, they'd made snide remarks about her bohemian appearance. Their words had hurt at the time, but now I realise I was far richer than those girls would ever be, because whilst they might have possessions, I'd been brought up with love and laughter by my extended family. Love was something some of them obviously lacked, if their ability to show compassion and empathy was anything to go by; not to mention their pompous, judgmental asses.

"At least going there meant I got to spend more time with you," I grin, peeling a mint out of the silvery wrapper.

"And for that I'll always be grateful, Lacey-Lou."

His eyes are misting up, and he examines the roses he'd been pruning particularly carefully.

"I'm going to see Uncle Lenny later, if you want to come?" I offer. "I'd be glad of the company."

It's still strange going back to Auntie Marilyn's house and seeing all her nick-nacks on display when she's no longer there. She collected all sorts of oddities; paperweights and ornaments and clocks that hadn't worked in years. Jumble, most people would call it. Or tat. Anything she thought was beautiful would be displayed for all to see, even if it had been unloved by its previous owner. Much like Uncle Lenny actually, who'd been divorced twice by the time Auntie Marilyn took him in.

"I've got a bottle of that whisky you like too?" I add, hoping the bribe might swing it.

"Go on then," he says with a roll of his eyes. "You know the way to win me over."

"Too right I do."

I lean in and plant a kiss on his cheek. He brushes it off with the back of his gardening glove, never one for public displays of affection, but he doesn't need my hugs and kisses to know how much I love and appreciate him. I tell him all the time, even though the bond between us is so strong we don't need words. Somehow we intuitively 'get' each other.

"Meet you there at eight?" I say. "We can watch that quiz show he likes then."

Uncle Carrick groans. "I can't bear that programme. The questions are too easy. I think that's the only reason he likes it, makes him feel clever when he gets the answers right."

"Think of the whisky!" I shout over my shoulder with a laugh.

"I might need a whole bottle to myself to put up with Lenny!" he calls jovially.

I smile as I head towards home, the thought of a fun evening with two of my favourite people bringing a spring back into my step. It's almost enough to make me break into a run.

Almost.

Fern

"Yes, Jasper, yes! That's much better!"

The door to the café has been propped open to let in some much-needed air. It gets stifling in here during the peak hours otherwise. That's why the rich tone of the Italian's voice is drifting in, clearly audible from across the park as he cheers on his enthusiastic young pupils.

Maggie's had a dopey grin painted on to her face all morning. It's obvious she's got a crush on him. She even left her usual spot in the kitchen earlier to peer out of the main window and watch the youngsters dribbling grubby mini footballs around a line of orange plastic cones. When I innocently asked what was keeping her attention she'd given a noncommittal response about how nice it was to see children enjoying the first truly warm day of the year. I didn't believe a word of it, of course, but hadn't questioned Maggie's reply, instead getting on with taking the plateful of fluffy scrambled eggs on toast over to the young man sat in the window, the sunniest seat in the whole café. He's waiting on a pot of coffee too, which Maggie's preparing.

After the eventful night at the hospital I'm glad to be busy. It stops me worrying about Luke and waiting for Kelly to turn up. Nerves are churning in my stomach. I don't know how I'm going to say what I need to say to her.

The scrambled egg on toast guy must be new to these parts: if I'd seen him before I'd have definitely remembered him. He's got this sort of edgy look that's slightly out of place in the park. Most of the people here are decidedly mainstream – not that there's anything wrong with that, I'm hardly Lady Gaga myself – but this lad stands out from the crowd. His blonde hair's a fraction too white to be natural, as though it's aided by a touch of bleach, and he has a small silver hoop pierced through his bottom lip. It keeps quivering as though he's moving his tongue against it in the hollow of his mouth, which is kind of distracting.

He's so far removed from the kind of boy I usually go for that I can't decide whether he's good looking or not. I never fancy anyone, except the same person I've had a painful crush on since the first day at secondary school. I'd fallen so hard and so deep that I'd never wavered. My heart had one not-so-careful owner who couldn't care less that he held it captive.

I cast my eyes around the café for the edgy boy's skateboard, assuming he's one of the hip kids that hangs out at the purpose-built skate park on the other side of the boating lake. The stuff they do is frightening: dangerous flips and tricks that look like they belong in a music video. Just watching them makes my stomach turn with fear. I can't see a board though, not even tucked under the table.

"Can you serve this to the gentleman in the window, please?" Maggie asks, snapping me out of my daydream. I carefully carry the gleaming silver coffee pot over to the man.

Ah, there's a flash of navy blue polo shirt peeping out beneath the red and black flannel of his shirt, a giveaway that he works in the park. All the sports coaches, maintenance staff and gardeners wear the same style. They're standard-issue, regulation and dull.

Memories of the uniform I wore at secondary school flood back to me. I'd hated it. The other girls had dressed in miniskirts that barely covered their tiny, shapely bottoms, with socks pulled up to their knees in a bid to look sexy. I hadn't. I'd worn a knee-length skirt with an elasticated waist, the only grey skirt on the High Street that fit my large frame. It was hideous and unflattering and saddled me with the cruel nickname 'Fernephant' for all five miserable years I was there.

Thankfully Maggie's stance on workwear is fairly laid back. As far as she's concerned staff at the café can wear whatever we like, so long as it's white on top, black on the bottom, and clean and pressed. I'm still fat, but black

43

trousers are easy enough to come by. School uniforms are difficult to buy for those of us who carry extra weight, unless you accidentally click on those dodgy fetish websites that pop up when your laptop protection expires. At least black trousers are a wardrobe staple.

I place the coffee pot down on the table in front of the guy, cringing at the dull clunk it makes as it lands on the shiny surface of the tablecloth. It goes right through me, setting my teeth on edge.

"Thanks," he says, not looking up from his phone. He's engrossed in whatever he's reading, silently mouthing words I'm unable to decipher. Lip-reading's not a skill I've mastered.

I stand awkwardly for a moment, shifting on the spot as I wait for eye contact that doesn't come. Most customers offer at least a cursory smile, but not this one. He doesn't even look up.

Eventually I give up waiting, but still smile politely even though I know he won't see. I wish I could be a bit less well-mannered, replying with a clipped "Enjoy," or something, because it's downright rude not to acknowledge the wait staff, but it's too ingrained. I've been brought up to be civil regardless of how I'm treated, which is probably why I was such an easy target for the bullies at school. They knew they could say whatever they damn well pleased because I'd never have the guts to fight back.

As I walk back to the counter I wonder about his role. Most of the staff at the park have been here for years, the same familiar faces as much a part of the landscape as the imposing bandstand and the large boating lake. I remember Carrick Braithwaite, the friendly gentleman who tends the walled garden near the main entrance, from when I was young. He'd share interesting snippets of information about the roses he carefully pruned, such as how there were over a hundred species of roses and that it was England's national flower. Maggie said he'd done the same for her when *she* was young too, and some mornings on my way to the café I see him passing on his wealth of knowledge to the next generation of curious children. The familiarity in the scene cheers me and although over the years Mr Braithwaite's hair has changed from mousey brown to silvery grey to the brilliant white it now is, he's still as friendly and upbeat as ever. He's part of the park. I selfishly hope he'll never stop clipping those plants with those secateurs of his, even though he must be closing in on retirement age.

I sneak one last look over at the edgy boy. It's likely I'll see him again if he's working here all summer. Most of the park staff are much older than I am, but he looks a similar age, twentyish. Even if we never become best buddies, it might be nice to have someone else around who knows about chart music and the latest films. If he ever bothers to speak at all, that is, I think sulkily. Maggie tries her best to keep up with the trends but it's not the same, and although Kelly helps out with the odd shift she's not around enough. She's always got her head down, revising for her exams.

I can't stop the sigh that escapes me. What's going to happen to Luke now? He won't be able to sit his exams if he's recovering from brain surgery, and without A-levels he'll not be able to take up his place at Nottingham. The letter had been very clear – 'conditional offer'. Will they let him defer until next year instead, if he's well enough? Or is that it, his one chance blown because of some freak of nature that he can't control? It doesn't seem fair, but having never had any desire to go to university I have no idea how it works. Maybe that's something I can ask Kelly when she arrives.

Moving towards the window, I tap Maggie on the shoulder with the tip of my index finger. She throws me a look, a warning, as she turns, spotting the knowing smile that's playing out on my lips. I can't help it. It's so cute how enamoured with the handsome coach she is. I can tell by the rosy pink glow of her cheeks and the sparkle in her eyes, so she can deny it as much as she likes – I still won't believe her.

"Tell me the truth this time," I say with a grin, "is it the kids you're watching or the coach?"

Maggie's cheeks flush further, until they resemble two

red apples on the sides of her face. That's my answer right there. She's smitten.

"No, no, I was just looking…" Maggie stumbles over her words, knowing she's been rumbled.

Peering out of the window, I follow her gaze to where the coach is patiently demonstrating to the kids how to pass the ball with the inside of the foot. His lean body moves nimbly, and his young students flock around him in admiration. He's a footballing Pied Piper. With a sweep of his hand he nonchalantly flicks his long, dark hair out of his eyes. It's like a scene from a shampoo ad, and although Maggie's trying to play it cool I hear her inhale sharply at the motion.

"I suppose he's quite good looking for an older man," I think out loud.

"He's probably only in his thirties, it's hardly like he's taking out his pension!" Maggie scoffs, fanning her face with her hand. She's still a bit pink. "Older man indeed," she adds, rolling her eyes.

"But he *is* older."

"Older than you, maybe. I'd hazard a guess I've got a good few years on him."

"He's in good shape too," I muse, hoping to coax her feelings out of her. "And those European men take good care of themselves. There was something about it on that breakfast show; apparently, men on the continent are more likely to cleanse, tone and moisturise than men here in Britain. Looking after your skin is vital if you want to keep a youthful glow."

My hand automatically reaches for my face. Fortunately, my skin is one of my best features. Even during the height of puberty I rarely suffered spots and blemishes. It's more the result of good genes and good luck than beauty products, though; Luke's been blessed with good skin too. It's probably just as well. I've neither the time nor the money to splash out on unnecessary, overpriced creams. Soap and water are good enough for me.

Maggie's eyes twinkle mischievously, the first hint of a crease wrinkling at their outer corners. "Are you trying to tell me I'm looking old?"

The thought I may have caused offence horrifies me. I don't want to insult anyone, and certainly not Maggie who's both a boss and a friend.

"No, no, not at all! You're always really well presented, but then you're one of those young, funky mums, not like mine. You're far more open-minded than either of my parents. And you don't look forty; if I didn't know you had a son my age, I'd think you were much younger."

Now it's my turn to flush red; I can feel the heat spreading up my neck and I silently curse as the familiar flaming sensation takes over. It's bloody annoying how I can't stop it happening. But thoughts of Joshua Thornhill have a nasty habit of turning me into a gibbering wreck, and add to that the fear of causing offence, my cheeks don't stand a chance.

"I'm teasing, Fern," Maggie replies, reassuringly placing her hand on my shoulder. "And although I'm delighted that you think I'm young and funky, my main concern is this place." She gestures around the café, to where the young man in the window is still engrossed in whatever he's reading and a group of middle-aged women are huddled around the long table near the door, sipping cups of tea whilst putting the world to rights. Her eyes rest on the large clock on the back wall. It's already twenty past eleven. "Speaking of which, the football mums will be coming in any minute now. Would you be a doll and fill up the water jugs? Those little ones look so tired after all that running about and it's so warm out there. I bet they'll come in desperate for a glass of water."

I hurry off, keen to please, but not before catching Maggie sneaking another discreet look at the coach.

She can deny it all she wants – my boss has a crush on him, I'm certain of it. I only hope it'll be more fruitful than the one I've been harbouring for years.

Maggie

I'm fussing, fidgeting with the collar of my frilly white blouse, but that doesn't stop me grasping the opportunity to steal one last glance out towards the football session before heading back into the kitchen to rescue a batch of fruit scones from the oven. The coach is smiling broadly as he holds open a large net bag and the boys and girls are gathering up the balls, helpfully putting them away as their training session draws to a close. His head lifts, his angular jaw and high cheekbones visible even from this distance, and I swear he's looking straight at me. Then he nods, a half nod of acknowledgement that causes me to quickly turn away in embarrassment. I busy my hands by sorting the condiments that sit in a small silver bucket on the table, checking the use-by dates closely although there's no need. I only bought them last week. If they're out of date already, the wholesalers will be getting an earful.

How can I let someone I hardly know affect me like

this? My stomach's knotted, my heart pounding wildly. All that over a man I've spoken to a handful of times, and then only to say 'that's £2.49, please'? What an absolute fool I am. It's ridiculously childish.

I make my way back to the kitchen, my haven, basking in the pleasurable aroma of the scones.

The kitchen is a safe place to hide, and being out here will give me a chance to regain my composure. I don't want to be caught eyeing up the toy boy football coach even if Fern does think I'm young and funky.

I know the truth. I'm far too long in the tooth to do something as ridiculous as fall in love.

The lunchtime sun streams in through the window, flooding the café with waves of light. The whole room looks cheerful and welcoming with the natural illumination. The off-white walls radiate warmth, the slivers of thin red curtain that frame the windows casting a soft rosy hue.

It's another moment that reminds me of how much I love The Lake House Café, and how much I've achieved. The place had been a boarded-up eyesore when I took it on. People had said I was crazy to try to turn it around, but I'd always believed it could be restored to its former glory and become a welcoming resting-place for everyone who used the park. I hoped it would become somewhere people could enjoy refuelling before heading back out on their merry way. I'd been right. These days the café is the most popular spot in the park, perfect for people-watching and enjoying a naughty treat. All those doubters had been proved wrong a thousand times over, and I couldn't be more proud.

The café's filling up again now. A glut of morning joggers have completed their circuit of the woods and are rewarding themselves with well-deserved lattes, and a young couple walking their two near-identical golden retrievers have popped in for two large sausage sandwiches slathered in generous lashings of tangy brown sauce. The man, a Dermot O' Leary lookalike with a devilish grin, is secretly feeding titbits to the dogs underneath the table whilst his partner hungrily wolfs her butty down, oblivious.

Then there's the football mums buying cupcakes with lavish, brightly coloured fondant icing for their ravenous offspring. I make a mental note to put another batch in later, because at this rate they're going to clear me out altogether. The chatter of the excitable children fills the building with joy, and their mucky boots cover the floor in a dusty trail of dried mud. Fern will have to do a quick mop round when it quietens down a bit.

"Excuse me?"

The interruption snaps me out of my thoughts.

"Oh!" I exclaim, blood rushing to both my brain and my cheeks as I'm face to face with the dishy football coach.

I should have guessed it was him by the exotic accent: even those two words were laced with a hint of Italian that reminded me of my current celebrity crush, TV chef Gino D'Acampo. The thought of Gino only makes me blush all the more.

"I'm sorry," I say, momentarily flustered, "I was miles away. What can I get you?"

I force myself to smile, hoping I look less worked up than I feel. My manic smile can be a bit much: I'm all teeth and gums.

"It's so hard to choose," he replies, his voice like a song. "Everything looks delicious."

Each word causes an excitable flutter low in my stomach, reminiscent of the butterflies I used to get when Clint and I first got together. That seems a long time ago. It *is* a long time ago, more than half my life. Surely by my age I should be well past crushes that leave me clammy-palmed and stumbling for words? The days of blaming my hormones for my lustful desires are long gone, and surely I'm not menopausal yet? Although that might go some way to explaining the obsession I've had with Gino of late...

"The scones are fresh out of the oven," I offer, "or the lemon drizzle cake is popular. It's a bit of a favourite with my regulars."

I immediately regret my choice of words, worrying my comment might come across as big-headed.

"Then I'll trust their judgement," he says with a smile. It's a wide, affable smile over a jaunty, stubble-coated chin, and his dark eyes manage to be both intense and friendly all at once. "A slice of lemon cake and an orange juice please, and one of the cupcakes for Pepe."

He turns, beckoning a small boy in a navy-blue tracksuit. The child is the spitting image of the man, a miniature version right down to the floppy almost-black hair and the large, lazy smile. The similarity is a timely reminder, a warning, and I immediately chide myself for allowing my far-fetched daydreams to get the better of me. Of course a man like this is married with a family. He's way too attractive not to be. Plus he spends his Saturday mornings coaching other people's children. A catch like that was never going to be single.

"Coming right up."

I busy myself with the order, placing a gleaming glass filled with ice cubes on to the smooth, round tray before adding a chilled bottle of juice and two matching small, white side plates. Reaching for the tongs to select a cupcake, I carefully clasp the frilly yellow bun case between them before purposefully placing it in the very centre of one of the plates. Picking up the mock-marble-handled cake slice, I carefully nudge one of the more generous slices of lemon drizzle along the cake stand, jimmying it on to its side to transfer it to the plate.

"I can already smell the lemon," he says as the cake balances precariously atop the cake slice. "I like it. It reminds me of home."

I look up to offer a smile and politely ask where home is, but before I can say a word the cake has slid straight on to the counter. It crumbles sadly as I exclaim "Oh!", hurriedly reaching for a serviette to tidy the mess, as though hiding the evidence will somehow undo my clumsy error.

Scooping the largest remnant of the cake into the white tissue paper, I exhale, feeling every inch an absolute idiot. But I don't have chance to dwell on it as an olive-skinned hand skims my own.

I jolt back, acting on instinct. It's as though a shock has been sent through my body by his fleeting touch.

"Let me help you."

Pulling his hand towards him, he brushes the rogue crumbs into the palm of his other hand.

"I'm sorry," I stutter nervously. "I'll tidy the mess, then I'll get you another slice."

The little boy, Pepe, is wide-eyed at the mere thought of his cupcake.

"Why don't you two sit down and I'll bring it over to you?" I say, mortification charging through me.

"It's fine," the man insists, brushing his hands against the silky black material of his shorts. Stray crumbs fall to the floor. "We're in no rush, we can wait."

His eyes lock with mine and I nod graciously. I throw the cake-filled paper napkin into the bin before washing my hands in the small sink that lines the back wall. This small act gives me a moment to regain my composure. Heaven knows I need it. Inside I'm a mess: a jibbering, cake-dropping mess.

"Anything I can do here, Maggie?" asks Fern, her rounded cheeks aglow after cleaning the tables. She's a delicate English rose with her creamy complexion, dark hair and natural blush, a real beauty. It's just a shame Fern can't see for herself how pretty she is, but that's the reserve of the confident. Shy, retiring people rarely appreciate how beautiful they are.

"This gentleman's waiting on a slice of lemon drizzle cake. I had one of my ditzy moments and managed to smash a slice to smithereens on the counter." I bring the heel of my hand to my forehead. "If you could finish serving him whilst I go and check on what's in the oven, please?"

Fern gives me a loaded look, one that shows she knows full well there's nothing in the oven and that I'm scrabbling for an excuse – any excuse – to escape the shop floor after my faux pas; but she takes over anyway, managing to slice and serve the cake in one effortless manoeuvre.

I'm very nearly in the kitchen when the man's voice calls out to me, polite and genuine. "Thank you, Maggie."

Twisting on the spot until our eyes connect, I pause before speaking.

"Thank you...?" I say, my voice trailing off questioningly.

"Paolo," he responds, his Italian accent stronger than ever. "My name is Paolo."

I push the swing door open just a fraction, peeping cautiously through the gap. I don't want to make a fool of myself yet again, but can't resist sneaking one last look at Paolo and his son. They're sat at the same table as the attractive young man with the pierced lip and dimples. I wonder how they know each other: they seem an unlikely friendship. Maybe it's nothing more than both working in the park.

The little boy is scooping the buttercream from the top of his cupcake with his index finger before deliberately licking it off, whilst Paolo is cupping his glass of juice as he talks. They are proper man's hands, big and protective, but even from here I can see it, the tell-tale gold band on the third finger of his left hand. It's thick and glistening and screams 'married'.

I close the door, disheartened. I refuse to allow myself to so much as daydream about a married man; it doesn't feel right. Those trollops who had affairs with Clint all the while knowing I was sat at home looking after Josh and Kelly, well, I don't want to be like them. What little froth of excitement I'd allowed myself to feel at this crush (or whatever it is) is starting to dissipate already. Even thinking about him is wrong if he's not available, and the ring, not to mention Pepe, show that available is something he most definitely is not.

Fern appears from nowhere, making me jump.

"What are you doing?" Fern asks curiously, her brow furrowing as she examines my face.

"Nothing!" I hiss, my heart still racing from being unexpectedly disturbed. "And stop sneaking up on me!"

"I wasn't sneaking." She looks put out at the suggestion. "I came to see if there was any more gingerbread in the kitchen, that's all. It's selling fast today."

"In the red tin in the cupboard. I made a double batch."

"And how was the cake?" Fern asks innocently. Her large brown eyes are wider than ever with exaggerated virtue but there's a knowing look on her face. Not quite a smirk – Fern isn't the sort to smirk – but almost. "You were in such a rush to get away, I hope you got to it before it burnt."

"All right, all right," I say, throwing my hands up. I know when I've been rumbled. "There was no cake. I wanted the ground to swallow me up and escaping into the kitchen was the closest I could get to disappearing."

"Thought as much," Fern answers with a quiet triumph.

"But don't you go getting any ideas," I say sternly, waggling my index finger in warning, "and don't you dare breathe a word either. He's a married man. That in itself means I wouldn't go near him with a bargepole, and you know how people around here love to gossip. I've been part of enough rumours to last a life time, so don't go fuelling any more."

"Hmmm," Fern replies noncommittally. "But what if he wasn't married? You must admit you're attracted to him."

"That's neither here nor there: he's a married man so there's nothing to discuss. And that's an end to it."

Jutting out my chin, I take a deep breath to prepare myself before walking into the café. Stealing one quick, stealthy glance at the Italian's table, I see the little boy high-fiving the young man with the sweeping blonde hair and pierced lip before stepping out on to the terrace area, following his stunningly attractive father like an obedient puppy.

Pearl

"Stop pulling, Mitzi!"

I should get that put on loop on a tape so I can play it whenever I need to. It seems to be all I'm saying at the moment.

I knew a puppy would be hard work, especially as I'm not exactly a spring chicken any more. It's eighteen years since Alf and I bought Bluey, our darling little Westie. He'd been a bundle of ruffled white fur, scruffy and cuddly and revelling in attention. Even as a pup he'd played on his cuteness, pricking his ears up and peering longingly at us with his head jauntily angled until we'd give him just one more titbit or allow him to sit up on the sofa with us. He'd been the baby we'd never had, although not for want of trying. Heck, we'd tried morning, noon and night for years. But it wasn't meant to be, and in the end we decided enough was enough. Bluey might not have been a child, but he was a dog with real personality and charm, one that everyone would fuss over when we walked him in the park. Even when he was older and his fur turned a more silvery tone he'd had this perfect mix of cheekiness and elegance that drew park-goers to him. And he'd had a lovely temperament, always eager to please. He'd been the apple of our eyes.

Mitzi, on the other hand, is an absolute minx. She's only six months old so has the excuse of still being a puppy, but she's a total tearaway. Who'd have thought a miniature dachshund would be able to do so much damage? My poor slippers look like they've been mauled by a wild animal. She might only stand an inch or so off the ground but she's a demanding little thing and hasn't yet learned how to take no for an answer. And that's not to mention the constant straining against the lead every time we're out on a walk. For such a small creature, Mitzi's surprisingly strong-willed.

She turns to look at me, all dark, wide eyes and open mouth, tongue hanging out like a strip of uncooked bacon.

"You can give me that look all you like," I say sternly. "You're a terror, and well you know it."

It's a warm afternoon. The sunshine reflecting off the lake causes me to squint and the ducks are dipping their heads under the water to keep cool. Mitzi's probably in need of a drink too. After we've done the lap of the lake we'll pop past the café, Maggie's got a bowl of water outside ready for any thirsty pooches who happen to be passing. She's thought of the lot, that one, which probably explains why the café's so popular.

Mitzi's still dragging me around, pulling the lead taut as her little legs scurry along the winding pathway. A young boy on one of those bikes without pedals comes zooming past and her head whips around in a flash. She's nosey like that, desperate to know what's going on.

The little boy's feet are pushing him along, first the right foot and then the left. He's going at quite a pace. He's like Fred Flintstone in his Stone Age car, feet whirring until he picks up speed, and his parents smile on proudly at his achievements.

There's an older girl too, probably around eight, but I'm terrible at estimating the ages of children. She's bouncing a tennis ball as she walks, the rhythmic thump, thump, thump getting ever nearer.

The tug on the lead is more determined now, Mitzi's long, lean body straining to play with the ball.

"Mitzi!" I chide. "For goodness' sake. Behave!"

But my words are too little and too late, because the round black handle of the lead is already out of my hand, trailing along the floor behind my bouncy pup.

I give chase as best as I can, but for a dog with such short legs Mitzi is deceptively fast. It must be that boundless youthful vivacity, something I myself am rapidly losing.

She's already sniffing around the little girl's ankles, hoping to get a chance to play with the fuzzy yellow ball, although the girl is holding it above her head at arm's length. Mitzi thinks it's all a game. Of course she does, everything's a game to her, but I can see the girl's nervous. Her body is rigid, her eyes large.

When I finally reach her, flustered and out of puff, I apologise profusely to the girl and her parents for Mitzi's exuberance. "She doesn't mean to scare you though, she just wants to play. In dog years she's still a child, like you."

The girl looks at me thoughtfully. "So she wants to be my friend?"

"That's right," I say. "She's not really used to being near children, so she gets excited when she thinks she's found someone new to play with." I smile. "Especially someone with a ball."

"Don't you have any children?" The girl's face crinkles up, as though that's almost inconceivable.

"No," I reply sadly. "There's only me and Mitzi."

I swallow down the lump of grief that lodges in my throat. It's still so very raw, being alone.

I can't believe I'm a widow. When I was young I thought widows were old women with walking sticks and purple rinses, people who lived in 'rest homes'. I'd laughed at that, thinking retirement would be a rest compared to the endless slog of first school, and then, in later years, work. I never thought Alf would die on me aged fifty-nine, when we were still wearing jeans and trainers and had all our proverbial marbles. My hair's not even grey yet, let alone purple. The box of dye I buy from the chemist each month sees to that and does a reasonable job, although being blonde helps too. The greys are less obvious; they blend in.

"She's cute," says the girl, crouching down and tentatively reaching forward to stroke Mitzi's smooth, brown coat. Mitzi's tail wags happily from side to side at the attention. "I'd like to be friends with her."

"Well, maybe we'll see you in the park again. We're here a lot, me and Mitzi. We only live over there."

I gesture in the general direction of my back garden, the same house Alf and I bought soon after getting married. We'd never be able to afford it now, prices have gone silly. It was a stretch even then, but we were both working so we'd decided to take it. The three-storey villa had a curb appeal that was too hard to resist. Everything about it was attractive, from the pointed gable that crowned the building to the climbing peace roses around the front door that reminded me of dreamy summer sunsets. The bay windows had been the clincher though, huge glass panes that flooded the front room with light.

The house's proximity to the park had been a draw too, back when we'd envisaged having a family of our own. We'd imagined lazy days in the sunshine with a picnic of jam sandwiches and savoury eggs. Alf and our children kicking a ball about. Hunting for squirrels as we walked through the wooded area at the far side of the park. As it turned out, children were never meant to be for us, but the park remained a blessing. It was perfect for dog walking for starters, a real community hub where I'd bump into people I knew, and on the rare occasions I cover a shift at the café it's only a five-minute walk back home. I like having the greenery to look at too. It's nice to be close to nature.

"See you," the girl calls, waving as she chases after her brother.

I wrap Mitzi's lead tightly around my hand, winding it twice so there's no chance of her running free again. She's a little Houdini, escape artist extraordinaire.

I'm thankful for the shade of the tall firs that line the pathway; it's slap-bang in the middle of the day and exceptionally warm. It's a little tricky with Mitzi pulling at the lead in my hand, but I manage to shuffle the sleeves of my blouse up so my forearms are exposed. I'm instantly convinced I can feel the heat prickling against my skin, despite the branches overhead offering protection from the scorching rays.

"Pearl!"

The voice rings out from the other side of the hedge in front of me and I spy the familiar face peeping out from over the dark green leaves.

"Oh. Hello, Carrick."

He's better prepared for the weather than I am, a floppy brown sun hat perched on top of his head. His skin's already looking tan, as though he's been away on his holiday already, but he's always that shade. It comes from working outside, I suppose.

"How's the tearaway?" he asks with a wink, nodding in Mitzi's direction.

The tearaway is desperate to keep walking rather than stop to chat, but I don't want to be rude.

"Oh, she's fine. Already managed to give me the slip once this morning though," I admit, lowering myself to scoop her silky body up in my arms.

He throws back his head and laughs. "She's not like your Bluey, is she? A real rascal, this one. I think she likes keeping you on your toes."

"She does that all right," I smile, as a wet doggy tongue laps at my cheek. "Even though she's a pain I can't imagine not having her. The house was too quiet with just me rattling around in it."

"It must be strange," he ponders. "Being on your lonesome after all those years."

"It's taking some adjusting to," I admit. "And it's harder still without Bluey. But I'm keeping myself busy, you know how it is."

He probably didn't. Carrick's the perpetual bachelor boy, and he's not had a lady friend for years.

Alf had spent more time with Carrick than I had over recent years. They'd both been in the skittles team and had shared games of darts at the pub of an evening. They weren't as close as they'd been in their youth, when they'd both represented the local cricket club, but they'd still enjoyed a chat over a pint. Alf said Carrick would fob off anyone who asked why he didn't have a woman by his side. He had wondered if Carrick might secretly be gay. I knew that wasn't the case.

"Well, if you're ever after a bit of company, I can always pop in for a cuppa after my shift?"

There's something in his eyes, a look that's hopeful. Maybe he's as lonely as I am. He doesn't even have a canine companion, as far as I know, and his nieces are all grown up now with lives of their own. I'd heard on the grapevine that the oldest one, Dina, was getting married soon.

"That'd be nice," I say as I pop a wriggly Mitzi down on the pavement, and I realise I mean it. Since Alf died I've done very little in the way of entertaining, but it's the kind of house that needs people in it. Maybe if Carrick came over I could get the good china out of the cupboards; it's been stashed away unused for far too long. "I'll check my diary." He needn't know I had nothing more exciting than dog walking scheduled.

Carrick beams as he readjusts his sunhat. "Let me know when best suits. I'll look forward to it."

Mitzi tugs impatiently at the lead, the cord rubbing uncomfortably against my hand as she does so. "I'm going to have to go. Madam here doesn't want to stand around chatting."

"See you soon," Carrick says with a courteous nod.

I have just enough time to hold up my free hand in a wave as Mitzi takes me on a walk towards The Lake House Café, probably longing to lap at the water that's in a shiny silver bowl near the doorway. Carrick's right back to work, secateurs in hand to deadhead the gorgeous dusky pink rosebush.

"We're having a guest come and visit us soon," I say breathily to Mitzi, who's charging on ahead. "So you'll need to be on your best behaviour."

She twists her body round to the direction of my voice and pops her slathering tongue out of her mouth. If I didn't know better, I'd swear she was making fun of me.

Fern

Kelly's blonde hair glimmers in the sun as she enters the café, a worried expression on her face. My stomach lurches. I'm not good at managing awkward conversations at the best of times and this is likely to be one of the most difficult conversations I've ever had.

I'd told Kelly the cold hard facts on the phone, and she'd seemed to take it well. At least, she hadn't broken down in tears or asked me questions I didn't know the answers to. She'd replied with a quiet 'okay' at the end of each sentence and then thanked me for letting her know. Talking in person was going to be much harder than talking over the phone though. There's something about seeing people's expressions that makes it harder to control my own emotions.

"I can't stay long," she says in a whisper, her eyes flickering around the café. "If Mum sees me here she'll go crazy. She thinks I'm at home revising. I *was* revising until I got your phone call. Now I can't think of anything except Luke."

Her expression is weary and pained and I can only imagine mine is worse. I had two hours of broken sleep last night, and my body can tell. It wants to curl up and shut down, but I'm not going to let it. I've got too much to do.

"I wish I hadn't had to tell you, and I wish I had better news, but all we can do is wait for him to get over this infection so they can operate."

"When I saw him on Thursday he was fine," Kelly hisses through gritted teeth. "He told me the headaches had gone. I thought they were stress-related because he's been working so hard lately. How wrong was I?"

I shrug.

"I don't know, Kel. Maybe Thursday was a good day. All I know is that last night he was screaming in pain. I was lying in bed reading one minute and the next Luke was crying out for me to come and help him. The panic in his voice..." I shudder at the memory. "He thought he was going blind, said he couldn't see anything but black. It was terrifying."

"I should have been there for him. I've known for weeks that he's not been right. If only I'd taken it more seriously..."

I hold my hand up to stop her mid-flow.

"There's nothing you could have done, nothing any of us could have done. Luke has a brain tumour. We couldn't have stopped it happening."

I appreciate how helpless she feels. I'd had all the same thoughts myself last night, the 'what ifs' and 'if onlys', and the guilt had eroded my soul until I'd finally snatched a restless sleep leaning on my dad's bony shoulder.

"I should have said something. Maybe if I'd told him to go to the doctor and get it checked out he'd have listened to me?"

"Kelly, please. Stop beating yourself up over this. If you'd tried to get him to go to the doctor he'd only have thought you were nagging. You know as well as I do that he hates making a fuss."

"I can't bear to think of him in hospital." Kelly looks so unsure, her usual confident persona nowhere to be seen. "Poor Luke. Hospitals are depressing, full of old people waiting to die. He must be so scared. Can I go and see him?"

She's looking at me with such hope, but I know there's no way she can come to the hospital. My parents would hit the roof, especially in their current emotional state. "He's not allowed visitors at the moment, because his immune system's so low and they really need to get him back to full strength so they can operate."

I'm not lying, but we both know it's only half the reason. My dad had walked in on Kelly and Luke kissing at Luke's eighteenth birthday party back in January. He'd been furious, despite both of them trying to explain that it was a typical drunken snog, the sort most teenagers have after a few too many alcopops.

I guess I've not been a typical teenager, holding out for someone who's way out of my league, so my old-fashioned parents haven't got experience in knowing what to expect from a hormone-addled adolescent. They'd already made it clear they thought it was outrageous that within Luke's gang of closest friends there was a girl who identified as bisexual, and rather than being ashamed of her sexuality, openly revelled in it. Finding Luke kissing her was a complete shock for my prudish dad, so when they announced they were dating he took it as a personal insult. In his mind, Luke wasn't seeing Kelly because he liked her, he was doing it just to wind him up.

Mum had inevitably sided with Dad in a bid to keep the peace, whereas I stood up for Luke. If it had been anyone other than Kelly that Luke had been dating there wouldn't have been anywhere near as much fuss; that was what got to me more than anything. Sometimes it's as though Dad's stuck in the dark ages. He didn't believe Kelly would be able to 'give up girls' as though being monogamous and bisexual was as mythical as unicorns or fat-free donuts, rather than a perfectly normal way of life.

It all came to a head last month after a blazing row where Dad forbade Luke to spend any more time with Kelly, and since then they've been seeing each other in secret. My parents don't have a clue that they're still together. No one does, except me and their closest friends. Even Maggie believes they parted ways. She's mentioned her fear of Kelly and miserable Mischa getting back in touch numerous times, and although I've wanted to reassure her there's no chance of that happening I haven't been able to. It's not my place.

Kelly's shoulders sink, as though she's physically deflating. I can tell how much she wants to be able to support Luke, how now more than ever she longs to be able to tell the world that she's his girlfriend.

"I wish I could see him. I wish I could give him a hug and tell him how much he means to me."

I fix my eyes on hers.

"You don't have to tell him anything. You've been together for months now, he knows how much you love him."

Kelly shakes her head. "He doesn't. He thinks I hate him."

I can see she's welling up and for one awful moment I think she might cry. I've seen enough tears in the past twenty-four hours to last me a lifetime, I don't think I can take many more.

"He doesn't think you hate him. He asked me to let you know what was going on. He wouldn't have done that if he thought you wouldn't care. You two have been through so much together already, and for what it's worth I think you're the perfect couple."

"The perfect couple no one knows about," Kelly replies sadly. "How am I supposed to support him when I'm not even allowed to be near him?"

"Bide your time. For now, I'll be the messenger for you and I'm taking Luke's phone to the hospital later too – we were in such a rush yesterday to get him checked out that we didn't even think to take it. And I'm sure that one day Mum and Dad will get over it. If they saw how much love you two have for each other I know they'd give you both their blessing. They might be old-fashioned but they're not monsters."

Kelly looks away, shamefaced, but her words catch me unawares.

"You don't understand. The last time I saw Luke we had this dreadful argument. He said he couldn't cope with the secrecy any more and that we should either tell everyone about our relationship or else call it a day. And I got so angry. Not angry at him, more angry at the situation. Angry that my sexuality has caused so many problems for us. Something inside me just snapped, and I took it all out on Luke. Do you know what the last thing I said to him was?"

I shake my head.

"The last words I said to Luke were 'drop dead'."

And then the tears do start to fall, both mine and hers.

"Oh Fern, what if he does die? What have I done?"

Maggie

The sun's shining for Fern's 21st birthday, the bright morning at odds with the current mood around The Lake House Café. Things have been strained recently for everyone, with Luke in hospital. Emotions are running high. There have been times lately where I've felt like I'm treading on eggshells, but even so I couldn't forget Fern's birthday.

May 15th.

It's Clint's birthday too, although I push that thought to the back of my mind. I don't want Fern's celebration to be sullied, and certainly not by thoughts of him.

I had come in early especially to decorate the café in Fern's honour, keen that our customers knew it was a special day. I'd pinned pretty bunting proclaiming 'Happy Birthday Fern' so the pastel triangles hung beneath the counter and wrestled with a canister of helium to fill dozens of shimmering lilac balloons. They were the centrepieces on each table, tied with silver florist ribbon that I'd painstakingly curled with a pair of scissors. It's a good job I'm an early bird because the whole process had taken longer than I'd anticipated, but the effort was worth it. If anyone deserves a fuss it's Fern.

I'd also, naturally, baked a cake – a gloriously rich red velvet cake topped with thick cream-cheese frosting. I'd known as I placed one spindly white candle at its centre what Fern's wish would be. Luke had been deemed well enough to have the operation yesterday – a gruelling ten-hour ordeal that had obviously been a worry for everyone. I knew unequivocally what Fern's wish would be for the operation to have been a success and for life to return to normal for the Hart family as quickly as possible. Thankfully early indications were that it had gone well, with the surgeon happy that the whole tumour had been successfully removed, but he'd been quick to remind Fern's parents that there were no guarantees. Luke would be carefully moni-tored, both during his immediate recovery at the hospital and as an outpatient when he was well enough to return home.

The bell above the door jangles as Fern enters the café and I grin from ear to ear at her reaction. Her jaw physi-cally drops in surprise. Individually the changes I made might only be small, but together they make quite an impact, transforming the café into a room worthy of a party.

We might not have a knees-up planned, but I'm going to make sure every person who passes through that door wishes Fern a wonderful birthday full of happiness. She needs to know exactly how important she is to everyone, and especially to me.

"Happy birthday!" I exclaim, a ripple of pleasure rushing through me at Fern's stunned response. She's giggling in embarrassment at the realisation this is all for her. "Twenty-one today!"

"I know," Fern groans. "Does this mean I'm officially a grown-up? Am I meant to suddenly have the answer to the meaning of life?"

I laugh. If only.

"I don't think so, but if you find it, let me know. I'm still searching for that one myself. Now come here, you. Let me give you a birthday squeeze."

Fern humours me, letting me wrap her up in a ginormous bear hug. Her body's warm and soft, a joy to cuddle.

"I've got a present for you, too," I say excitedly.

The younger girl's eyes light up.

"You didn't have to get me anything. I wasn't expecting a present."

"I know you weren't, but I wanted to," I insist. "Plus, I thought you might not have much to open. Your family have a lot on right now."

There's no point skirting around the issue. This has been

a matter of life and death for Luke and as special as a big birthday is, I didn't blame Fern's parents for being distracted. Naturally Luke is at the forefront of their mind at the moment, being as poorly as he's been.

Reaching beneath the counter, I pull out a neatly wrapped box. It's not quite square (but near enough) and wrapped in tastefully ruched white tissue paper tied with a silky, pale purple ribbon that matches the balloons. What can I say? My eye for detail is impeccable. Handing it over with a grin, I watch as Fern carefully peels back the layers, waiting for the reaction.

As the birthday girl takes in the robin's-egg-blue box, I know it was the perfect choice. Her eyes widen, she giggles nervously, and her hand reaches for her mouth, shocked.

"No way," she stutters finally, her voice a trembly, squeaky mess. "This is too much. You got me a present from Tiffany's?"

"Open it up and see for yourself," I tease.

Fern carefully prises the lid off the box, gasping as she sees its contents. Nestled inside is a delicate silver chain with a small round disc hanging from it, engraved with an 'F' in swirling twirling script. It's understated yet beautiful just like its new owner, a perfect keepsake for a milestone birthday.

"It's too much," Fern says, but I can tell she loves it. She's gently fingering the charm, feeling the weight of it against the pads of her fingertips.

"Nonsense," I pooh-pooh. "You're only going to turn twenty-one once. It's worth celebrating."

I smile and nod towards the cake on the counter in case it's been overshadowed by the jewellery. The cakes are the showstoppers at The Lake House Café.

"And naturally there's a sweet treat too. If you want cake for breakfast then that's fine by me – your day, your rules – or if you'd rather take it home to share with your family that's perfectly okay too. I can easily box it up."

Fern looks genuinely moved by all the fuss. She's been graciously in the background for so long that it's almost as though she's forgotten how it feels to be the centre of attention.

"Thank you," she manages, finally regaining her composure. She shakes her head in disbelief. "I'll have a slice in a minute."

"You're more than welcome," I assure her, placing my hand on her arm. "You've been such an asset to the café and more than that, you're a good friend to me too, and to Kelly." I take a deep breath before talking again. I need to choose my words carefully. "She told me everything last night, you know, about how her and Luke have been seeing each other in secret because your mum and dad can't handle the fact she's had girlfriends in the past."

Fern gasps.

"I've got to admit that hurt me, to think my daughter

can't be open about her relationships, not even with me, because of other people's prejudice. It's hard to accept, especially as her sexuality has never, ever been an issue to me. But she also told me how supportive you've been of her and Luke's relationship even when your parents have disapproved, and I can't tell you how much I appreciate that, Fern. You're a good friend and a wonderful sister, and now more than ever the pair of them are going to be grateful for having you on their side."

I'd been shocked when my daughter had broken down yesterday evening, initially thinking it was the exhaustion of her self-imposed revision timetable causing her to go into meltdown. It turns out it was good old-fashioned matters of the heart, and we'd both struggled to keep our emotions in check as she poured out her feelings. I'd been tempted to go round and give Mr and Mrs Hart a piece of my mind, tell them how Kelly's an amazing girl. How her past relationships are none of their bloody business and have no bearing whatsoever on the love she has for Luke. I'd only restrained myself because of the enormous stress they're under right now, although Kelly had looked wary when she'd seen me cracking my knuckles as though preparing to go to battle. If it hadn't been for Luke I'd have gone round all guns blazing.

"Things are different now I know they're together. It explains a lot about how erratically Kelly's been behaving.

She hates not being able to go to the hospital to visit, but she told me you'd been keeping her in the loop. She's lucky to have a friend like you, Fern. We all are. Happy birthday, sweetheart."

Fern fans her hands in front of her eyes, her lips pursed tightly together as she struggles to hold back tears.

"I'm so sorry for my parents," she says. "They're not bad people, they just don't understand." She examines the necklace once more, draping the disc over her fingers. "Can you help me put this on? I struggle when they've got fiddly clasps. I'm such a butterfingers."

"I thought you'd never ask," I jest, before gladly fixing the necklace around Fern's neck. When she turns to face me, hands outstretched in front of her as though inviting opinion, I nod my approval. "It looks lovely."

"Whoever bought it must have had exceptionally good taste," Fern teases back, and in that one moment she looks more carefree than she has in the past fortnight. It's lovely to see, and I wish I had a camera to capture a picture of her happiness in what has been a difficult time. "Speaking of taste, let's get a knife and make a start on that cake. It looks scrumptious. In fact, almost too good to eat."

I tut with modesty as I retrieve a knife from the drawer, a smart silver blade with an ornate handle that's saved for special occasions. I hand it to Fern.

"You do the honours, birthday girl."

Fern giggles. As I give a solitary and somewhat off-key rendition of 'Happy Birthday', she pushes the knife into the airy sponge. I'm not sure if it's my bum notes or that she's had her fill of time in the spotlight, but I notice her catch sight of the clock hanging on the far wall amid a multitude of dangling, lilac-coloured heart decorations. "We should have opened up already!" she exclaims.

"No one's banging the door down, so I'm sure it's fine," I assure her. "Stop worrying. Now, let me have a tiny taste of that cake before we open that door..."

The slice she hands me is enormous, but I don't complain. Just this once, the punters can wait.

Lacey

My heart's pounding in my chest and my mouth is uncomfortably full of saliva. My bedraggled hair's sticking to the sweat on my face and neck too, and that's not to mention the unpleasant sticky sensation under my armpits. Every part of me feels grimy. No wonder everyone I passed on my last lap of the park kept a wide berth. I must look like some kind of wild beast, a freakishly unkempt animal that's escaped from the circus or something. Ick.

I thought I'd be finding this running malarkey easier by now. That once I'd got past the first few horrific runs it'd suddenly fall into place and I'd be like a victorious athlete heading into the stadium at the end of a marathon – tired from the physical exertion, but with that athletic glow and built-in grit that compels the naturally sporty to push themselves until the bitter end. In reality I'm a hot mess of sweaty exhaustion. Whoever made up that crap about women 'glowing' rather than sweating obviously never saw me doing laps around the park when it's already scorching hot.

I flop on to the bench that marks the end of my route. It's nothing much to look at, just a simple slatted wooden bench with a small rectangular brass plaque on the uppermost plank of the backrest, but to me it's a welcome sight. Every run ends here, with a breathless me collapsing on to this bench. No one ever comes and sits next to me. I'm not surprised. On top of looking a right state, I'm panting like a dehydrated bulldog in a heatwave. In fact, looking down I can see the rings under the arms of my t-shirt, dark grey patches of sweat spreading out in circles where my body has cried salty tears of pain. Yuk.

I'm so tempted to reward myself with something crammed full of calories and saturated fats. I stare longingly out across the grass towards the café, its whitewashed walls shimmering under the perfect blue sky. It's calling out to me, 'Lacey, Lacey...come and stuff your face...' I'm tempted, too. I could really go for a doorstop wedge of coffee cake and a full-fat Coke right now, even though I know it'd undo all the hard work I've been putting in.

Stay focused, Lacey. Eyes on the prize and all that jazz.

Virtuously, I unscrew the cap on my water bottle and glug back its contents. The now warm liquid does little to cool me down, but I guzzle it regardless. It's become part of the routine. Run three laps of the park, sink on to Olwen

Adams' bench and then drink the remainder of my water whilst berating myself for how unfit I am. That's how my training sessions pan out, every single time.

"You should do a warm down, you know."

The voice surprises me. Using what little energy I've got, I pull my head up and lock eyes with its owner.

"I will."

I can barely manage to speak right now, let alone muster up the will to stretch. Quite frankly, I'm a bit annoyed about being disturbed. I deliberately set off early so I'd see as few people as possible, and I certainly don't want to interact with strangers when I'm as disgustingly sticky as this. All I want is to get my breath back, cool down and head home to jump in the shower. There's a new bottle of fruity shower gel all ready to crack open waiting in the bathroom, part of a gift set Uncle Carrick gave me for my birthday. I've been focussing on it the whole time I've been running: I needed something to help me stay motivated. The thought of that lemony wash kept me going during the difficult last leg and I can't wait to get home and slather it all over my achy body. It smells like bliss in a bottle.

"You need to do it before you rest," he continues. Bloody know it all. "It's no good otherwise. Defeats the object."

"I'll be fine."

I look purposefully away, over towards where the football coach is lugging some small white goalposts across the park. Some Saturdays, the ones where I have a lie-in, the children are already here kicking the balls about by the time I reach the bench. I quite like watching them, but the glamorous types on the sideline make me feel self-conscious. They're so well-groomed, like they've spent the morning going for manicures with some top-notch beautician or been to have their hair blown out just for the occasion. Maybe they have, I don't know. And they wear those neutral shades of brown – tans and camels and chocolates – as though it's in some yummy-mummy dress code, and hide behind ridiculously large dark glasses like they're celebs hiding from the paparazzi. They make me feel like a scruff in my smelly running gear with sweat dripping off my forehead. Those are the kind of women who probably *do* glow rather than sweat. They're like a whole other species.

"Nice morning though," the man continues. He doesn't seem to realise I don't want company. "Local radio said today could be the hottest day of the year so far." He sits down, just a few feet away from me at the other end of the bench. "I'm not good in the heat. I've got that fair skin that burns easily."

I look at him properly for the first time as he examines his speckly arms. He's got a scruffy mop of gingerish hair and cream-white skin with more orangey freckles sprinkled over the bridge of his nose. Definitely the type that'd need factor fifty. If I had to hazard a guess, I'd say he's a similar age to me. Maybe a year or two older, but mid-twenties at most. And he's small, in both height and build. Kind of scrawny, as though he needs a good meal.

"I'm lucky, I go brown quick."

My breath's coming back to me now, so I can just about hold a conversation without fear of collapsing with heart failure. Not that I really want to talk, but I don't want to come across as rude either.

"You're looking pretty pink right now," he says, nodding at my blotchy arms.

Whenever I run my whole body goes red. I literally look like a lobster boiling in a pan, flailing and waiting to die. Heaven knows what my face looks like: probably like I've got a whopping great tomato instead of a head.

"Let's just say running's not my forte," I reply drily.

Understatement of the century, if not the millennium.

"You're out doing it though. Good on you. Most people are laid on the settee watching hangover TV at this time on a Saturday."

"It's not really through choice," I admit. "I agreed to do a run to raise money for charity. In two months' time my family are expecting me to do a half-marathon. They've already sponsored me so I can't back out."

His mouth forms a tight O. I can't tell if he's impressed or gobsmacked by my foolishness. "A half-marathon. Ambitious."

"Stupid, more like. I don't know what I was thinking."

I shake my head and feel a drip of sweat creep down the back of my neck from beneath my hairline. Grim.

"No, no. It's great. Sometimes you have to do something totally out of your comfort zone, it's good for the soul. Is it for a charity close to your heart?"

I tense, forcing my shoulder blades together and cricking my head to either side. It's still a bit raw.

"A cancer charity."

It's all I can manage. If I say any more I'll start to cry.

"Cancer's a bastard of a disease," he spits.

I tilt my head up, taken aback by the sharpness in his tone.

He continues as he clocks my reaction, "It killed my Nana Olwen. Breast cancer." He exhales, a long audible breath escaping his lips. "It's two years since she died now, but it doesn't get any easier. I still miss her every day."

He runs his finger along the brass plaque on the back of the bench and although I've seen it many times, I read it properly now.

In Loving Memory of
Olwen Adams
Who Was Happiest at Fir Tree Park

"Oh," I say awkwardly, registering the connection. "I'm sorry, I didn't realise this was your bench."

"It's not really mine, it's Nana's," he says with a shrug. "My mum had it put here as a memorial after she died and I come here sometimes. I prefer it to the cemetery. It helps me feel closer to her, if that doesn't sound weird."

I think back to Auntie Marilyn's funeral, to them lowering the dark wood coffin into the hole in the ground as we stood helplessly watching. She'd have hated everything about that day: the gloom, the misery. How I'd clung to Uncle Carrick's arm because I was scared if I let go I'd crumble. We all wore black, scared to stray from tradition for fear of upsetting Uncle Lenny even though Auntie Marilyn was one of the most colourful people in town. She'd had bleached blonde hair and a collection of butterfly tattoos on her arms. She was a walking rainbow, until the cancer came.

"It doesn't sound weird. I hate cemeteries."

I'd not been back since that grey November day, not ready for the finality of seeing the headstone to hit. I'd rather bury my feelings than my beloved auntie any day of the week.

"Yeah, they freak me out too. Too quiet. And I hate leaving flowers, because I know by the next time I go they'll be dead. I prefer it here, where there's life and nature. Somewhere I knew Nana Olwen was happy." He smiles and his face lights up, emerald eyes shining like gemstones. "She used to bring me here on days out when I was little.

We'd bring a kite and try to fly it, but it barely got off the ground. Then I'd nag and nag until she'd give in and take me on the pedalos. I always wanted to go on the blue one, number five. I was convinced it went faster than the others."

I shake my head. "Nuh-huh. Number three, every time."

He stares at me.

"The orange one?" he says in disbelief. "The pedal was stuck half the time! That was the worst of the lot!"

I laugh despite myself.

"Quite the pedalo connoisseur, aren't you?" I joke.

"I've not been on one in at least fifteen years," he says with a chuckle. "But I know number three was a waste of space."

"Orange is my favourite colour."

Not that I'd really thought about my favourite colour since primary school when we were obsessed with making those origami fortune tellers where you had to pick which colour you liked best, but it probably still is. Cheerful, uplifting and bright, the same colour as the walls in Auntie Marilyn's living room. Plus, it was impossible to be miserable when you were wearing orange. That's why I'd plumped for the tangerine trainers. I'd thought they'd encourage me to keep on running even when I didn't feel like it. A small reminder to myself of why I was doing this in the first place.

"Mine's green," he says, brushing down his khaki t-shirt. It's camouflage effect, as though it's army issue, but I can't imagine he's the military type. He seems too little for one thing, and not quite tough enough for another. His shorts are the same colour but a tad darker. He'd blend in with the surroundings, but for his dazzling hair.

There's a lull in the conversation, a silence falling between us, but it's not uncomfortable. The birds are still chirruping away in the trees and the sound of chattering children arriving for football practice is background noise.

"Well, that was a conversation stopper," I say finally, picking up my water bottle from the bench.

"Which bit? Cancer or favourite colours?"

"Both, most likely. Anyway, it's time for me to head off. If I don't get in the shower soon I'll stink like this for a week."

"Nice," he says with a smirk, but he doesn't look mean. I don't think he could look mean if he tried. He's like a little ginger hobbit, or a red-headed Mark Owen. Cute and smiley and totally unthreatening. Ed Sheeran! That's who he looks like, but scrawnier. "Maybe we'll run into each other again?"

"Maybe," I say. "I'm here most Saturdays."

"Good to know," he replies before offering his hand. "I'm Warren Jones."

"Lacey Braithwaite." I smile, holding out my own hand in return. Thankfully it's a bit less sticky than the rest of me.

"Lacey Braithwaite," he repeats thoughtfully as our palms connect. "Nice to have met you."

I hold up my hand in a wave before walking across the grass past the immaculate row of football mummies, wondering if I'll ever see him again.

"See you around," Warren calls after me. "And don't forget – cool down next time!"

Pearl

" Come on in, Carrick, for goodness sake. You're putting me on edge hovering on the doorstep like that."

He's twitching, shifting his weight between his feet like a toddler needing a wee. Jigging, that's what he's doing. His dark green trousers are swaying from side to side and he's got a shy little smile on his podgy round face. Well, what I can see of his face, which isn't much. It's hidden behind the enormous bunch of flowers he's holding out; beautiful open blooms which I'm guessing he's cut fresh from the rose garden in the park. Lemon yellows, pastel pinks and delicate peach shades mixed haphazardly together, reminding me of the ice cream carts at the seaside with their colourful fruity cool-me-down treats. It's as though Carrick's brought a handful of summer with him.

"These are for you," he says, self-consciously thrusting the bouquet at me. "I know it's a bit old-fashioned, but I think it's nice to give a lady flowers. Especially since I cultivated them with my own fair hands."

"Thank you," I say, slightly overwhelmed. "They're beautiful."

No one's given me flowers since Alf died, and although I've pottered about a bit in the garden and cut back the fuchsias, which threatened to go berserk if I left them to their own devices, I haven't bought myself any either. They'd become so entrenched with the horrific memories of the funeral that I couldn't face buying them, having their fragrance filling the lounge and bringing back all the sadness of that day.

These flowers are different though. Whether it's their delicate scent, fresh and light, or their warmth, or that they're not presented in a rigid, pristine way like the funeral wreaths had been, I don't know. All I do know is that they're not scaring me, causing a metallic tang to fill my mouth in the way it does when I pass the small shop on the high street that dealt with Alf's funeral flowers. These lift my spirit, bringing the beauty of nature back into the house after a long, cold winter.

"They're not much, I know," he says modestly as I usher him through. He brushes his work boots on the coarse mat in the hall and I can't help but think his feet must be sweltering in them on a hot day like today. I'd contemplated flip-flops when I'd taken Mitzi round the block for a stroll earlier.

"Don't do them down," I shush. "It's a long time since I've had a gentleman bring me flowers, let me tell you now." I clutch them protectively to my body, the pleasant floral fragrance dancing in my nostrils. "I love them. In fact, I'll put them straight in a vase, if it's not terribly rude of me to desert a guest. It's so humid in here, even with the windows wide open, and I'd hate them to wilt through carelessness."

"Go ahead." He smiles warmly, scooping the hat from his head and ruffling his hair. It's thinning on top, like many men his age. Alf had been receding for years and by the time he passed away he was bald as a coot; Carrick had a lustrous head of hair in comparison, even though it was now a pure, brilliant white. I remember it from years ago, a sandy colour: the same as manila envelopes or sanded-down wood.

I rummage in the cupboard under the sink for a suitable vase. There's quite a collection gathering dust down there. Tall, slender flutes for a single stem, a red-glass square vase that had been a gift from my sister-in-law one Christmas past, a cut crystal bowl that is far too pretty to be hidden away, but has never been on display as the glass cabinet is fit to burst with sentimental souvenirs and the tea set Alf and I were given by his parents on our wedding day. I'd very nearly got it out today in preparation for Carrick's visit, but it didn't feel right to do so. Although I knew there was nothing untoward about his visit, nothing more sinister than two old friends having a catch-up, I couldn't quite bring myself to use the best china, instead using the everyday Cornishware teapot, the familiar blue and white stripes which coordinated with the country-style kitchen feeling more appropriate. It meant we'd have to drink from mugs – I'm not even sure if they make cups and saucers to match the teapot – but Carrick's not the sort to have airs and graces. Anyway, we've known each other long enough. It's not as though I've got any kind of impression to make.

Carrick strolls through as I'm filling a wide-necked marbled vase with water and shuffling the roses into a loose arrangement.

"They look all right in that, don't they?" he beams, pulling out a dining chair and settling himself down. I'd already set the table, laying a fresh white cloth with broderie anglaise trim over the well-used surface. Not that either of us would care, but it made the kitchen look a bit more presentable, and I'd laid out an array of cakes on a two-tier cake stand. It almost looked like a proper little tea party for two.

"I'll pop the kettle on," I say, filling it with water and flicking the switch at the wall to kick-start it into life before placing the flowers in the centre of the table. They brought a sparkle back into the kitchen, made it seem more lived-in. I'd forgotten what a difference it made having more than just myself in the house, too – well, myself and Mitzi. The whole energy of the place was different.

"You must be gasping after being out in that heat all day."

"Maggie's made sure I've not gone without," he says, patting his belly. "She filled my flask twice this afternoon and threw in a gingerbread man for good measure. It's not like I need fattening up."

"Oh, give over. You look fine to me, and you're working all day lifting and carrying. You get plenty of exercise going about your everyday business. One little gingerbread man's not going to do any harm."

He shakes his head ruefully. "The doctor said I should try and lose a few pounds, but it's not easy at our age."

"And here I am tempting you with even more cake," I say with a grimace, taking in the cake stand laden with temptation. "Don't feel you have to have some just to be polite. I won't be offended."

"Don't be daft, this is quite the spread you've put on." I notice him eyeing up the chocolate chunk shortbread and the generous wedges of banana loaf piled high on the cake stand. "And everything looks delicious. I hope you've not gone to too much trouble."

I can't hold back the laugh and it rings loud around the kitchen.

"What's so funny?" he asks.

"It was no trouble at all," I explain. "I went to the café and had Maggie bag up some of her finest supplies to bring back. It's not as though I've been slaving away over a hot stove all day."

"And there was I thinking you'd been baking up a storm," he says, shaking his head with mock disappointment. There's a glint in his eye that shows he's only joking. "Not worth the effort, am I?"

There's something about the flirtatious nature of the comment, that and the fluttering low in my stomach, that makes me relieved when the kettle noisily clicks off. I reach for the mugs from the wooden mug-tree on the work surface and bring them to the table, ignoring his question for as long as possible.

"We go back a long way, Carrick." I make a conscious effort to keep my tone light. "It's not like I have anything to prove to you after all these years, is it?"

"I suppose not," he agrees amiably.

It's strange having a male in the house. Carrick's so at ease, his enormous smile filling the room and his worn old boots comfortably attached to his feet lounging under the table. He can't feel the atmosphere in the same way I do, surely? If he did, he wouldn't be looking so relaxed, so totally at ease. It's not like the atmosphere is bad, it's just so definitely *there*. The past, hanging unspoken between us.

"Anyway," I continue, "everyone loves Maggie's cakes. It's

less of a gamble than me having a go at making something and then setting the house alight in the process."

I laugh, recalling some of my previous baking disasters. There was the time I put self-raising flour *and* bicarbonate of soda in a cake mix and the whole lot erupted in the oven like Mount Etna in her heyday, not to mention the rock cakes, which lived up to their name so well that they caused Alf to lose a tooth. He'd never let me live it down, grumbling good-naturedly about how my baking had resulted in dentistry fees that almost bankrupted him.

"I'm no Mary Berry. Even those packet mixes are a stretch for me. Let's just say I'm fine at cooking, but baking is a different matter entirely."

"Oh, I'm sure you're not so bad."

"Honestly, I'm terrible. You're far safer in Maggie's capable hands."

I've filled the teapot now and I'm going to have to sit with him. I really need to pull myself together. I'm a grown woman! I was married for thirty-seven years, so it's not as though I'm not used to being in the company of a man. But this is Carrick, and there's always been that undercurrent. There's so much we don't talk about. The distant days we've brushed under the carpet in the hope that by hiding them away we'll be able to forget about them all together.

"I'm partial to her lemon drizzle," he admits with a smile. It's the same smile as back then, easy and generous. It was the very thing that had caught my eye in the first place, back when we were naïve teenagers without a care in the world.

"Everyone's partial to Maggie's lemon drizzle," I correct. "It had completely sold out by the time I got to the café, I'm afraid. And Maggie, bless her, was so apologetic. She even offered to make another and drop it round on her way home from work, but I told her not to be daft, that as long as we had something sweet and calorific it'd be fine."

"She's a good girl, Maggie," Carrick says fondly. "Kind. Nothing is ever too much trouble for her."

"I'm so glad she's doing well for herself at last. When she had all that trouble with that bastard Clint..."

My voice trails off, but my jaw tenses at the thought of that cruel, cruel man. He'd not had an ounce of decency in him, Clint Thornhill. He used to strut about like he was better than everyone else and all the girls swooned as if he was something special. In reality he was a grubby good-for-nothing; he'd proved that with the string of women and the crime. I'd been glad when he'd been locked up: the world felt a safer place for it.

I mustn't be doing a very good job of hiding my anger, because Carrick's watching me with caution. He's probably afraid my temper's going to make one of its appearances and I'll fling the whole contents of the table across the room. Heaven forbid that cake goes to waste.

"He's locked up," Carrick says sensibly. "He can't do any harm from behind bars, Pearl. Anyway, I thought this was meant to be a pleasant evening. Let's not spoil it by talking about him."

"Yes, yes. I know you're right." But I'm still shaking as I pour the tea, my hand trembling despite my best efforts. Clint's sentence was almost complete. He'd be out next month, and then what would happen?

I feel Carrick's hand close in over mine and I automatically tense. Although we see each other regularly it's usually in public places like the park or down the pub on quiz night. We're never alone like this.

I can't remember the last time our bodies touched. The skin on his hands has aged now, weathered. All those years of digging and pruning and spending baking hot days exposed to the sun have left them rough, and his skin a good few shades darker than it was in his youth. He squeezes gently, and I can't help but wonder if he's noticing the physical change in me too. The skin on my hands is different now, thin and papery, and the grey-blue veins are raised and closer to the surface. They look ugly, old.

"Come on," he says. "I'll be mother."

My heart heaves in my chest as he takes the teapot from my hand. I hadn't realised how tightly I'd been gripping the handle, my knuckles rigid, until I relax. I lean back against the upright back of the chair. It's hard and uncomfortable, but reassuringly sturdy. With my swimming head and my tight chest I need that security, something to make me feel present in the world.

He pours the tea and all I can focus on is the absurdity of the situation. The roses on the table, so ordinary and extraordinary all at once. Mitzi asleep, a rarity in itself, along the door frame like one of those sausage dog draught excluders, except she's an actual sausage dog, not some nasty cheap prize you might win at a funfair. But most of all Carrick, sat in my kitchen as though it's the most normal and natural thing in the world.

"Calm yourself down and have a cuppa," he says reassuringly as he places a sugar-loaded tea in front of me. It's as though he can read my mind, see the weight of my troubles pressing down on me.

"I don't know if I can." It sounds melodramatic, but the whole situation is bubbling up inside. "It's all just so much, you know? Having you here brings it all back."

"I'd never have come if I'd thought it would upset you like this, Pearl. That's the last thing I'd ever want."

There's that softness in his eyes again, and something else I can't decipher. Sadness? Pity? Love?

"People say time heals, but I don't know if I believe that it does."

A wave of sorrow washes over me and my own eyes are moistened. I reach blindly for a napkin and dab at them, breathing deeply to try and regain composure. I can't break down like this. I must remain strong, stoic.

"We did the right thing." He looks straight at me, almost as though he's looking into the depths of my mind. "It wasn't the easy thing, not then and not now. But we knew that, didn't we? We did what we had to do." He's wearing a serious expression now and his hands cup the mug so I can no longer see the iconic design.

"Do you ever wonder how it would have been? If things had been different?"

I hold my breath as I wait for his answer, hoping he feels the same as I do. I wouldn't wish the long nights of heartache on anyone, but there would be a crumb of comfort in knowing that it's not been me solely bearing the pain and longing all this time.

He sighs, a long heavy sigh as though he's breathing the past out of him. If only it were that simple.

"Every day. I wonder 'what if' every single day."

Hearing him say it out loud doesn't make me feel better like I expect it to; if anything, I feel worse. The tears that had been welling up crash against me, streaming down my cheeks so any decorum I've been fighting to maintain is lost.

"Sssh..." he says, drawing me in close to his chest. He smells of the outdoors, freshly mown grass and mulch. His enormous hands stroke my hair and I feel like I did when

I was a little girl, when my mum would stroke my hair to help me get to sleep. "There's still time, it's not too late. And it's up to you, I'll do whatever you think is best. Just please don't cry, Pearl. Whatever you do, please don't cry."

But as I bury my head in Carrick's broad shoulder, I can't help myself. These tears have been bottled up for far too long and as his t-shirt dampens with the pain I've kept in me for all these years, I know something is going to have to change. He's right, there's still time.

Pulling back, I bring myself to say the words I never thought I'd hear myself say.

"I think it's time to be honest. Time to tell them the truth. We're not getting any younger, and I can't go to my grave with this gnawing away at me."

The colour drains from his cheeks, but he doesn't argue. He pulls me in tighter and places the faintest of kisses on my forehead.

"If that's what you want, sweetheart, then that's what we'll do."

I can see the cakes in the background, untouched. I wonder if they'll keep. I don't think either of us will have much of an appetite after this. We've got a lot to talk about, Carrick and me.

June 2017

Maggie

"I hate being late. It throws me for the day." Fern places her hands on her cheeks and shakes her head, presumably in a bid to refocus. Her ponytail sways from side to side behind her. "I can't calm myself down."

"Come on," I encourage her. "You're not even late, not really. Talk to me. You know anything you say goes no further than here. 'A problem shared is a problem halved', that's what they say, isn't it? So go on. Halve your problem."

Fern sighs heavily. She looks totally and utterly defeated by life. "It's Luke," she says finally. "Things are worse."

"Worse? I thought he was out of hospital now?" I'd been foolish enough to assume that him coming home meant he was on the mend, but then again I know nothing about brain tumours, other than that they're serious and potentially deadly. I've no idea about recovery times or relapses, secondary symptoms or anything else. Who does, unless they're unfortunate enough to be affected by it? I hadn't liked to pry, so although I'd listened when Fern had explained the operation and the follow-up care Luke would be receiving from the hospital, I hadn't pressed for information.

I certainly hadn't brought it up with Kelly. She's mostly taken to shutting herself in her room under the guise of revising, but I can see her heart's not in it any more. Her whole outlook has changed. She's lost her charming-yet-infuriating backchat, and she's far more solemn.

Fern nods glumly. "He's home, but Maggie, he's so miserable. He's exhausted, half the weight he used to be and he feels like a failure because he's not well enough to sit his exams. It doesn't help that he's not got the energy to go out because all he wants to do is see Kelly. He's so *down*. He doesn't look like an eighteen-year-old: he looks like a frail old man on his deathbed and it scares me."

A single tear trails down Fern's cheek, although her large hazel eyes are brimming with them. Her lower lip trembles and my maternal instinct kicks in as I bundle Fern into an all-encompassing hug. Neither of us speak, our pain-soaked silence saying more than any amount of meaningless words. I just hold her, and hope that will be enough.

The chirruping birdsong wafts in through the open window, the skittish blue tits ignorant of Fern's heartbreak, and the coffee machine makes its familiar loud gurgle, like a giant's stomach calling out for food. There's a yappy bark of a dog, probably Mitzi, the sausage dog that belongs to Clint's Auntie Pearl. Pearl's always up bright and early on a Saturday so she can let the frisky pup off her lead before the swarms of youngsters claim the park as their own. We might be peaceful, Fern and I, but the noise of life goes on around us. It reminds me how the world keeps on turning, even when we don't believe it possibly can.

"Is there any way I can help?"

I wish I could wave a magic wand to make Luke's pain bugger off once and for all, but in the absence of witchcraft and miracles, I'm hoping there's something – anything – I can do to make life easier for the Hart family. I thank my lucky stars that neither Josh nor Kelly ever had any health issues to speak of. A few nosebleeds, the usual list of childhood illnesses and a broken thumb was as bad as it ever got. I can't even begin to imagine how it must feel for Fern's parents, to know their child has a brain tumour. It must be every parent's nightmare.

"Nothing."

"If you think of anything, you just ask, promise? I only wish I could do more."

Fern's lips are pressed tightly together, as if she's putting all her efforts into not giving in to the tears that threaten to fall. Her breathing is heavy and deliberate, her hand clutched over her heart, bobbing with the rise and fall of her chest.

"At the moment we're in limbo. We don't know whether the surgery has got rid of all the aggressive cells or not and all we can do is trust and hope, but no one really knows."

Fern looks exhausted as she stares, fixated, at a point on the far wall. She's been put through the emotional wringer lately, her whole family has. She clamps one hand between the other, vigorously massaging her fingertips into the back of her hand.

"I'm scared he's going to die, Maggie. He's my little brother! He should be doing all the things teenagers are supposed to do – drinking cheap cider down by the river and getting a tattoo on a whim. Scaring my parents half to death by not coming home until four in the morning. He shouldn't be having his head sliced open and worrying about whether or not he'll make it through the night."

"No," I reply sadly. "He shouldn't. But he's being cared for by world-class specialists who'll do all they can to make sure he's as well as he can possibly be. And everyone's willing him on." I smile. "Having family like you by his side must be an enormous comfort to Luke. Don't underestimate the power of love. It's not a cure, but it's a brilliant painkiller."

Fern reaches for a serviette from the silver dispenser on the table and uses it to dab her eyes before loudly blowing her nose. She shakes herself down and plasters on a smile, which I know is little more than a brave face.

"Come on, we can't sit around all day," she says, her voice clipped. "There are hungry people in that park and they all need feeding. Let's open up."

She strides purposefully to the door, flipping over the wooden sign hanging on its glass panel to indicate The Lake House Café is open for business.

I watch on, impressed by the younger girl's strength of mind. Fern's more resilient than she realises, but then maybe we all are. When Clint had been sentenced I'd thought my world was ending – suddenly I found myself a single mum with no income and no qualifications. It had seemed hopeless at first. Then slowly but surely I'd learned to cope. More than cope, in fact. The children had thrived in the safe home environment I'd provided and when I'd opened the café they'd been delighted. (Their popularity had soared overnight. All their classmates were desperate to come in to taste the creamy milkshakes Kelly and Josh promised were the tastiest in the area, not to mention the cakes.) And now my children are maturing into well-rounded, polite adults and I'm the one who's delighted. They're my greatest accomplishments. I survived the days where I could have torn my hair out, the ones I'd willed them to stop with their incessant bickering or endless streams of 'whys'. I did what I'd never thought possible – rode the storm and came out the other side.

I say a silent prayer that Luke will too.

Fern

Surprisingly, I feel better for talking. The strain of keeping Luke and Kelly's secret from my parents is still weighing heavy but at least by having Maggie to confide in I've been able to offload some of my worries. No one I've loved has ever been seriously ill before, and I never would have thought it possible to be so exhausted. It's impossibly hard watching someone you love fade before your very eyes, to feel helpless and guilty and selfishly relieved that it's them going through this not you. But voicing my troubles helped. No wonder people pay vast amounts of money to talk to therapists. Not everyone's fortunate enough to have someone like Maggie Thornhill on hand to share their burdens with.

I watch on with interest as my boss balances a stack of plastic beakers on a tray. She pours some raisins into a bowl and adds that to the tray too, placing it alongside the tall, clear jug of water.

"That's a nice gesture. For the football lot?" I enquire. I'm sure my boss is just looking for an excuse to talk to the coach, but I keep my suspicions to myself.

"I didn't have enough oranges to slice into the traditional quarters for a half-time refreshment, so this'll have to do," Maggie replies modestly, confirming in not so many words that it definitely *is* for the footballers.

I can see right through her tactics though. Any excuse to spend time with that Italian stallion she's been mooning over.

"I'm sure the children will be delighted at the thought of a bonus snack midway through their training session."

Maggie beams as she picks up the tray.

"I hope so."

Taking extra care not to slip as she walks down the ramp in the café's doorway, my eyes follow Maggie as she makes her way towards the children. They're squealing excitedly as they play a team game, weaving between the ankle-high cones with the ball at their feet, cheering their friends on with as much passion as any Manchester United or Liverpool supporter.

Paolo looks up, surprised to see Maggie standing on the touchline bearing unexpected refreshments. Blowing the silver whistle he has on a string around his neck, the children obediently freeze.

I can see Maggie swooning from here. She can protest

all she likes, but I'd recognise that look anywhere. It's the same one that's in all the films, the music videos, on every TV programme; the one my brother has when he talks about Kelly, and her when she talks about him. The one I have when I think about Josh.

Bewilderment. Yearning. Desire.

Maggie

"I thought your sporting protégés might want some fresh water. It's a hot day. We don't want anyone keeling over."

I crouch to place the tray on the freshly-mown lawn, grass cuttings tickling my fingers as I do so.

"That's very kind," Paolo says, brushing his dark hair out of his eyes before tucking one of the wayward strands behind his ear. "Come on, team," he says, gesturing for the swarm of children to come and get a drink. "We're lucky today, Maggie's brought us all a drink and a snack from her café."

I swallow hard.

He's gorgeous.

And he remembered my name.

The group is mainly made up of boys keen to emulate the latest Premier League stars, but there are a few girls too, hair scraped back off their bright red faces into severe pony tails.

It's lovely to see children so passionate about sport and exercise. Neither of my two had ever been bothered, especially not Kelly. She wouldn't have wanted to spend her Saturdays playing football. Even as a young girl she'd been all about hair and makeup, begging me to let her paint her toenails electric blue or to buy her a stick of tinted lip salve. (The teachers would let her use that on medicinal grounds, whereas a lipstick would be confiscated. She could be so wily at times, could Kelly.) Josh had only been interested in experimenting, taking apart the TV remote and trying to work out how to successfully piece it all together again. His logical, scientific mind had wanted to discover how things worked and he didn't have a sporty bone in his body, then or now.

The children gulp down the water with relief, happy to take a short break from their physical exertion, and Paolo smiles. "They've been working very hard today so they're ready for a drink."

"That's what I thought. It's hotter than it looks." Not as hot as you, I want to add, but of course I don't. That'd be ridiculous. Far too forward.

Pepe's in the middle of a group of boys, all wearing identical Réal Madrid kits. It surprises me that he's not wearing one belonging to one of the top Italian teams, but then again, kids are always attracted to the most successful teams. I pity the poor mothers who have to try and keep them gleaming white – and it's nearly always the mother's, not the father's, job to stay on top of the mountains of washing their children produce. The boys have already managed to cake their knees with mud and get streaky grass stains on their shorts. The kits will be in need of a hot wash after training. The kids too, most likely.

"Some of the mums stay to watch and they might have a drink for their children. But a lot of them forget," Paolo says with a wry smile. "Everyone's in such a rush to get here that they don't think about staying hydrated. They just want to make sure they don't miss out."

I inadvertently look over to a cluster of women sat on the bench observing the green. They might not have time to pack up a drink but they've found time to style themselves, I think grimly. They're flawlessly dressed in crisp blouses, Capri trousers and killer heels, oversized handbags in muted shades of tan and beige resting at their feet. And they've all got a full face of make-up on and none of them have so much as a hair out of place. Kelly would approve of the attention to detail, but I find myself immediately wishing I'd put on at least a sweep of mascara and a dab of lipstick. Compared to these beauties I'm practically naked, facially at least.

"Gabrielle has a drink for Pepe," he continues proudly, waving at one of the glamorous women.

A beautiful young woman beams back in response. She's

wearing a ridiculously large pair of sunglasses with huge black lenses that cover the majority of her face, but I can see from the caramel highlights in her dark hair that she's one of the young, glamorous mums. The queen bee, most likely, going by how the other mums are fawning over her.

"She's so organised. Pepe and I are incredibly lucky," he adds affectionately.

I stiffen. Jealousy is an unattractive trait, but the familiar sensation builds within me, making me feel uglier still. It's coursing through my veins as the realisation hits that this stunning woman is not only Pepe's mum, but Paolo's wife.

"Incredibly lucky," I echo, before smiling half-heartedly, making my excuses and quietly retreating to the sanctuary of the café. After seeing Gabrielle, all I want to do is run and hide. I couldn't compete with a woman like that, even if I wanted to.

Pearl

The sun is still shining overhead, but the heavens have suddenly and unexpectedly opened. I wish I'd brought a brolly. So much for an evening stroll and an opportunity to talk. With the warm rain falling, Mitzi's more skittish than ever and desperate to get back home.

"I'd put money on there being a rainbow later," Carrick states with confidence. "They often follow these summer showers."

"Maybe," I reply noncommittally.

We're not here to talk about rainbows, he knows that full well. We've got far more pressing issues to discuss. Since our conversation a few weeks back I've been struggling to focus on anything. It's just as well I took early retirement, as I'd have had no chance keeping my mind on the job. It was hard enough focussing on the Antiques Roadshow on Sunday night, let alone anything that'd require I engage my brain.

Carrick links his arm through mine and I automatically flinch, casting my eyes across the park to make sure no one's seen us.

He can obviously sense my discomfort as he removes his arm with a laboured sigh.

"People will talk, Carrick."

"If you're serious about us telling people the truth, they'll be talking anyway. Us walking through the park arm in arm is small fry in comparison to what you're proposing."

He looks pinched; stung.

"Are you sure you want to do this?" he continues. "Because I've been thinking, and I'm really not sure it's for the best, Pearl. It's not only us it affects, is it? There are so many people who could potentially get hurt..."

My patience wains. I can feel my blood pressure rising.

"So we keep our mouths shut and pretend it never happened, is that what you're saying?" My voice is snappy in tone, not my usual light and airy sing-song. The beginning of bad-tempered Pearl. "What happened to you saying you'd do whatever I wanted? Have you forgotten that?"

"I've not forgotten," he says patiently, "but there are other people to consider. People who are already vulnerable. I've been spending a lot of time with Lacey since Marilyn died and she's fragile. She doesn't need any upheaval right now."

My heart weighs heavy in my chest. Carrick's sister

Marilyn had been one of those people who had an enormous presence. She was carefree and wild, a bohemian free spirit. The community was duller without her, in every sense. She'd had compassion and verve, and a way of connecting with people as though she could see deep into their souls. Spiritual, that's the word. She'd been spiritual.

"It's hard, I know, especially for Lacey. You, Marilyn and Lenny pretty much raised her. But can you really keep it a secret forever? Would you be able to rest going to your grave with something like this on your conscience?"

"I don't know." He looks tired, I note. "It's been forty years, Pearl. It's a long time – a lifetime. And what's to gain by opening a can of worms now?"

I stop, fixing my gaze firmly on his. A raindrop slips down my jawline to my chin, irritatingly itchy.

"I can't go on living a lie, Carrick, and what's more, I'm not willing to. People look at me and see Alf's widow, I recognise the out-and-out pity in their eyes. 'Poor Pearl, all alone with just the dog for company', that's what they're thinking. But that's not the whole truth. I've got a family ready and waiting, and if they only knew I might not be 'poor Pearl' any more."

"We made our decision all those years ago, and rightly or wrongly we have to live with that. We can't change the past. Heck, I wish we could. There are so many things I'd do differently, given half the chance."

My stomach fizzes at his words. Does he mean me? The baby? Both?

"Really?"

"Really. We didn't know what we had back then, did we? We were too young to appreciate it."

Yet again, I'm not sure what he's referring to.

"Well, I'll tell you something for nothing," I say, the fire within me showing no sign of dimming. "We're not young any more, Carrick: in fact, we're getting old. Every month I'm crossing out another name in my address book. Alf, Marilyn, Olwen…similar ages to us. That's why we've got to live for today, because we don't know how many tomorrows we've got left."

He's mulling it over, I can tell, and although I hate myself for stooping so low, I angle my head so I'm gazing up at him through my eyelashes. I might not be nineteen anymore, and Carrick Braithwaite's torch may not shine as brightly for me as it did back then, but it's worth a try. I can't do anything without his support, and I wouldn't want to. Getting him on side is the only way, and I'm not above using my feminine wiles. Let people say whatever they want. He's right, they'll have plenty to gossip about soon enough.

"I suppose," he grumbles, admitting defeat. "But give me a bit of time, a chance to talk to Lacey. I won't tell her everything yet, but I want to prepare her gently. It's going to come as an almighty shock to her."

"Not only her," I reply. "I think there are a lot of people around here who are going to be shocked when they hear the truth."

As the sky brightens and a familiar arced glow of colour emerges, Carrick slips his arm into mine once more. This time I don't shrug him off.

Lacey

"Come on in," grunts Uncle Lenny, nodding in the direction of the front room, as though I've not been in this house hundreds, if not thousands, of times before.

He's looking thin, and his face sallow. I wonder if he's eating enough. Auntie Marilyn had always done the cooking, enjoying experimenting with flavours. She came up with some strange concoctions from time to time, but usually she'd throw together something that would set tastebuds flickering with pleasure. She just had the knack: maybe it was her creative flair. I can't imagine Uncle Lenny being as adventurous now she's gone. Who knows what he's eating? Probably nothing more than fish-paste sandwiches and half a tomato.

"Thanks, Uncle Lenny."

I wipe my feet on the doormat before stepping inside, the pang in my chest as tight as ever as the emptiness I anticipated feeling as soon as I entered the house hits me.

As much as I knew she wouldn't be here, Auntie Marilyn's absence all but winds me – but I make a conscious effort to slip off my sorrow along with my shoes. If she were still alive, she'd berate me for bringing negativity into the house.

The house itself isn't much to look at from the outside – a mid-terrace covered with grey-and-white pebble dashing – but the trailing hanging baskets and large clay plant pots filled with riotous shades of cerise, marmalade orange and sunshine yellow add much-needed bursts of colour. It warms my heart that Uncle Lenny asked Uncle Carrick to make them up. The locals have come to expect the summer floral extravagance, one of Auntie Marilyn's little quirks that delighted the children in the neighbourhood, along with the hideous garden gnomes she'd collected from car boots and jumble sales over the years. She'd loved their cheeky expressions.

"Is Uncle Carrick here yet?"

Uncle Lenny nods. "Got here half an hour ago. He's already helped himself to two rounds of toast. With jam," he adds pointedly, as though that makes all the difference.

"I bet he's been too busy to stop for lunch again," I say, shrugging out of my cardigan. It's warm in here. "He never takes a break; he works too hard."

"He's a dedicated soul, just like Marilyn. Your family are grafters, that's for sure."

He doesn't mention Dad. They've never seen eye to eye,

what with Dad and his delusions of grandeur. Uncle Lenny is as far from grand as you can get, but he's got a good heart beneath the sullen exterior. He's a deep thinker, which is his strength and his weakness. It makes him both empathetic and prone to bouts of heavy-hearted depression. Uncle Carrick thinks that's why Uncle Lenny loved Auntie Marilyn so much. Her exuberance was enough for the both of them and helped him remain on an even keel. He's not been the same since she died, although I'm not sure any of us have. Someone with her presence and personality is a major loss for us all.

"Speaking of grafting, you'll never guess how far I ran today."

His eyes light up.

"Go on..."

"Nine miles!"

My chest puffs out with pride. It was my longest run yet, and although my body was telling me I'd pushed it to its limit by mile eight, with Warren jogging alongside me for the final mile I'd managed to keep propelling myself forward somehow. He'd been more out of breath than me by the end, and he'd only covered a fraction of the distance I had.

"That's fantastic. You've almost cracked it, haven't you? It's that Braithwaite spirit. You're not just grafters, you're bloody stubborn, the lot of you."

I grin, knowing he's right. "I think you'll find 'determined' is the word you're looking for. Once we put our mind to something we go out and do it. That's not such a bad attribute to have, is it?"

He reaches out and places his hand on my cheek.

"It's not bad at all. She'd have been so proud of you."

I swallow down the lump in my throat, gently but firmly pushing his hand away before walking into the living room, where Uncle Carrick's slouched in an armchair, cup of tea propped on the arm, half-empty packet of chocolate-coated Digestive biscuits placed on the other.

He jumps up like he's been shot. "Lacey! We've been waiting for you."

I look at the clock on the sideboard, nestled in amongst the statuettes and photographs and other odds and bods. Half past seven, just like we'd agreed.

"I'm bang on time," I point out. "It was you that got here early."

"Maybe you're right." He wraps me up in a hug, holding me so tightly that I'm sure my bones are cracking. Or perhaps that's just because I'm feeling fragile after today's exploits. "How're you doing, anyway? Did I hear you say you ran nine miles today?"

He looks impressed, and it pleases me. With my parents so far away, the approval of Uncle Carrick and Uncle Lenny has always been important. Never mind that I'm a fully grown woman who shouldn't need an ego boost. It's nice to know there are people rooting for me, people who're proud that I'm trying to make a difference, no matter how small.

"You did. Every muscle in my body is reminding me of it too," I joke. "I've no idea where I'll be able to pull another four miles from. I was running quite literally on empty today. And I'm sorry, but I'm going to have to sit down. My legs are like lead weights."

I sink into the sofa, sighing with relief as I flop back into the soft pile of cushions.

"You're amazing." Uncle Carrick beams. "You've really committed yourself to this training, and I know it's not been easy. I'm surprised you've managed to keep the momentum going. Work all day and then running in the evenings, not to mention the morning runs on weekends. You've put your heart and soul into it. No one can say you've not tried your best."

"Well, I don't want to make an idiot of myself," I say bashfully.

I don't tell him there had been many a moment when I'd considered throwing in the towel. That all changed when Warren started coming to the park to support me though. Knowing he'd be there spurred me on.

"We're proud of you, aren't we, Len?"

Uncle Carrick widens his eyes and nods at Uncle Lenny, prompting him to add to the words of encouragement.

"More than proud. And that's why we wanted to give you this."

He pulls out a long rectangular envelope from behind the clock and hands it to me. It's thick, stuffed full, and as I open it I gasp, the wedge of bluey-green five-pound notes glinting cheekily at me.

"Where's this come from? There must be a hundred pounds here!"

"Hundred and fifty," Uncle Lenny corrects.

"But you've already sponsored me, both of you." I'm at a loss for words, something that doesn't happen often. "You didn't need to do this."

"We wanted to," Uncle Carrick assures me. "It's the least we could do. You're doing the hard work, what with all the training."

I fold the envelope flap down, although it's so full it immediately springs open again.

"This is brilliant. I've got over a thousand pounds in sponsorship now! You two are full of surprises, you know that?"

Uncle Lenny laughs. "I'd hardly say that. It's not like we've got any skeletons hidden in our closets, is it, Car?"

As I bend to put the donation safely into the inside pocket of my bag the room falls quiet. The clock ticks, the heartbeat of the living room echoing in the new-found silence.

I look expectantly at Uncle Carrick, waiting for him to come back with one of his usual quick-witted one-liners, but he doesn't say a word. Instead he twitches, then picks up the packet of biscuits from the arm of the chair, noisily untwisting the wrapper.

"No skeletons," he says finally, with a quick flicker of a smile.

He takes a wheatmeal biscuit and offers me the packet.

"Biscuit?" he asks.

But I can't help feeling something has distracted him, and whatever it was has made him jittery.

I bite into the Digestive as Uncle Lenny turns on the TV, the opening credits for his favourite quiz show blaring out into the room.

I'm glad of the interruption, however banal. For reasons I don't understand, the atmosphere has changed.

Uncle Carrick looks uncomfortable, fidgeting.

Uncle Lenny looks as puzzled as I am by the sudden shift in mood.

And although Auntie Marilyn's lounge is filled with colour I can't push aside the uneasy feeling that I'm being kept in the dark.

Fern

It's a glorious June day, the type where people laze in the sun on the central expanse of grass that cries out to picnickers and children alike. Although it's early, the park is already buzzing with families and couples making the most of the good weather. I wave to Paolo and Pepe, who are setting up for the coaching session. At least, Paolo is. Pepe's dribbling a football with apparent ease whilst his dad calls out a warning to him not to stray too far.

I'm feeling brighter today too. Physically Luke's recovering beautifully, and although everyone's keen to keep reminding us not to get ahead of ourselves, seeing the relief on the faces of the medical staff who've been caring for him is massively reassuring. Compared to the grey, sombre expressions they'd been wearing around us when he was at his worst, they were practically glowing at his last consultant appointment. We can't help but feel quietly optimistic. Luke himself has been more upbeat over the past week or so, too. Kelly told me that the two of them have been texting and making plans for the future, and it wouldn't surprise me if that's what's bolstered his positivity.

It's blooming hot though. I know it doesn't help that I'm significantly bigger than most of the other girls my age and would never dare to dress in the skimpy clothes everyone else seems to clamour for as soon as we get a bit of warm weather, but I sometimes wish I had the guts to. The trouble is, I care far too much about what other people think. They'd all be laughing at me if I turned up in a strappy sundress or short skirt that exposed my chunky legs, or passing comment on my roadmap-like stretchmarks.

"Are you all right?" Maggie asks, gingerly picking up chunky slices of steaming hot flapjack from a silvery baking tray and transferring them to the wire cooling rack.

"Fine," I reply, reaching for the apron that's hung over the door. The thought of putting on another layer of clothing is mightily unappealing, but as it's part of my work attire I don't have a choice. "Ready and raring to go. What have you got prepared for today? I can see there's the flapjack, and is that ginger cake I can smell?"

Maggie nods in response. "I was going to make a Victoria sponge, a treacle tart, some white chocolate blondies and of course some cupcakes. It looks like it could be another busy one. There are plenty of people milling about already."

"Warm too," I mutter under my breath, fanning myself

with a glossy laminated menu. I feel like a potato roasting in its skin.

"However busy we are, I'm sure the ice-cream kiosk will be busier still," Maggie states. "Hopefully the footballers won't all defect over there for a vanilla cone instead of here for the cupcakes."

I shake my head vehemently. "No fear of that, they're loyal to you. I bet even if they do have ice cream they'll still be pouring in here for their usual cakes."

Maggie grins, flattered. "I hope you're right. Now come on, let's get set up and those doors open wide. There are already people passing and we've got enough cakes to start off with so we might as well make the most of it. Can you fill up those large jugs with iced water please, Fern? If it stays as hot as this people will be needing plenty of fluids."

"Don't I know it," I reply. "I'm boiled."

I push the sleeves of my blouse up slightly, revealing the pure white flesh of my forearms, before thinking better of it and pulling them straight back down. I'm sure Maggie notices, but she doesn't comment. She's much too polite to tell me how ugly my soft, sausage-like arms are.

Ten minutes later, The Lake House Café is ready for business. Matt, the scrambled-egg-on-toast guy with the lip-ring, is pulling up the shutters to the kiosk at the boat-house. He catches my eye and nods a greeting as I turn the sign on the café door to 'open'.

He is good-looking, I decide, shyly raising my hand in acknowledgment. That's what's strangely intimidating about him. He already has a tan of sorts, he's obviously one of those people that holds their colour all year round despite the exceptionally fair hair. He's not as aloof as I'd first thought either, and we've made small talk about the food on the menu and how rubbish TV is at the moment when he's been in the café. He's all right. Not as classically good looking as Josh, but then I've loved him forever, with his angelic fluffy hair that I desperately want to reach out and touch, and pinprick dimples that appear as if by magic when he smiles. But he's friendly, the guy from the boat-house, and although it saddens me to admit it, I've probably said more to him in the last few weeks than I've said to Josh in the whole ten years I've known him.

As he moves into the small wooden hut, brightly coloured bunting strung over the gabled roof, I set to work in the café. This is no time to be idly daydreaming about Josh Thornhill. There's plenty to do, and not a moment to waste.

The morning whizzes past and we're as busy as Maggie had anticipated, the constant flow of customers streaming through the door keeping both of us on our toes.

"If it carries on at this rate I'm going to have to phone Kelly and see if she can come and give us a hand," Maggie says, cramming a generous handful of pure white serviettes into the stainless steel dispenser. "I'd rather not disturb her because she's trying to get her head down and revise with her final exam coming up on Tuesday, but this is even busier than I'd thought it would be."

"We'll manage," I say quickly, placing a steaming hot teapot on a tray alongside a miniature jug of milk, a cup and saucer and a small pot filled with perfectly cubed sugar lumps. Kelly's got enough on her mind right now. "It'll probably quieten down after lunch," I add, although as the first group of football mums walk in, their enormous bags draped over the hooks of their arms, I doubt it'll slow any time soon.

The excited babble of the muddy-kneed children fills the café with as much warmth as the mid-summer sunshine, and Maggie quickly moves to her spot behind the counter to take their orders. We know a lot of these families now, they're our Saturday regulars. Maggie jokes they're as much a part of her weekend as *Britain's Got Talent* and a bottle of Chardonnay, but I know she's got a soft spot for one parent in particular – Paolo.

"Hi, Marcus," Maggie says cheerily, beaming down at a little boy of six or seven with mousey hair slathered in gloopy gel. Freckles are liberally scattered over his nose and he boasts a prominent scab on his chin where he's obviously had a fall. "What can I do for you today – your usual chocolate cupcake with rainbow sprinkles?"

The boy nods, his tongue peeping out of the corner of

his mouth in anticipation at the thought of Maggie's rich chocolate delights.

"He's a creature of habit," Marcus's mum replies with a laugh, reaching into her bag and pulling out a smooth black leather purse with a keyring of a terrier hanging from it. "And a Diet Coke too please, Maggie. I'm dying of thirst after standing out there for an hour. We're not used to these temperatures at this time of year, are we? Not used to it at any time of year!"

"Don't grumble about it!" jokes Maggie, pulling the iconic silver and red can from the fridge that lines the back wall of the café. "It's supposed to be raining again on Monday, so we need to make the most of the good weather while we can."

The lady groans, pushing her over-sized sunglasses on to the top of her head to find some money in her purse before handing a note to Maggie. "Don't say that, we're visiting family in Scarborough next week. I'd hoped for at least a bit of sunshine. Marcus has been saving his pocket money for weeks and I'm a bit concerned I won't get him out of the arcades as it is. If it's miserable weather, I'll have no chance."

"These weathermen and women aren't always right," Maggie says hopefully, counting out the lady's change. "Have a lovely break whatever the weather. Make the most of it and enjoy every moment. They don't stay this small for long."

She's reminiscing, I can tell by the faraway look in her eyes. Probably thinking about when Kelly and Josh were small.

Josh. He'll be back soon, and I feel sick at the thought of seeing him. The last time I saw him was Christmas, at the annual carol singing event on the bandstand across the park. He'd looked undeniably gorgeous wrapped up in his woollen black scarf and beanie hat, mumbling along to 'O Little Town of Bethlehem', his nose bright red from the biting cold.

When he gets back he'll be in the café trying to cadge free food and drink all day, looking all floppy haired and gorgeous as he hogs both a table and my attention. My heart races at the thought. He has that effect on me. He always has, and I couldn't avoid it if I tried. It's too ingrained. I'm like one of those dogs, the ones that salivate when they hear a bell because they associate it with food, except I salivate at the thought of Josh.

The phone rings, forcing me to snap out of my thoughts, and I quickly dab the back of my hand against the corner of my mouth in case any drool has actually escaped. How embarrassing would that be, slathering everywhere?

"Thanks, Maggie, we will," the lady smiles, before handing the cupcake to the eager boy by her side and snapping back the ring-pull on her can of pop. "We'll see you when we get back."

Maggie has such an easy way with everyone who walks

through the door. She knows how to make everyone feel welcome. They're each a valued customer in their own right, and not just because they're choosing to spend their hard-earned cash at the café rather than down the department store or at one of the boutique bistros that have sprung up on the high street. She manages to make everyone feel good about themselves, it's a God-given gift.

I wish I could have a smidge of her confidence, not having to think about every word I say before I say it, not worrying that everyone's looking at your body and thinking it's gross. It must take so much pressure off, knowing you aren't socially inept.

"Good morning, The Lake House Café, Fern speaking. How may I help you?" I say, switching on my best telephone voice. It's not like I have much of an accent, but I find myself speaking more clearly on the telephone, and with more grace.

"Fern, it's Kelly." She sounds relieved. "Is Mum there?"

I glance over to Maggie, who's serving another one of the mini footballers his post-training snack.

"She is, but she's serving. I can get her to call you back in a minute?"

"No, no, it's you I wanted to talk to. I only asked about Mum because I didn't want her to overhear."

I lower my voice. "She won't hear. What's the matter?"

"Have you spoken to Luke this morning?"

"No, he wasn't awake when I left. I came in early because I was up and ready. Why?"

"He's just rung. He told your parents he's been seeing me."

"Oh."

I can't imagine that went down well. They've been trying to wrap him up in cotton wool since the operation and even though the consultant said he's fine to carry on going out and seeing his friends so long as he doesn't overdo it, if my parents had their way he'd be under lock and key.

"Yeah, it's fair to say they weren't happy." She laughs bitterly. "They told him in no uncertain terms that they disapprove of us being together and that they can't support our relationship. Your dad seems to think I'm going to dump Luke for a girl any day now, as though being bisexual also makes me promiscuous."

"Dad doesn't understand. I'm not sticking up for him, because he's wrong about this, but it's nothing personal. He just doesn't understand what bisexual means."

"That's what I wanted to speak to you about. I wondered if you might have a word with him."

"What do you mean by 'have a word with him'? Try and get him to see things from yours and Luke's point of view?"

Kelly sighs. "Yeah, I suppose. Every time Luke tries to explain that our relationship is just like any other your dad puts up his defences. He might listen to you though."

The thought of trying to talk to my parents about this makes me squirm. I can't bear the thought of inciting confrontation, but equally it doesn't seem fair that they're passing judgement on Kelly and Luke's relationship purely because Kelly's last relationship was with a female.

I know what I have to do.

"I'll talk to them," I promise. "I can't guarantee they'll listen, but I'll try my best to get them to understand."

"Oh Fern, you're a diamond! Thank you so much for doing this, for even trying to do this. I know it's been hard for you being stuck in the middle."

Kelly's voice is so full of joy that I don't have the heart to tell her my words will most likely fall on deaf ears. Instead I let her enjoy this moment.

"No problem," I say. "I know you'd do the same for me."

"I would. I owe you a massive favour for this."

"You don't owe me a thing," I reply. "You've given my little brother something to live for. That's more than enough."

As we say our goodbyes and I put the phone back into its cradle, I mentally prepare for the conversation I'll be having with my mum and dad. It's time for me to put on my big girl pants and stop pussy-footing around. For once I'm going to say what I think and blow the consequences. This time it's not about me. It's about Luke, Kelly and their future happiness, a happiness they have as much right to as anyone else.

Maggie

The steady influx of families flooding through the café has kept me busy all morning, almost too busy to wonder where the handsome football coach is. Almost, but not quite. I'd seen him across the park earlier, tidying up the equipment as the children streamed back to their parents, but that must be almost an hour ago now. Perhaps he wouldn't come in today after all. I'm surprised by the hollow emptiness that sits in my stomach at that thought.

Absent-mindedly, I hum along to the song that's playing on the radio, a jaunty eighties tune about holidays that reminds me of school discos and family weddings. There's certainly something about this good weather that lifts my mood. Of course, it helps that business is booming and the park's coming into its most colourful season. The fir trees that give the park its name don't change much throughout the year, but the flowerbeds are beginning to spring to life after a restful winter, adding a depth and brightness to my surroundings. I'm lucky to have this right on my doorstep.

It's when I look through the window, daydreaming as I lower myself to my haunches to take a tray of steaming hot sausage rolls from the oven, that I see him crossing the park, holding his little boy's hand. He's coming from the direction of the playground, and I smile at the thought that Pepe had coerced his dad into an impromptu visit to the swings. Paolo's strides are long, unsurprisingly as he's so tall, and his son's skipping at his side to keep up. I'm so engrossed in my thoughts that it isn't until it's too late and the red-hot metal of the baking tray is burning my hands that I realise my painful mistake. The oven gloves are lying redundant on the work surface where I'd left them earlier and a searing pain shoots through me as I instinctively pull back, my reflexes kicking in too late. The pastry-cased sausages fly up into the air along with the baking tray they'd been cooking on, landing on the floor with a clatter, which would be deafening if it weren't drowned out by my high-pitched scream of pain. Angry red burns are already flaring up on my palms, straight lines of scarlet that look like they've been drawn on with a Sharpie. Tears spring to my eyes. The pain is an intense tingling that hurts so much that I bite down on my tongue as a temporary distraction.

I flinch as I look at the compact green first aid box hung

next to the door. I'm going to need help. The pain is unbear-able.

"Fern!" I call, wincing at the agonizing burning sensation on both my hands. My fingertips are blistering where they'd been in contact with the tray. Shit, it hurts.

"FERN!" I shout again, more loudly this time. "CAN YOU COME BACK HERE FOR A MOMENT, PLEASE?"

I hope the urgency in my voice will be apparent to my colleague but not to the customers. The last thing I want is to cause a scene.

Fern's head bobs around the door, her face like a still from a Hitchcock movie as she takes in the scene.

"What happened?" she gasps, pushing the door wide and making her way fully into the kitchen.

I hold out my upturned palms. They're looking more inflamed by the minute. Fern, ever a sensible head, is already reaching for the first aid kit and that's when I hear the voice calling from the café.

"Hello? Is anyone serving?"

I'd know that voice anywhere. Paolo.

"Go," I instruct Fern. "Customers can't be left waiting."

That's what's at the forefront of my mind, not the pain, which has me wanting to reel off every swear word I know. All I'm bothered about is making sure everyone's orders reach them in quick sharp time. Both the café and I have a reputation to uphold.

That's when his head pops around the door, long hair streaming behind him.

"It's fine," he says calmly, nodding his head at Fern. "I'm trained in first aid. You go and serve and I will look after Maggie."

His voice soothes me, the tone of it flowing over me as my head continues to spin.

He takes my hands in his, his touch delicate and gentle as he examines the burns. "They looks sore," he observes. "But we can treat it. First, let's get them cooled down."

Turning on the cold tap, he thrusts my hands under the running water. I instinctively whistle in through my teeth. It initially stings, although it only takes a few seconds before the skin begins to feel less angry and inflamed.

He searches in the cupboards as I bathe my hands. "Where's the cling wrap?" he enquires.

I'm puzzled for a moment until I realise he means cling film. It's in a low drawer, stored with rolls of greaseproof paper and a stash of paper bags for customers who want takeaway. "Down in the bottom drawer," I answer, nodding to the cupboard next to the fridge.

He retrieves the thick roll of cling film and expertly tears a strip about two inches wide off with his bare hands. He doesn't even consider using that weird jagged edge on the box, the one that looks like a row of crocodile teeth and has caught me unawares on many occasions.

"Let me wrap your hands."

His hand holds my wrist steady and a surge of electricity races through me at the contact. His grip is tight, to ensure I remain perfectly still so he can carefully cover the burn with the transparent coating. I close my eyes as he bandages me up, first my right hand, and then my left.

"Are you okay? You don't feel dizzy or cold?"

I shake my head.

"I'm fine, honestly. Just embarrassed about trying to take things out of the oven without gloves. I was in such a rush that I didn't even think…"

I can't believe I was so stupid. How many times a day must I have retrieved baking from the oven without incident, and then today, when Paolo's here no less, I forget the basic safety equipment and come across as a fool. If only the ground could swallow me up.

He looks right at me, his eyes boring deep into mine. Those mesmerising chocolate eyes make me want to melt on the spot.

"I was worried when I heard you cry out. And I know I don't belong in here…" he pauses, gesturing around the kitchen, "…but I had to see if you were okay."

"I'm fine," I repeat.

I am. Yes, my hands hurt, but it's my ego that hurts more than anything. I wonder what Paolo must think. Yet again I've managed to come across as a ditzy airhead, not an independent woman with my own thriving business. I inhale deeply in a bid to regain my composure and suddenly frown as I remember Pepe.

"But what about your little boy? Is he out in the café?" My voice is high and pitchy. "You should go to him, he'll be worried. I'll be out in a minute and I'll get you one of the cakes he likes – on the house of course, as a thank you for this."

He holds his palm out to stop my stream of words. "Shh. Pepe is fine. He's with Gabrielle."

"Ah." I relax in the knowledge that the little boy is safe, but can't stop myself feeling sadness – maybe even envy – at their perfect little family unit. I'd never been able to offer that to Josh and Kelly. It eats away at me that I've failed to give them that stability. "Your wife's with you today."

Paolo throws back his head and lets out a loud belly laugh.

"My wife? No, Gabrielle's not my wife." He chuckles again. "She's Pepe's nanny. Normally she doesn't work on a weekend, but she's been coming to the park to run lately. She's taking part in a race for charity next month and all the time she's out running. She takes it seriously. When Pepe saw her on the way back from the playground he demanded she join us for one of your cakes as a reward for her hard work."

I can tell I'm turning pink.

"Oh."

There's nothing more to say. So the dark-haired beauty isn't his wife after all.

"Pepe's mother's in Italy," he continues, and I wonder if he can read my mind. It feels as though he knows what I'm thinking. "She works for a big fashion house in Milan."

"It must be hard," I muse. "Being away from her."

"Pepe is used to it."

I wonder how their marriage works with them based in different countries. Maybe I'm too conventional: people have all sorts of weird and wonderful relationships nowadays. All I know is that if Paolo were mine there'd be no chance I'd let him live in another country. I'd never want to let his gorgeous face out of my sight.

"It's just the way it is for us," he says with an indifferent shrug. The movement is so totally European, it makes me smile.

The tinkling of a little boy's laughter rings out from the café, causing Paolo to beam. "My son means everything to me."

"So you do most of the parenting," I say, trying and failing to keep the surprise out of my voice. It's still rare to see a dad shouldering most of the childcare. "My situation was different, but I brought up two young children almost on my own as well. It's hard work."

"Some days I'm so tired I want to cry," he says emphatically. "And Pepe has so much energy, it's like he'll never stop talking and running and jumping. I took him to the park after football hoping it'd tire him out. It didn't work."

I smile, remembering Josh at that age. He'd been an unstoppable ball of energy, but with him it was constant talking, non-stop reeling off facts and figures.

"My son was like that too. He calmed down as he got older though. He's twenty-one now."

"No! You are not old enough to have a son who is twenty-one."

Paolo looks genuinely shocked and I instantly regret revealing anything that could give away my ample age.

"I had him young," I say. "Let's just say parenthood hasn't been an easy journey for me."

My chest tightens as Paolo catches my eyes.

"I don't think it is for anyone," he says evenly.

Somehow, coming from him it makes me feel a little bit better about my shortcomings.

"You're a good woman, Maggie. You work hard and have a smile for everybody. That's why everyone loves the café. You make people feel good about themselves. I'm sure your children know they're very lucky to have you."

My heart thumps at his kind words. Surely he can hear it?

"Thank you," I mumble. "And Pepe is lucky to have you, too."

"He won't be thinking that if I don't get him his cake." Paolo laughs. It's a joyous belly laugh that makes me smile in response. "If your hand is all right I should get back to him, he's probably driving Gabrielle crazy by now, begging for food. He's got an enormous appetite at the moment. I think he must be having another growth spurt."

"I've monopolised your time far too long, I'm sorry. My hands are stinging far less now though, you've worked wonders."

My heart, on the other hand feels like it might explode. I wonder if his training covered CPR. And mouth to mouth...

"I don't know how I can repay you," I say, tentatively moving my fingers beneath the swaddling. Both hands throb angrily in response.

"A slice of your lemon drizzle cake would be wonderful."

I smile, putting on a brave face. "I think we can manage that. I might even be able to stretch to two..."

Lacey

"Keep going, you're nearly done!"

Done in, more like.

My legs are barely lifting off the floor with each painful jog-step forward. There's a burning sensation down my right side that's some sort of monster stitch and I can barely breathe, not to mention that with only four weeks until the half-marathon, my self-doubt is at an all-time high. Four more weeks of this torture, and then I can banish the trainers to the bin and never, ever have to run again.

"You're doing great!"

Whatever I am, it's not great. It's painful and horrific and yet another reminder of how stupid it was to decide to run a half marathon on a whim. I'm not an athlete. I'm not even a fun-runner, this being as far from fun as I can imagine. But I keep putting one blistered foot encased in an overpriced orange trainer in front of the other, determined not to let Auntie Marilyn down. She'd have thought

I was absolutely off my rocker for even trying to do this, saying I'd have been better doing a sponsored head shave and having done with it, but I know she'd be delighted to see me challenging myself to raise funds and awareness. She was always fighting for some cause or other – better recycling facilities in the town, campaigning against animal testing, safer crossing facilities outside the local school. She wasn't happy unless she was trying to make things a little bit better and she made things a lot better actually, not just for me but for everyone in the community. Her drive and ambition was infectious and encouraged everyone to think about what they could do to keep our town such a special place to live.

"And you're done!"

I want to hug him and slap him in equal measure. It's all well and good standing there with a stopwatch and some invisible pompoms, calling out the odd buzzword to try and keep my morale up, but Warren's been sat on Nana Olwen's bench the whole time I've been running around the park, soaking up the sunshine. He's got the easy job.

I collapse into the space beside him, pulling up the cap on my water bottle with my teeth. I feel like my whole body's in flames, every part of me sore beyond belief. The water is warm and tastes vile but I don't care, I knock it back anyway like it's a tequila slammer. I could do with something to give me an instant buzz: I don't think I'm going to have the energy to make my way home.

"You did it, Lace. And you're getting quicker too. With a bit more training you'll be able to manage those last two miles."

"I don't think I can," I gasp, patting at my flaming cheeks.

"Of course you can," Warren assures me. "You're getting better all the time. Faster and fitter. On the actual race day it'll be easier too, you'll be swept along with the atmosphere."

"And adrenaline?" I say cynically.

"Exactly, and competitive spirit. You'll see everyone else kicking on and it'll spur you to push yourself that bit harder."

I roll my eyes. This goes to show how little he knows me, because I'm the least competitive person I know.

"I won't."

"You will," he says with a grin. "It'll be like on sports day at junior school where you magic up a bit of extra energy from somewhere to run just that little bit faster when you're on the last stretch. You'll pull it out of the bag, I know it."

I shake my head, determined to prove him wrong. "Never did the running races on sports day."

"Everyone did the running races on sports day at my school," he says with a frown. "Teachers said the taking

159

part was the most important bit and those that finished first had to cheer the stragglers at the end over the finishing line."

"What were you?" I puff. I still feel like an elephant's sitting on my chest. Maybe I'm going to have a heart attack.

"What do you mean?"

"A runner or a straggler?"

He looks sheepish.

"A straggler," he admits finally. "I'm a terrible runner now and I was even worse back at school. All I cared about were science and maths."

"Ah, so you were one of the geeks." I could imagine him as a geek, drowning under a starched white lab coat with round wire-rimmed glasses perched on his nose as he held bubbling test-tubes over Bunsen burners. In my mind it's like potions class in Harry Potter, although Warren's more Ron than Harry. He's got that reddish, ruddy Weasley vibe going on.

"Of course I was a geek," he says, motioning to the outfit he's wearing. It's not the most fashionable, but he manages to carry off the loose-fitting white t-shirt and faded jeans, sort of. "I doubt you expected me to be the cool, sporty type did you? Small gingers don't tend to be the star of the sports teams."

"I don't think ginger hair ever stopped anyone from excelling at sport," I correct. "It's about self-belief, not whether or not you've got a recessive gene. I totally lacked coordination as a kid – my mum says I didn't start walking until I was twenty months old – and even the teachers used to get frustrated by how bad I was at PE. That's why I never got to take part in the proper races on sports day. I had to do the comedy ones instead."

He looks quizzically at me, raising a jaunty eyebrow. "Comedy races? Sounds interesting. Egg and spoon, sack race, that sort of thing?"

"I wish. No, it was stupid stuff. Three-legged races and this awful one where you had to put on stupidly large clothes as you ran around the track. By the end you'd be wearing some 'hilarious' outfit. A flowery nightie with a pair of flip-flops, goggles and a jester hat, that kind of thing."

It had been so humiliating and I can still hear the mocking laughter from the other kids as I tripped over the ridiculous flippers they'd expected me to run the last five metres in. I'd landed with a hollow thwack on the rock-hard grass, my knee stained deep-green and scarlet with the vibrant mix of grass and blood.

"Doesn't sound so bad," he mused. "I can imagine you totally rocked that flowery nightie."

His cheeks flush slightly, as though he realises he's admitted to thinking of me in bedclothes, even if the me he's imagining is only ten with gangly legs and arms.

"I didn't," I confess. "The whole thing was one massive embarrassment, I ended up sprawled helpless on the track crying my eyes out. By the time I got into the last year they didn't even let me do the comedy race. Not worth taking the risk. I think they thought I'd end up with a broken neck or something."

"All the more reason to be proud of what you're doing now then, if you ask me. It's easy to do something when you're good at it. It shows much more character to do something that's a proper challenge."

There's a bubble of pride swelling in me at his words, realising that he's right. I could have taken an easy route. Organising a fun day would have been a piece of cake and I could have roped in all the party planning contacts I have through work. I could have exploited the connections I've built with the local press to drum up more support too. It probably would have raised more money in the long-run, but this was about me physically pushing myself in Auntie Marilyn's memory, going out of the cosy safety of my comfort zone. In a weird way it's been therapeutic. Empowering.

"You should be really proud of what you're doing, Lacey. Really proud. I bet you anything your aunt would be."

Tears prick my eyes, threatening to fall on to my already sweaty cheeks. Maybe if I cry I can pretend it's a delayed reaction, some kind of freaky after-sweat thing.

"I need to warm down," I say eventually. "You're always on about the importance of stretching out after a run."

"One time! I said it one time." Warren laughs. He looks cute. "But it is important. You can't go getting injured after all the work you've put in. Imagine how awful it'd be if you couldn't run on the day."

"Don't even joke about it," I say firmly, thinking of the generous sponsorship I'd already collected. "I'll be running this half-marathon if it kills me."

Wincing as I bend into a deep lunge, one knee cocked skywards and the other quivering an inch above the floor, it wouldn't surprise me if it did. Every muscle in my body is screaming at me.

"It won't kill you," he says. "You've got this. I can feel it in my bones."

I switch my position.

"You're right," I say. "I've got this. Thanks, Warren. Thanks for believing in me."

It's funny how even when I'm doubting myself, if Warren tells me I can do it, for some unknown reason I believe that maybe – just maybe – 13.1 miles is within my capabilities.

Pearl

The café is teeming with people. There's a group of mums bouncing chubby, drooling babies on their knees whilst their frothy coffees go cold; they barely get a chance to take even the smallest sip of their drink because their offspring are demanding every bit of their attention. These exhausted, bleary-eyed mums sacrifice their hot drink to hunt for a tub of dimply rice cakes that's at the bottom of their enormous changing bags, or to pick up a rattle from the floor for the hundredth time that day, because the babies seem to think it's hilarious to do the same thing over and over again. The babies' gummy grins morph into belly laughs as their mum, who's probably been up half the night and not had time to brush her hair, let alone wash it, resignedly bends down to rescue the plastic toy from the floor for the umpteenth time.

Then there are the elderly couples, cute little grey-haired pairings who've probably been planning their day out all week as a break from watching daytime TV on loop.

Outside at the newly opened water park are toddlers running through the fountains in their underwear, splashing about without a care in the world, the only thing they have to worry about being whether or not their mum will treat them to an ice cream from the candy-striped kiosk next to the boating lake before home-time.

Families, everywhere.

Families of all shapes and sizes and make-ups.

Perfect, love-filled families.

"You're a star for filling in like this," Maggie says with a smile of gratitude. "Fern rarely misses a day, but she needed to be with her family."

"Is it Luke? I'd heard he was recovering well from his operation."

"He is, but he's got an important appointment at the hospital today so Fern wanted to go along to support him. They're really close, you know."

"It's nice to have that bond. He's lucky to have such a devoted sister."

I think of Vivienne, of how strange it is to now be the lone sibling after a lifetime of togetherness. Of how much I miss her.

We'd drifted apart, especially in the years leading up to her death, but she'd still been my sister and I'd loved and admired her, even if I hadn't always agreed with her reasoning. She'd stood by Clint despite his unforgivable actions – loyalty he hadn't deserved.

"Kelly's pretty devoted to Luke too," Maggie confides. My ears prick up: this is news. "They've been seeing each other on the sly, even though Luke's parents don't approve. You know how old-fashioned they are."

I snort. "That's the trouble with the Harts. They're a nice family, but they think their way of living is the right way."

"Oh, I don't know. We're all guilty of that from time to time."

"I can't understand why anyone would have an issue with their son dating Kelly. She's beautiful and spirited and bright as a button. You should be proud of the young woman she's turning into."

"I am. She's got her head screwed on properly, which is a relief. Maybe I managed to do something right along the way."

"You did plenty right, Maggie, and you didn't have the easiest ride. You had those children when you were little more than a child yourself. Don't do yourself down. Many women would have panicked at the thought of a baby so young, but not you."

Many women like me.

"I remember you crying when Clint and I came to tell you and Alf we were expecting Josh. You were in such a state." She laughs at the memory. "We thought it was because you disapproved at first: it was only after you'd calmed down enough to talk that we realised they were tears of happiness."

I don't tell her the real reason I was crying was because I knew that the baby she'd been carrying would never know who I really was. I don't tell her that it was a deep-rooted sorrow from keeping such a huge secret from the man I'd loved with all my heart. I don't tell her any of it. Instead I do exactly the same as I did that day in my lounge, brush it off with humour.

I roll my eyes to heaven and light-heartedly say, "What am I like?"

Fern

"Luke messaged me again this morning."

The colour in Kelly's cheeks is natural this time, not her usual sweep of dusty-pink blusher across her high, jaunty cheekbones.

"He told me he's feeling much better. I think it's relief after the positive feedback from the hospital."

Kelly clutches her hands together like a fairytale princess making a wish. She's radiant with love, and it's my brother who's making her feel like that. It's strange, especially when it's her brother making me feel so broken.

"He's doing well," I confirm. "His appetite's coming back now and he's not looking as weak, although he still spends most of the day lying on the settee. Gives him an excuse to hog the remote," I add jokingly. It shows how far I've come; just a few weeks ago I'd not have been able to entertain the idea of laughing at anything relating to Luke's health concerns.

"I can't wait to see him. It feels like forever since we were last together. I just want to squeeze him tight and tell him I love him."

I look at her quizzically.

"Love? That's a strong word."

"It's a strong feeling," she fires back. "I know we're only young, but this past month has shown us how much we mean to each other. We don't care what your parents think any more. Luke could have died. Surely what matters most is being with people who make you happy?"

She's got a wise head on those young shoulders and I can't argue. Love wins out, every time.

"That's why I'm going to speak to my parents for you. I wanted to do it sooner but it never seems a good moment."

"We really appreciate it," Kelly gushes. "Both of us."

"You're lucky. I know Luke's my brother, but he's a good catch. Look after him."

"Don't worry, I plan to, if your parents ever let me within a ten-mile radius. But what about you? No love interest at the moment?"

I almost laugh. No love interest ever, more like.

"I'm not really looking."

"What about the guy from the boathouse? Matt, is that what Mum said he's called? He's good-looking, if you go in for that skater-boy type."

"No!"

Kelly looks up, amused by my rapid response.

"He's not *that* bad. I prefer my boys to look well-groomed, neat. My girls too, for that matter. Mischa's the only one who's not been my usual type. But Matt...he's got more going for him than most of the singles around here."

"It's not that he's not good-looking, it's just..."

My voice trails off. However lovely Matt from the boat-house may or may not be, he's not Josh, and it's Josh that has my heart.

Kelly sighs.

"Don't waste your love on my brother. You're worth a million of him, Fern."

Kelly had realised years ago how I felt about Josh and it hurts to hear her say what I know – that he's not the nicest person. He was one of the people who called me names at school, who laughed at my mottled tree-trunk legs poking out from under a bright red PE skirt the time I was forced to play goal defence for the netball team when there was an outbreak of chicken pox in my year group. Everyone had jeered, both at how unathletic I looked and how unathletic I *was*, and that was just for starters.

But despite everything, I can't help it. I'm like one of those prisoners who falls for the people who keeps them locked up. What is it they call it? Stockholm Syndrome?

Josh knew I liked him. I'd had his initials scratched into my pencil tin since Year 7 and had taken a photo of him on a school trip to Wales off the display in the corridor in the geography block so I could carry it in my purse. But to Josh, having someone like me fancy him was an embarrassment, and I've tried to hide it of late, to protect him. He's made me feel bad about my feelings – and bad about myself – for years, but I've loved him for so long that I can't imagine not having him on my mind.

"Let's talk about something else." I'm keen to divert the subject away from my non-existent love life. "How does it feel to have finished your exams? I bet it's a relief."

"It's weird, knowing I'm finished with school for good."

"It's a big thing; it's been part of your routine for so long. And all that revision you were doing too. I've never known anyone work so hard for their exams."

"I put so much effort in to get the grades for uni. It's been hard. I'm not the brightest crayon in the box and when you've got a brainbox like Josh for a sibling..." She bites her lip, realising she's mentioned him again. There's no escaping him, even when he's miles away.

"Your mum thinks the world of you," I assure her.

"Josh is the golden boy. I know Mum loves me, I don't mean that she doesn't. But how can I compete with him? With his brains and good looks everyone falls at his feet. It's like he can do no wrong. I'm not expecting you to slag him off," she clarifies. "I know you still like him, and that's fine. I get it. When you like someone, you overlook their flaws. They're magnified for me because he's my annoying older brother. That's the difference."

"How did you know I still liked him?" My voice is barely there, little more than a whisper. "I didn't want anyone to know."

"I wasn't sure if you still did, not until you reacted just now. I thought maybe you'd have grown out of it."

A bitter laugh escapes.

"I only wish I could. He's been gone three years, except for the summers. It'd make sense that I'd stop wasting my time thinking about him. What's it they say, 'out of sight, out of mind'? I wish."

"There's always Boathouse Matt…"

"I've seen him watching that woman who comes and paints those watercolours of the lake, so I don't think he'd be on the lookout for anyone even if I was. Have you seen her? The willowy one with the blonde hair? Dresses in long floaty skirts with mirrors on, like a hippy from the Seventies?"

"My art teacher?" Kelly scoffs. "Don't be daft. He's about half her age! Why would Miss Archibald be interested in him?"

"She could go in for younger men," I argue. "Be one of those cougars. Like your mum with that football coach…"

I draw my hand to cover my mouth as Kelly gasps at my revelation, although surely she must have had her suspicions. The way Maggie gets flustered each time he comes into the café is a major giveaway.

"Are you saying she's after a toy boy? Seriously? Mum's never shown any interest in anyone, not since Dad."

"Well, I don't know for sure, but I think so." I shrug. "You must have noticed how she looks at him, as though she's going to need the smelling salts at any moment. And I can see why. All that dark hair and olive skin."

Kelly giggles as I fan myself dramatically. He *is* pretty hot for an older man.

"But he's married," I say, "so she's obviously decided he's off limits. No harm in her looking though, is there?"

I know that's not really true. There's plenty of harm in looking at something you want but can't have. All that time I've wasted mooning over Josh, the misplaced love that could have gone to someone who'd boost my confidence and spirit has taught me that. I don't want Maggie to end up getting hurt by falling too hard for someone she can't be with.

"I don't know. It's hard not being able to be with the person you love."

She's thinking about Luke. "Well, you'll be off to university in September. You and Luke won't get much chance to see each other then…"

She interrupts. "I might not go. I haven't decided for sure."

I'm surprised. All that time and energy spent poring over revision schedules and cramming in as much study as possible to get the grades needed to get on the course she had her heart set on, and now she might not go? It doesn't add up. Surely she's not thinking of hanging back just for Luke?

"Oh?"

"I might stay at home for a while and save some money." She smiles, her eyes brightening. "Me and Luke are hoping to go travelling together next summer. If I can save enough to be able to afford it."

"Well I'm surprised, but you have to do what you think is right. Trust your gut. People told me I should have gone to university, but I didn't want to be lumbered with a load of debt and there was nothing I cared enough about to want to study for three years. I've been happy enough working in the café, and as it turned out my family would have needed me here right now, so I'd have dropped out before my finals anyway. Life has a funny way of working out for the best, even though we don't always realise it straight away."

She holds up her hands, both with fingers tightly crossed. "I really hope you're right, Fern."

I hope I am, too. Especially as the more I think about how I've promised to talk to my parents, the more nervous I'm becoming.

Maggie

Coming into the café early this morning was a good idea. It's given me a chance to clear my head, as well as the cupboards. Both were in dire need of a good old sort-out.

I've been distracted lately, what with everything going on. Josh showing no sign of coming home. Kelly twitching about the future. I've been concerned about Fern too, because she's seemed out of sorts as well. With Luke out of hospital I thought she'd be a bit brighter, but if anything she seems more distracted than ever.

My own worries are going nowhere either; there's a feeling of helplessness looming over me as I wait for the inevitable to happen. I keep expecting Clint to turn up now he's out of prison, demanding to see the kids and wanting to talk to me. Josh and Kelly are old enough to make their own decisions now and I trust their judgement. I wouldn't tell them they couldn't see Clint, even after all the hurt he caused. But I never want to lay eyes on him again. The thought he could walk through the door at any point is unsettling to say the least.

Still, the café won't run itself, so I do my best to push my ex-husband to the back of my mind, concentrating instead on the ingredients I need for today's cakes. I'm keeping it simple, I decide. Three large cakes – a classic Victoria sponge, a rich chocolate orange and the ever-popular lemon drizzle, a batch of cupcakes, flapjacks and oat and raisin cookies. That'll do for starters.

I pull what I need out from the cupboards, methodically lining up the packets and jars, and then, concentrating on the task in hand, I begin to bake.

It's been a bit quieter today, the grey clouds looming overhead obviously putting some people off venturing to the park. We've still had a steady flow of customers, but with me, Fern and Kelly all scheduled to work there have been moments when we've been twiddling our thumbs. There's only so many times you can check the salt and pepper mills are full before you begin to wonder if you really are going doolally.

I've decided to use the opportunity to clean the windows, although knowing my luck it'll start throwing it down with rain the minute I get started. Anyway, I've found the bucket and filled it with hot water, and I have a chamois ready to go. Just elbow grease needed and those windows will be gleaming in no time at all.

Turning up the radio, I set to work, finding myself enjoying it much more than I should. It's rewarding, watching the smudges disappear to be replaced by sparkling clean glass and although it's a big job – the windows are almost floor to ceiling on three sides of the building – I'm enjoying doing something practical.

All too often I'm dashing in and out of the kitchen, whereas here I can say hello to the passers-by and make small talk with the customers about their plans for the holiday season. I try not to be envious of those jetting off to warmer climes, such as the couple who are getting married next month and then honeymooning in the Maldives, but I've got a serious case of wanderlust.

I've not been out of the country since my one and only trip to Paris, a long and arduous coach journey followed by a whistle-stop tour of the main sights during a secondary-school trip. It hadn't been what I'd expected, nor what it had looked like in the pictures I'd pored over in anticipation. The Eiffel Tower was smaller than I'd imagined and the paintings in the Louvre less inspiring, except for the main attraction of the Mona Lisa, which was captivating even then as a fourteen-year-old. But again, it was so small, not much different in size to the posters I'd torn out of *Smash Hits* to put up on my bedroom walls, even though Mum complained that the sticky tack left greasy circles on the paintwork. I'd argued back that it didn't matter, I had no intention of taking them down, but it hadn't been long before my attention had moved from Matt Goss and then I'd found the dark patches where the sticky tack had left its mark ugly and irritating. I never quite forgave Bros for that.

Eventually we'd painted over the marks. The whole room had transformed from a little girls' pink palace to a classy neutral shade of cream, but the room had never felt like my own after that, as though by getting rid of the familiar baby-pink walls my whole childhood was erased. Not long after that I'd met Clint, taking him back to my new grown-up bedroom when my parents were out so we could spend all day snogging without being interrupted. I'd been so in love back then, so utterly blinded by him, that I'd have done anything he wanted. He had been my dream come true, for a while.

Squeezing the excess liquid from the cloth, I wipe my sleeve across my forehead. It's surprising how hot I feel, especially on this overcast day. I'm not so unfit that a few windows can beat me: at least, I hope not. I can't deny I'm in need of refreshment though, so I climb down from the stepladder and ask Kelly to get me a glass of water with ice. It's exactly what I need, cool and invigorating.

"You look like you've been busy," Paolo says, sitting down next to me. He has a habit of appearing from nowhere. "How are your hands now? All better?"

I smile as I hold up my palms, showing him the pale

white crinkled stripes where the burns were healing nicely.

"See for yourself. They're much better now; they don't hurt at all anymore. Must have been the first-class treatment I had, stopping any serious damage."

I don't mean for the words to sound as flirty as they do and immediately wish I could retract the comment.

"It's only first aid," he says, brushing away the compliment. "I have to have the certificate to be able to run the football sessions. It's required, in case any of the children get an injury."

"Well, I appreciate it. I don't think I'm going to have any lasting scars. It's my pride that's damaged the most. I can't believe I was stupid enough to take the tray out of the oven without gloves."

"It'll teach you to use protection," he says with a smile, and for a fleeting moment it sounds suggestive, as though he's flirting with *me*, but I quickly dismiss the thought. He's Italian, it's probably an innocent comment that's lost in translation. Heaven knows, if I was trying to speak to him in his first language I'd be useless. 'Gelato' and 'arrivederci' are about as far as my Italian stretches. "That's what gloves are for."

I suppress my snort. It's obviously been way too long since I've had any kind of action if the merest hint of innuendo is enough to get me thinking sexy thoughts.

"I've been especially careful," I assure him. "I'm not taking any risks."

"Good to hear. I think your customers would cry if your hands were so damaged you couldn't bake."

I don't tell him that for the first three days after the accident I'd not been able to close my hand into a fist. It had hampered my cake-making ability no end and I'd resorted to getting Kelly to help me out. I've never been one for using a mixer, instead favouring the good old-fashioned bowl and spoon, but I'd dusted down the Kenwood Chef that week. My daughter's cakes always seem to be heavy regardless of how much air she whips into them, solid blocks of stodge that thick layers of jam and buttercream might hide from view but wouldn't fool the regulars. The light texture they'd come to expect just wasn't there and so I'd had to resort to machinery for a few infuriating days.

"No Pepe today?" I observe. "It's not like you to be in here on your own."

"He's with his mother," Paolo replies with a smile. "She's here for a long weekend. They've gone to the cinema to see that new superhero film. He's crazy about all those men in capes. He hardly slept last night with excitement, and she promised him popcorn as well. I told her it'll leave him bouncing off the walls, but I bet when they get back he'll have had one of those massive buckets. She spoils him."

"Mums should be able to spoil their children. We only want to see them happy, and as long as it is a treat and not every day..."

Goodness knows my two had practically been raised on sugar, certainly when I was perfecting the recipes. There were days we'd not even bothered getting a knife out to cut the singed-around-the-edges cakes, instead grabbing a spoon each and getting stuck in, leaving the burnt patches and focussing instead on the more appealing-looking sections.

"I don't mind Pepe having sweets. You know I let him have his cupcake every week after training and we go to the sweetshop after school on Fridays."

His comment brings happy memories of taking Josh and Kelly to the small sweetshop right next door to the primary school to mind. The jars of brightly coloured sweets lining the walls like jewels. Strawberry bonbons, cherry balsams, cola cubes…each week it'd be something different that Becky, the owner's teenage daughter, carefully measured on her scales before expertly pouring the treats into a white paper bag. She must be heading towards thirty now. Scary thought.

"It's when she gives him fizzy drinks that I get cross; it makes him go hyper." He rolls his eyes back in his head and flaps his arms wildly by the side of his face as though to demonstrate his son on a sugar rush. "I wouldn't mind but it's easy for her. They have all the fun and she's the kind one that lets him eat as much junk food as he wants, but it's me that has to get him bathed and calm before bedtime, even when she's here in the UK."

"I bet she's grateful for it. Sadly there are some men out there who still think it's down to the mums to do all the work."

I'm a sucker for a hands-on dad. It's probably down to Clint being absent for so much of Josh and Kelly's life, firstly through choice, where he'd always find something to put before spending time with his children, and then later when he was behind bars and everything fell to me by default. Seeing the dads who came to the park with their children made my heart melt: the ones cheering their daughters as they mastered the art of riding a bike or racing their son across the grass, letting the child win at the final moment. I can tell Paolo's a good dad; seeing the bond between him and Pepe is enough to assure me of that.

"She's not here most of the time."

He looks up through thick dark eyelashes, and for a moment I could drown in the dark pools of his eyes. He's film-star handsome, rugged and masculine, but I need to switch these feelings off and sharpish. It's inappropriate to be talking about his wife and all the while fantasising about him.

"We don't see her very much," he continues. "Not as much as Pepe would like to. Not as much as he *deserves* to. I think that's why she spoils him: she tries to make up for not being there."

"It must be difficult, her being so far away. You must miss her terribly."

He looks at me blankly, his brows lowering into a crinkled frown.

"Pepe does, yes. But me and Antonia...we haven't been a couple for a long time."

My mouth drops open as I digest his words. Could it really be that I've been beating myself up about having an inappropriate crush for so long when he's been single all this time?

"I thought you were married."

It sounds like a question. It *is* a question, and one I have a burning desire to find out the answer to as quickly as possible.

"We were," he says. "Still are, really, but only on paper. We got married far too quickly, and only because we were expecting Pepe. It was the wrong reason, and we learned that very quickly." He squashes his lips together and shrugs his shoulders. "Me and Antonia are different people – she is all work, work, work. It's always her career that's her priority. I enjoy my job, I like going to the schools and teaching the children about the importance of exercise and being here on a Saturday with them is so much fun, but Pepe is the most important person in my life. I want to make sure he's happy and safe, that he believes he can do anything he dreams of. He will always be *my* priority. Wherever he is, I'll be right there. I couldn't be like her, only seeing him for a few days a month."

I want to defend Antonia because I know first-hand that it's entirely possible to be both a mother and have a career, but it's hard not to side with Paolo. He's so passionate about doing the right thing for Pepe, and although being a mum shouldn't be the only thing that defines a woman, I can't imagine living in a different country to my children, especially during those formative years. It's hard enough now with Josh and Kelly reaching the point of flying the nest, but there's no way in the world I'd have missed out on seeing them grow from babies to toddlers to back-chatting children. A wave of pity washes over me for Pepe, not having his mum with him every night to read him a bedtime story.

"It's not a normal situation, living in different countries," he admits. "But neither Antonia nor I could see the point in staying together for show, and it wouldn't have done Pepe any favours. This way he gets to spend time with us both, enjoying two cultures, learning two languages. It's the best of both worlds for him."

"How did you end up here?"

Although I love Britain, especially the glorious greenery, I imagine Italy can rival its natural beauty, plus the warmer weather gives it an advantage for starters.

"My mum is British, it was my father who was Italian. When he died, Mum came back here to live nearer to her sister. She loved Italy, but she missed her family. So I came too, and Antonia for a while. But she wasn't happy, and went back to Italy the week after Pepe's first birthday."

The way he says it is so matter-of-fact. I suppose when anything is your reality it becomes your normal after a while. Heaven knows my own situation would seem strange to most, but it's the way things have been for so long that I can't imagine them any other way.

"So you've got family who live locally?"

"My mum lives near the tennis club, in one of the houses on the new estate."

I nod, knowing where he means. They're gorgeous houses with beautiful large gardens. Square houses with a central door and pointy roof, the kind of house children draw in infant school, with smoke billowing from the chimney and curtains tied into neat bunches at the windows.

"My cousins live close by, they both have children a bit younger than Pepe. It's nice for them to be able to play together, especially for Pepe. I sometimes feel bad that he's an only child. I was lonely growing up and swore I'd never just have one child, but sometimes things don't work out as you plan them."

"Kelly and Josh are complete opposites," I sigh. "They're hardly an advert for siblings. It's not quite as bad now, since Josh went to university and they're not living in each other's pockets. When they were younger though…" I shake my head at the memory of it, the constant tale-telling and bickering, "let's just say they're very different people."

"But they'll always have each other. That's what I think must be nice about having brothers or sisters. Knowing you've always got someone there for you."

"That person could just as easily be a friend though, or a cousin. And of course, I think every parent hopes their child will find love and settle down. I know I do. I wouldn't want them to be as lonely as I've been."

It's not very often I admit to just how lonely I've been all these years, and I don't know why I'm opening up to Paolo. Maybe I'm quietly hoping he'll scoop me up in his arms and we'll live happily ever after. Now I know he's separated it's a possibility, even if it is unlikely.

"Maggie," he tuts with a shake of his head. "A woman like you shouldn't be lonely. You're a beautiful and successful woman. I'd think men would be wanting to snap you up."

His fingers click as he says the word 'snap'.

I laugh at that. I wish!

"Not quite," I say, when I've managed to rein in my giggles. "I've had offers of a few dates, but nearly always turned them down. It's hard when you've got children, I didn't want to have to explain to Kelly and Josh. I haven't been out with a man for years."

The last time had been with someone I'd known back at school who'd gone into insurance. He'd spent the whole date offering advice about policies I must take out 'in case the inevitable happened sooner than expected', as though I might keel over and land face-first in my two-for-a-tenner lasagne any minute. We hadn't seen each other since, and he'd not convinced me to sign up either – no commission coming his way.

"But they're adults themselves now, you said it yourself. Surely they don't expect you to be on your own forever?"

I think back to Kelly, to her comment about me having everything I wanted except a man. Now the business is firmly established I probably *could* make a bit more time for myself.

"I think they'd like me to find someone. It'd take the pressure off them, knowing someone else was looking out for me. It's not that easy though. People don't ask each other out face to face any more, it's all those dating apps where you swipe right." I cringe. "It seems a bit brutal to me. I'd be scared no one would like my photo."

He makes a funny noise, a 'pppfff' as he puffs air out through pursed lips. "Now you're being ridiculous."

"When no one has asked you out on a date in five years, your confidence takes a bit of building up again."

I look down at the tablecloth, ashamed to admit I'm so unwanted.

"We can easily fix that." Paolo places his thumb under my chin, lifting it up until our eyes meet. My heart races at the contact and my lips feel so dry that I have no choice but to lick them. He watches my tongue as it moves over my lip, his eyes lowering only fractionally before focussing back on mine. "Can I take you out, Maggie? We could go out for dinner, tonight if you're free..."

He's still talking, but I don't hear the words. My head feels like it might explode, because I can't quite believe it, but Paolo – beautiful, kind-hearted Paolo – is asking me out.

"I'd love to," I blurt, talking over him. "Dinner sounds perfect."

And as he smiles back at me, all perfect teeth and bright pink lips, I feel like I might float away with happiness. Because I, Maggie Thornhill, am going on a date.

I'm dancing on cloud nine for the rest of the day, so much so that Fern and Kelly think it's hilarious. Playing it cool isn't an option when you're buoyed up by flattery, and a humungous grin keeps appearing on my face as I replay the conversation.

"It's good to see you looking so happy," says Pearl heartily. "Kelly mentioned there's a new man on the scene?"

She's dressed smartly today, not her usual dog-walking jeans and fleece, and her hair is styled into soft waves, a look which suits her.

I could strangle my daughter at times. She couldn't keep a secret if her life depended on it. At least Pearl's family, and I know she has my best interests at heart; I don't want Kelly telling all and sundry that I'm finally going out on a date. It'd be the talk of the park, if not the town, and I really don't fancy that.

Surely with all the drama surrounding Clint I've had my fifteen minutes of local fame? It had felt like much longer than fifteen minutes, when everyone was looking at me with either anger or pity. It had felt never-ending at the time. Being honest, it's only since the café's taken off that I feel confident I'm known for something other than my cheating, criminal ex-husband.

"I wouldn't say he's on the scene," I begin tentatively, "but I do have a date to look forward to."

I'm sure I'm going pink again. Either that or I'm starting on the hot flushes. Mum had had an early menopause, but I thought I had a few more years until that delight caught up with me. I'm not ready for night sweats and weight gain just yet.

"With that drop-dead gorgeous Italian, no less." She looks on approvingly. "If I were twenty years younger I'd be fighting you for him. He's an attractive young man."

"I think I'm probably a bit old for him myself," I admit quietly. "I'm worried he only asked because he felt sorry for me."

"Oh, stop it," Pearl shushes, adding a sugar lump to her tea and rapidly swirling her spoon in the liquid as it slowly dissolves. "You're gorgeous. He should be thanking his lucky stars you said yes!"

I laugh. I was hardly going to turn down Paolo, all muscular thighs and rippling arms.

"I don't think so, but thank you. It's done wonders for my confidence, if nothing else."

"I can see, and good for you. Nothing like a bit of flirting to give you a much-needed boost."

"Speaking of which, I was going to ask you about Carrick," I say, raising my eyebrows suggestively.

I'd seen the two of them walking together, Mitzi giddily running in circles around their feet as they'd strolled towards the rose garden. They'd seemed very comfortable together, but then they've known each other for years so maybe that explains the ease of their companionship. It might be nothing, especially as Pearl is still grieving for Alf, but the glow on her cheeks makes me suspect there is something between them.

"Is there a possible romance on the cards for the two of you?" I ask.

I could imagine them together, a pair of walking smiles, and hoped they'd get a chance at happiness. Carrick was too nice a gentleman to be single: how he'd been a bachelor for so long was puzzling to many of the older women who frequented the café. There were rumours he'd had his heart broken when he was younger, which had left him cautious and alone, but no one knew anything about the mystery woman who'd made him so wary.

"Don't be daft," Pearl scoffs. "I'm far too old for romance, and even if I wasn't, there's nothing between the two of us. He was Alf's friend."

She says it with a wistful tone, and I almost wish I'd not mentioned anything that reminded her of Alf.

"I'm sorry for prying, it's none of my business. He's such a gentleman, that's all. He'd be a real catch for one lucky lady."

"I'm sure he would," Pearl replies patiently, "but that lady isn't going to be me."

She carefully slices her scone – still warm, fresh from the oven – then spreads a thick layer of raspberry jam across its surface. She's so precise, making sure not a milli-metre of the circular surface is left uncovered by the tart red gloop. It's as she adds a dollop of clotted cream that she surprises me.

"We were an item once, many moons ago. We were only young: we didn't know what we wanted from life. It was fun, going dancing together all dolled up in our glad rags, and Carrick is a lovely, lovely man – he always was – but needless to say, it didn't last."

I'm surprised and immediately wonder if Pearl could be the mystery heartbreaker. Maybe she'd finished with Carrick to get together with Alf, ditching one man for his best friend? Or perhaps it had been something as simple as the timing had been wrong, they'd been one step ahead of the beat.

"I didn't know you'd been a couple."

"Oh, not many people do," she says, waving her hand dismissively. "It was such a long time ago now, I think even our friends have forgotten." She bites down into her scone and lets out a small moan of satisfaction. "This tastes absolutely delicious, as ever."

"Scones are easy enough to rustle up," I say, playing down my baking skills. "Most things are, if you work at them enough." I thought back to the nightmares I'd had with certain recipes over the years. Some of my first attempts had been all-out disasters that had left me crying into my pinny in despair and it had only been my determination and stubborn nature that had helped me overcome it.

"Maybe in baking, but sadly not always in life," Pearl replies cryptically. She takes another, smaller bite of scone, but places what's left of it down on her plate as though she's lost her appetite. "Some things aren't meant to be and however much you fight, you'll still end up the loser."

I'm not sure if she's still talking about Carrick, if there's a nostalgic glow for the overwhelming experience of young love, or if she's talking about something else. She's right though, I think grimly. When it came to Clint, for example, I was never going to be anything other than a desolate loser.

I force myself to laugh, once more willing thoughts of my ex-husband to leave my mind in peace.

"You're right," I say finally. "That's why it's easier sticking to cakes."

I hope I'm not making a huge mistake by laying my heart on the line again. For all that I'm a strong woman, I'm not sure I'm durable enough to survive the pain of heartbreak. Not again.

By seven o'clock I'm a wreck. I'd left Pearl to lock up the café, with strict instructions to ensure it was spick and span before dropping the keys round. Now she's oohing and ahhing, her hands clasped together as she admires my appearance.

"Oh Maggie, you look fantastic!"

"Don't scrub up too badly, do I?"

I do a little spin to show off, the skirt of my unimaginative yet trusty little black dress flaring out as I do so.

"You're a sight for sore eyes. Look at those legs! I'm so used to seeing you hiding in trousers that I didn't realise they were so shapely."

"Oh, stop it," I say modestly. "It's not like I exercise or anything. It's probably because I spend all day on my feet."

"Which is hard work in itself. My calves are aching after one shift! The shifts were long when I was working at the bank, but at least then I was sat down."

I look to the floor, brushing barely-there flecks of dust from the dark fabric of my dress.

"Anyway," she says, obviously sensing my discomfort, "I won't stop. I just wanted to hand the keys over rather than push them through the letterbox."

"I really appreciate it. Thanks, Pearl."

I relieve her of the large bunch of silver and copper keys. It's got as many keyrings on it as it has keys, my way of ensuring I don't leave them anywhere. The easier they are to see, the less chance of them going walkabouts, that's my theory.

"You have a lovely night," she calls as she reaches the gate. "Let that hunk spoil you. You deserve it."

"I will, don't you worry."

I close the door, wondering how I can fill the twenty minutes until Paolo's due to arrive to collect me. Examining my hands, I decide I'll splash out and paint my nails: Kelly's bound to have some spangly polish I can use. Yes, for once I'm going to put myself first, because Pearl's right. I deserve a lovely night.

Lacey

"That was your best session yet."

I flop back on the bench, exhausted but exhilarated. Maybe I'm getting the hang of this running thing after all. It's still difficult and I can feel myself wobbling around when I get tired – Warren says my head starts lolling like a bobble-head on the back ledge of a car when I'm on the final lap – but my legs are aching less and my heart doesn't pound quite so much. My body still turns scarlet though, that's not changed.

"You say that every time," I pant.

Warren hands me my water bottle and I gladly swig it back. He bought me a new one, a proper sports bottle with a phallic pink cooler section that you pop in the freezer. It looks so rude that it gives me the giggles every time, but I have to admit it makes the water taste a million times better. Lukewarm water was losing appeal.

"Because you're improving every time."

"Thanks. Having you here with the stopwatch is an incentive for me to push myself."

He'd taken it upon himself to become my personal trainer, cheering me on with words of encouragement and timing each lap so I can see the splits. The last one is horrifically slow, but my pace has picked up since he's been encouraging me. I'm less inclined to slack off knowing I'm being watched.

"Nice to know I'm good for something." He pats his hands down on his knees. "I'll get going then if you're done. Stretch yourself out though, yeah?"

"Can't you stay a bit longer?"

I look up, my eyes connecting with his. He's been here for over two hours already, watching me move around the park from a distance like the blue dot on Google Maps, but we've barely spoken. I'm not ready for him to go.

"I'll treat you to brunch at the café?" I raise my eyebrows hopefully, but silently pray that I'm not looking desperate.

The truth is, I like him. *Really* like him. And now the run is just a fortnight away I'm petrified that once it's over and I stop running past his Nana Olwen's bench I won't see him again.

He smiles, seemingly happy at the thought. More likely the thought of food than the thought of me, but I'll take whatever I can get if it means a bit more time in his company.

"Sure, brunch sounds good. But you're not paying a penny towards it – this one's my treat."

"No!" My voice comes out too loud, totally unladylike. "It was my idea so I'm paying."

He shakes his head from side to side. "It's on me this time. I insist. You worked so hard, you deserve spoiling, and I bet you're ravenous."

"I am a bit," I say sheepishly. My stomach is churning with hunger, especially as I'd not even had my usual pre-run cereal bar. "And thank you. That's really generous. I wasn't dropping hints to try and get you to pay," I add.

"I know," he says. "But I was when I said 'this time'. It was my way of making sure you owe me a meal so we have an excuse to go out together again."

He looks me up and down and I suddenly remember how dishevelled I must appear.

He coughs, embarrassed. "Maybe one evening? We could go for dinner?"

"Maybe," I say with a smile. Hopefully I'm coming across as though I'm playing it cool, but inside I'm screaming. Dinner with Warren sounds like the perfect night out. But first I'm doing these lunges so I can have my greasy fry-up. I feel as though I've earned it.

Pearl

"On your own today, are you?"

There's a hint of teasing in Maggie's words and I tut in response, before pretending I don't have the foggiest what, or rather who, she's alluding to.

"I've left Mitzi at home. Not that she's much of a guard dog. If a chancer decided to try and break in the worst she'd do is lick them to death! But she's already been around the block once today so I thought I'd give her little legs a rest."

"I wasn't talking about Mitzi and well you know it. I'm talking about a certain gentleman friend who you've been spotted with on numerous occasions lately. Tall, friendly, dab hand at gardening? Is there anything you want to admit to, Pearl?"

My heart races at the words. There's so much I want to admit to, but not yet. The time's not right, it's too soon. It won't be much longer now though. If there's one thing I've learnt from Alf passing away, it's that you never know when your time is up. I couldn't bear it if I never had the chance to tell her the truth.

"I've told you before, Carrick and I are friends and that's all there is to our relationship. There's nothing going on between the two of us."

I sip at my latte, the rich, milky liquid warming me from the inside. The caffeine does the trick in settling my nerves.

"Oh." She sounds disappointed, as though she'd actually thought Carrick and I were going to embark on an epic romance. She *looks* disappointed too. "So you're not waiting for anyone?"

I shift awkwardly in my seat.

"Well, Carrick did say he might pop in if he finishes trimming the bushes that back on to the road."

Her eyes light up at the revelation. "Really? That's interesting."

"The last thing either me or Carrick want is a relationship. It's all well and good being loved up at your age, but we're much too old for starting over. It'd be too messy anyway. By the time you get to our age there's a lot of baggage. I've got enough mistakes in my past that I want to try and tidy up before my last breath without making any more."

I've said too much, but Maggie doesn't seem to notice. She's already waxing lyrical about her date with Paolo –

how the restaurant they went to had fresh rose petals sprinkled on the tablecloth as decoration, and how Paolo insisted on buying champagne to go with the meal. How he held the door open for her and repeatedly told her she looked beautiful.

"He's got impeccable manners, Pearl. A proper gentleman. I don't know if it's from being brought up in Europe, but he's different to the other men I've dated. And certainly different from Clint."

I almost choke on my coffee.

"Well, it wouldn't take much for a man to treat you better than he did," I say as levelly as I can. "You really deserve a bit of pampering, you know. It's great that you've found someone to treat you like a princess. I know the youngsters all go on about equality, but I don't think there's anything wrong with being spoiled once in a while. Let your young man do the spoiling, you hear?"

Maggie places her hand on mine for a brief yet loaded moment. My skin burns with the contact.

"Thank you. We're not rushing into anything, but it's nice to have someone to talk to. I spend all day in here gossiping, but it's not the same as having someone to share in-depth adult conversation with, is it? Paolo and I have got a lot in common, actually." Her voice lowers, and she adds, "I'm not going to deny I enjoyed having a kiss and a cuddle too."

I almost blush at the revelation. "Good for you. You enjoy it."

I'm distracted by Carrick raising his hand in a wave as he passes the window.

"Here's your date," Maggie says with a smile, nodding at Carrick as he bundles into the café. "Or companion, whatever you want to call him. Tell him I'll bring him his tea over, with plenty of milk, just as he likes it."

"You're an angel, Maggie."

Sometimes I really feel she is other-worldly. Despite everything she's been through she always manages to find time for people and only rarely does she ever have anything less than a beam of a smile on her face.

As she heads back behind the counter, readying herself to prepare Carrick's weak-as-dishwater tea, I let out a long, exhausted sigh.

"You sound like you've got the weight of the world on your shoulders," Carrick quips as he sits opposite me.

"Sometimes I really feel like I do." I take another sip of my coffee, hoping the rush will hit quickly. "I can't hold it in much longer. It's getting harder and harder all the time. And people are questioning why we're spending time together. The rumour mill must be going bananas."

"Whatever they're saying, I bet they're a million miles away from the truth," he says, glancing around the café before his eyes linger on a table of youngsters in the corner.

There's the young man who works in the boathouse sat with Fern and Kelly.

Maggie appears at my side, placing Carrick's tea in front of him, and I hope she didn't hear our exchange. It's not yet time.

"Look at them," Maggie says with a laugh filled with fondness, as she follows Carrick's gaze. "Putting the world to rights." She shakes her head with affection. "The young people spend all their time drinking coffee these days. They must be high as kites on all the caffeine."

I nod politely and find myself calling out, "Kelly's a lovely girl, Maggie," as she heads back to the counter. She gives me a warm smile as thanks.

"What did you say that for?" Carrick hisses. His eyes are unnaturally fiery. It's normally me that struggles to control my temper.

"Because they're good kids, Kelly and Josh. Bright, and attractive, and well-mannered..." My voice is abrupt. Snappy and defensive. "She's done a fabulous job with them, and I think she deserves to hear that. It can't be easy being a single mum."

Carrick is still looking at the group, who are now all laughing loudly. Whether she feels the weight of his stare or if she's caught his eye, I don't know, but Kelly nods in our direction, her angular features softening.

His eyes fix on mine, brimming with tears.

"She's our grandchild, Pearl. Our own flesh and blood, and she doesn't have a clue." He sighs. "It's easier for you. At least she knows you're family. Whereas me? I'm nothing. To her I'm just the old man who prunes the roses."

I swallow down another sip of coffee, before stealing one last glance at the teenagers. They seem so free from care, as they should be.

"I know it's hard," I whisper. The coffee tastes bitter in my mouth now, the aftertaste unpleasant. "I know. That's why we've got to come clean. And soon."

July 2017

Lacey

I've been telling Warren about Uncle Carrick, and in particular Uncle Carrick's strange behaviour of late, for the past quarter of an hour now. Bless him, he's done a good job of listening to me rabbiting on. It's just a pity he doesn't know how straightforward my uncle usually is, so he has nothing to compare his new, evasive behaviour to.

"And he keeps twitching, like he's nervous. I can't put my finger on exactly what's up, but there's definitely something going on."

"And you're sure you're not just imagining it? You do have a vivid imagination."

I stare him down. "I do not have a vivid imagination."

Warren laughs. "So that achy muscle that you insisted was a pulled hamstring and the sore foot that you thought was a broken metatarsal were all in my head, were they?"

"You try training for a half marathon," I huff. "It's one niggle after another."

"But that's all they are – niggles. Not breaks or strains or heart attacks." He smiles, and I know his words are an effort to placate me. "You've had a tough time lately, but life's not all secrets and drama."

The look he gives me is drenched in affection and my heart skips a beat. Warren's one of the good guys. He gets it. He gets me.

"It's horrible losing someone you love," he continues. "Grief shakes us, makes us reassess our own place in the world. You know that yourself, you wouldn't have been training for the run if it wasn't for grief. But it's not only you that your aunt dying has affected. Your uncle lost his sister. From what you were saying they were really tight too, so it must have hit him hard, even if he is putting on a brave face."

Warren's words make me realise how selfish I've been. No, maybe not selfish. *Self-centred*. I've been so focussed on how difficult I'm finding it adjusting to life without Auntie Marilyn's vibrancy to buoy me along that I haven't stopped to consider how difficult it must be for Uncle Carrick.

"You're right. They were like two peas in a pod. Not so much in looks, but in their ways and their outlook. Always positive and friendly, always putting others first. He must miss her as much as I do."

"I'm sure he does." Warren reaches out and traces his

finger along the back of my hand. It causes a ripple to charge through my body and for a moment I almost forget how to breathe. "Don't read so much into it, Lace. He might be being quiet because he doesn't know what to say. Maybe you doing the run is bringing back some of the pain of losing your aunt, or maybe he can see flashes of her in you. From what you said she was a real go-getter, just like you are."

I pull myself taller, happy that I might be even a bit like Auntie Marilyn. She'd been my hero, the one person I most wanted to be like when I grew up.

"I never used to be like that," I admit. "But I'm starting to realise that life's short. I don't want to have regrets, unsaid things."

He looks at me quizzically. "What sort of unsaid things?"

"Oh, you know. Questions I could have asked, stuff like that. There's so much I'd love to know about Uncle Carrick when he was growing up, about what life was like here when he was young. My parents too, of course, but they're harder to talk to."

"You should reach out. Just ask him."

I shrug. "Maybe I will."

"Ask all the questions. Hundreds of them, to everyone." The look he gives me is briefly intense, then with a twitch of the mouth becomes mischievous. "Anything you'd ask me?"

I catch my breath. There's a lot I'd like to ask Warren. Until today we'd only ever spent time together at the park. There's a lot I don't know about him. There's only so much I can read into his personality by knowing his favourite colour's green. (Although the colour website I'd logged on to suggested it meant he longed for security in relationships. I'm not sure how accurate it is though.)

"Why do you help me train? What do you get out of it?" I say finally.

His eyes are alight as he replies. "Firstly, I help because I want you to succeed. You've put a lot of time and energy into this and you deserve to have someone cheering you on. Secondly, I like spending time with you."

"You do?"

He nods. "I do. In fact, Lacey Braithwaite, I'd go as far as to say I don't just like spending time with you. I like *you*. A lot."

And as he looks expectantly at me, I don't know how to respond.

"Oh," I manage finally, but inside I'm bouncing, because despite my shyness stopping me saying it out loud, I like Warren too. A lot.

Fern

I shouldn't be surprised that I hear him before I see him. He's been like that forever, over-the-top loud.

Kelly tuts in annoyance, sassily flicking her hair like Beyoncé to try to hide how bothered she is by Josh's homecoming. Her words give her away though, I can hear her muttering under her breath as she refills the fridge, "He's always got to be the bloody centre of attention."

Maggie's whooping with delight, over the moon to see her precious firstborn child, and a palpable surge of jealousy is shooting from Kelly's eyes. I recall what she said before about how she felt Josh is Maggie's favourite.

Meanwhile, I'm trying to calm my racing heart-rate. It picked up speed as soon as he spoke, and now that I've seen him it's no better. He's exactly how I remember him. Definitely better in real life than he looks in the pictures he posts online.

"Stop fussing, Mum," Josh says gruffly as Maggie affectionately ruffles up the long, dark curls that flop down past his eyebrows. He's all hair. He looks like a poodle. A beautiful prizewinning poodle. "I wouldn't have come home if I'd known you were going to be like this."

He might be playing it cool but I can tell from his face that he's loving being made a fuss of.

"Josh is only happy when it's all about him," Kelly grumbles. "I bet he planned the grand entrance. He couldn't just wait at home like any normal person would, oh no. He had to waltz in here and make a scene. Typical."

Maggie stands back and drinks him in. Her eyes narrow as she notices his t-shirt hanging loosely off his frame.

"You're looking a bit thin. I hope you've been eating properly," she chides. "I know cooking isn't your strong point but still...I hope you've ventured beyond beans on toast and Pot Noodles."

Josh tuts. It sounds remarkably similar to the annoyed 'tsk' Kelly had made when she'd realised the prodigal son had returned. "I've been eating tons. Stop worrying."

"He's always shovelling something into his mouth," says a tall blonde girl by his side. "Usually chocolate or crisps."

She's wearing the skimpiest pair of shorts I've seen in real life, little black hot pants that look like they should be worn by a backing dancer in a music video and a thin white t-shirt that's a size too small. The outline of her bra is clear through the material and although I don't want to judge her on her clothes I can't help it. She stands out like a sore thumb, surrounded by people in their conservative outfits.

"You must be Candy," Maggie says, her lips pursed together as she appraises her son's girlfriend. "And I'm Maggie, Josh's mum. It's lovely to meet you, although it would have been lovelier still if Josh had warned me you were coming," she adds.

She casts a judgemental look Josh's way, a rare moment of disapproval. I know why though – she'd have gone all out to impress if she'd known Candy was coming. It would have been like it was on my birthday, with decorations and spangles.

"Nice place you've got here," Candy says, gesturing around the café. Her blonde hair swishes behind her as she moves. I wonder if it's real or if they're extensions. I can't tell from this distance.

She's got a full face of make-up on, although it's obvious she's gone to great pains to look natural. It's the overdone mascara which gives the game away, the thick black lashes too dark with her fair colouring. She'd be better with a brown, I think critically. Kelly's expertise has obviously rubbed off on me. I've never been fussy, buying the same trusted products that I've used since school, but seeing Candy makes me consider branching out. Although no amount of make-up would transform me into her. She's like a Barbie doll.

"Oh!" Maggie looks both surprised and delighted by the compliment. "Thank you so much. It's taken a lot of hard work over the years, but it's all worth it."

"People travel from far and wide for Mum's cakes," Josh says with a smile. "Her lemon drizzle is to die for. You'll have to try a slice," he adds.

Candy looks horrified at the prospect. "You know what I'm like with sugars," she says, rubbing the flat of her hand against the bare skin of her stomach. "I blow up like a balloon." Looking at her slender frame, I'd be very surprised if that was the case, unless she has some kind of food intolerance. There's not an ounce of fat on her. "You'd not fancy me if I was the size of a house, would you?" she adds, fluttering her over-caked lashes flirtatiously.

The comment stings. Am I really unfanciable because I'm bigger than average?

"You'd never let yourself get out of shape," Josh replies. "All that dancing keeps your muscles toned."

He drapes an arm possessively around her shoulder. That cuts too, because as much as I hate to admit it, they make an eye-catching couple.

Maggie's already ushering them to a vacant table under the awnings outside, instructing a dejected-looking Kelly to wipe down the table. I can see the hurt in my friend's face. It's etched into a hint of a frown, hidden in empty eyes. She's scrubbing at the table with all her might even though it looks clean enough to me. It's as though she's taking out her anger on the shiny silver surface.

When she comes back through to the counter I make sure to ask if she's okay.

"I've been better," she replies grimly.

Small beads of sweat pepper her forehead, the lunchtime rush in the midday heat, along with the anger-fuelled table wiping, taking its toll.

"Did you know he was coming back today?"

Kelly's mouth drops open. "What? No! Don't you think I'd have told you if I did? After everything we've spoken about, I can't believe you honestly think I'd have kept that to myself."

I sigh, my shoulders sagging. "I'm sorry, I shouldn't have accused you. It's a shock, that's all. I didn't expect to see him. And I didn't expect to see *her*." I emphasise the word as though I'm swearing. "Who is she anyway?"

Kelly looks down at the floor, as though she wishes it'd swallow her whole.

"Her name's Candy. He met her in a club. They've been seeing each other for a couple of months."

"Oh."

"I didn't think it was anything serious, that's why I didn't mention it. I certainly didn't expect him to roll up here with her on his arm."

"A bit of warning would have been nice, that's all. I could have prepared myself."

"I told you, I didn't know! I wasn't deliberately keeping anything from you. I assumed it was a fling that'd fizzle out when he came back over the summer."

Outside, Josh wraps his lips around a thick black straw. Maggie's obviously made sure he's got his strawberry shake, his absolute favourite. Always with an extra scoop of ice cream to ensure it's really rich. Candy's got water. Probably scared of bloating if one single grain of sugar passes her pouty lips.

"She's beautiful, isn't she?" I say sadly. "The total opposite of me."

"You're beautiful too," Kelly replies. "She's a bit...obvious."

"I can't compete with someone like that. She's like a Victoria's Secret model. All she needs is the wings. Look at me. I'm twice her size."

"Stop being so hard on yourself, Fern." She reaches forward and places her hand over mine. "You've got loads going for you, but you only ever talk about the things you don't like."

"There's not much I like about myself."

"Well, you need to learn. Start looking in the mirror and seeing yourself the way everyone else sees you. You've got a gorgeous complexion, I've never seen you with a spot. Your teeth are straight and pearly white. Your curls are gorgeous, especially when you wear them down. You've got so much going for you, don't compare yourself to anyone else."

I wonder for a moment if I might cry, but instead I find myself sniffing before untying my ponytail and shaking out the curls. I know I can't keep it like that – health and hygiene regulations forbid it – but I feel prettier with my hair down. My moon face isn't as obvious, maybe that's why Kelly says it looks better. I pull my hair back up on top of my head, twisting the spirals into a loose bun. "All these years and he doesn't even give me a second glance. I really should try harder to get over him, shouldn't I?"

"I know it sounds harsh, Fern, but you really should." She smiles encouragingly. "In fact, I'm going to make it my mission."

Maggie

"Josh, this is Paolo. Paolo, this is my son, Josh."

It's strangely nerve-wracking, introducing them to each other. I don't think Josh expected me to find another man after Clint, and in many ways he'd stepped up to fill his dad's shoes. I hadn't expected it, and I certainly hadn't asked for it, but he'd thought it was his responsibility to be the man of the house. When Clint went to prison Josh took it upon himself to mow the lawn and trim the hedges, and take out the wheelie bins on a Monday morning before the refuse collectors came. He learnt where the trip switch was, and watched Internet videos on how to change a tyre, in case it might come in handy one day. Not because he thought I couldn't do it – by that point I'd been doing so much by myself anyway, having been practically a single parent for years – but because he thought I shouldn't have to do it alone.

As for Paolo – well, it must be hard for him too. He

looks twitchy as he offers his hand out to Josh. I had it easy – Pepe took a shine to me straight away. It was easy enough to get him onside, especially once I realised how much he adored chocolate cake, and he welcomed me with open arms. It didn't seem as if he thought of me as a threat, someone who would take up his dad's time and affection. Instead he saw me as a friend to both his dad and him.

"Nice to meet you," Paolo says affably, a wide grin spreading over his face. "Your mum has told me so much about you."

"All good, I hope?" Josh replies. The comment is jokey, but the harsh line of his mouth makes it sound more like a threat.

Paolo doesn't seem to notice. "All wonderful," he responds. "She's so proud of you, and naturally so. A degree from Oxford is a real achievement."

That acts as the ego boost Josh responds well to. "Thanks," he says, breaking out in a smile. "Mum always encouraged me to push myself, and seeing how she turned the café around from a disused shell into a viable business – well, let's just say it was a real inspiration. She's a special woman. I hope you know that."

His eyes narrow as he makes his point clear. There's no two ways about it, this is a warning.

"I do," Paolo says, with a nod. "I've not met anyone quite like her before. Someone so full of love and goodness."

Embarrassment takes over and I swat him on the shoulder to shut him up. Josh might like compliments, but I never quite believe anything nice anyone says about me. Years of Clint's snide put-downs saw to that.

"Just look after her," Josh adds. "When I'm not here."

I almost interject, almost say I don't need anyone to look after me. But it's like Josh said, it isn't that I can't manage alone. I've proven that I can, time and time again. But maybe I shouldn't have to. And maybe, just maybe, I don't want to. Not any more.

Pearl

I do a double-take at first, wondering if it's just my old eyes playing tricks on me. He looks so different, more a young man than a boy. I suppose he *is* a young man, twenty-one and preparing to graduate; and he's got a girl-friend too, if the glamorous blonde at his side is anything to go by. Maggie hadn't mentioned he was seeing anyone, but then when she talks to me about Josh it's usually to grumble about how infrequently he picks up the phone. It's rare to get any real insight into the man he's turning into, especially since he's been away.

"Pearl, look! Josh is back from Oxford!" Maggie's voice brims over with excitement, much to Josh's embarrassment. "He didn't even tell me he was coming back, just appeared out of the blue." She shakes her head, but I know there's no real disapproval in the action. She'll be over the moon to have him home.

"Hi, Auntie Pearl." Josh smiles, wolfing down his cake.

I reach out and hug him, breathe him in, but most of all I want to correct him. I want to tell him he's more than a distant relative. He's my grandson, all grown up. But instead I say, "Good to see you, Josh, what a lovely surprise for your mum! And you've brought a friend back, too?"

He nods.

"This is my girlfriend, Candy. We've been together for three months now." He says it like it's an eternity.

"Nice to meet you, Pearl."

Candy smiles, revealing gleaming white teeth and a trace of a dimple.

"So where did you two lovebirds meet?" I ask, keen to make the most of this opportunity to spend time with the youngsters. "Online? That seems to be how all your generation do it."

"A club," Josh says. "Candy works there."

"Oh, a barmaid?"

She looks the sort. Brassy and brash, like the landladies in the soaps on TV.

Candy throws her head back with laughter.

"Not quite. I'd be terrible at all that, I'm no good with money. I'd probably put the club out of business by giving the customers too much change."

"She's a DJ," Josh says proudly. "Saturday nights at The Red Room are legendary, and that's all down to Candy."

"Oh, shush," Candy replies, rolling her eyes. "Don't make

it out like I'm world class." She turns to look at me. "I used to cage dance at the club when I was a student, it was an easy way to make some money."

I try to keep the surprise from my face. "What's cage dancing? Stripping?"

Now it's Josh's turn to laugh. "No!"

"Normally the club give the dancers costumes – matching outfits, sometimes with headdresses or glow sticks or whatever. It's the dancer's job to enhance the atmosphere," Candy explains.

"I see." I don't. "Why do they call it cage dancing?"

"Because we're in cages above the dance floor so people can watch."

"I don't think I'd like that. I'd feel like a goldfish in a bowl."

I didn't used to like people watching me dance in my youth, let alone now. That phrase 'dance like no one is watching' wasn't one I could live by.

"It was fun," Candy insists, "but I did it for the money, really. The DJing's what I've always wanted to do. I'm at my happiest behind the decks."

"What sort of thing do you play?"

I'm remembering the music they used to play on nights out when I was young. Prog rock and disco, mainly, and there'd be a slow song at the end of the night to have a smooch to. It was usually 'The First Time Ever I Saw Your

Face', Roberta Flack's melodic voice the backing track for many a steamy clinch. It was the song that was playing when Carrick and I shared our first kiss. It was the song for the first dance at my wedding.

"Mostly house and garage," she replies with a shrug.

It's like another language, but I smile politely.

"I don't think it'd be your scene, Auntie Pearl," Josh says with a laugh, scrunching a handful of hair between his fingers. "Some of it's quite loud."

"Your Auntie Pearl was quite the party animal in her day, so I hear," Maggie interjects. "There's a lot you young-sters don't know about us. We've all been wild in our time, haven't we?" She winks playfully at me. "I bet you could tell a few stories…"

My blood runs cold at her words as Maggie, Josh and Candy teasingly make comments about my former party lifestyle. I force myself to paint on a smile, yet behind the mask all I'm thinking is 'if only you knew'.

I wouldn't be thought of as boring or past it if they knew I'd been an unmarried mother before I'd even left my teen years. They'd probably think me a rebel, or a wild child. They might even think I was loose, rather than that I was a daft so-and-so who fell head-over-heels in love and got caught out on her first time.

My chest constricts as Maggie ruffles Josh's hair. Yes, he shrugs her off, immediately bringing his hand to his curls in an attempt to put them 'right' after his mum mussed them up, but it doesn't matter. She can do that, because he's her boy and the whole world knows it. I could too, I suppose, although I'd probably be seen as the overbearing great-aunt.

I'd never even done it with Clint, although I'd often longed to inhale his white-blonde hair to see if he still smelt the same as he had the day he was born. Sweet and salty and fresh, like a day at the coast. Newness personified.

When I think of how I held him in my arms on the day he was born, it's hard to believe I could ever have let him go. He was beautiful. Beautiful and perfect and blemish-free, an innocent babe with his whole life ahead of him. When I think of my son, that's how I think of him. That's the son I want back in my life. But that helpless child is long gone, replaced by a heartless criminal who tore his family apart. When I look at it like that I can see why Carrick was so resistant for so long, because whatever happens now, we'll never have our son back, not the one we knew. Our beautiful baby boy has gone forever, and nothing can bring him back.

Fern

I hadn't been prepared, that was the problem. If I'd known he was going to waltz in, all perfect curls and toned legs poking out from beneath knee-length shorts, I'd have been all right.

Josh Thornhill. Every bit as gorgeous as ever.

It had taken me a minute to notice he had company, because I'd been so busy examining every part of him.

But I'd noticed her eventually. How could I not? She was perfect, full-on stereotypical beauty. It must be nice not to worry that everyone's talking about you behind your back, and the ones that are are most likely saying it through jealousy or admiration. Whenever I overhear my name I become a Paranoid Patty and withdraw into my shell.

I should have known he'd have a girlfriend. It's a miracle he's not brought anyone home before actually that I've not had to listen to Maggie talking about a long line of possible future daughters-in-law. I don't count Claire Montague, the girl he'd gone out with in Year 13. It had been painful watching them playing tonsil tennis all night at our leavers' prom whilst I sat in a corner alone, shoehorned into a plain navy dress that I didn't even like, but they were never going to be the love story of the century. Bringing Candy back is a different matter entirely. It's a big deal. It suggests it's serious.

I'm glad it's my break time. It's a relief to be able to escape from him squeezing her bare leg right in my eyeline, the way he catches her eye and smiles as they joke with Maggie and Pearl. My heart feels like it's splitting a little bit further in two with every moment I watch them together, and although it hurt so much I couldn't tear my eyes away from them. It was compulsive viewing, like one of those reality shows that you know is hideous and exploitative but has you hooked regardless.

At least I'm away from it all now, watching the giggling children whirling their legs as quickly as possible to power up the pedalos on the lake. There are some remote-controlled boats too, ones that have been brought down by a group of hobbyists – older men mainly, although there is one girl of about nine or ten furiously moving a joystick around a control pad as her mustard-coloured ship moves jerkily around the lake.

"What's that saying? 'You look like you've lost a pound and found a penny?'"

I frown at being disturbed: I'd enjoyed being miles away from all thoughts of Josh and Candy for a moment. Matt, the guy from the boathouse, is grinning at me.

I want to tell him to leave me alone to wallow in peace, but at the same time I'm scared of coming across as rude. The park's a public place, after all. He can sit anywhere he wants.

I decide to take the small talk route instead. "On your lunch break?"

He waves a small Tupperware container at me. There's chopped cucumber and carrot jiggling inside the clear container, along with some crackers.

"Yeah. I'm ready for it too. It's been crazily busy today on the lake. How's it been down at the café?"

"Good. Busy."

There's a pause as he takes the lid off his container. It clicks. He picks up a stick of carrot and bites down on it. It crunches. Click, crunch. I'd rather hear a click and a crunch than have to talk.

"What's got you looking so down?" he says finally. "Maggie working you too hard?"

I smile despite myself.

"Maggie's great. She's the best boss I could wish for, and although it's non-stop it's not too bad now we've got Kelly helping out. We're busy, but it's a good busy, you know? The day flies by."

"So it's not work that's given you that long face," he deduces. "In that case I reckon it's boyfriend troubles. Love life woes." He looks at me expectantly, bright blue eyes waiting for my response. They glint as I sigh resignedly. "Ah, I thought as much. Come on then, spill. You can talk to me."

"It's not a boyfriend. Not an anything really. Just someone I like, that's all." Which is a massive understatement, I know, but I have to downplay it. It makes me sound like a sad loser to say he's the only person I've ever loved.

"That's the worst," he says with a grimace. "There was someone I liked a while back and I was too scared to tell her. Drove myself mad in the end replaying what I'd say to her if I ever worked up the courage to ask her out." The smile he gives me doesn't seem like that of a heartbroken tortured soul. If anything, it's a fond, nostalgic glow. I can't imagine I'll ever look like that when I think of Josh. "I never did though."

"Maybe she liked you too. You could have missed your chance."

He is attractive, I think critically. His face is all angles, a pointed chin and sharp cheekbones, a long, thin nose above that pierced lip. Then there's the hair, fairly long and pushed up into a peak. I bet he gets plenty of attention: there are loads of girls into that look. Grungy but clean. Like he wants to be a bad boy but he doesn't want to upset his mum either.

"She was out of my league," he says, biting down onto

a cucumber stick. "Older woman. I knew it was pie in the sky, but it didn't stop me thinking about what it'd be like to be with her."

My eyebrows raise, wondering if it could be the painter he's referring to. Either way, it feels like a big thing to share, seeing as most of our previous conversations have been about food or the weather.

"Sounds intense."

"It was. I thought she might have liked me too, at one point. Some of the things she said were flirty, you know?" He shrugs. "But it wasn't worth the hassle of saying it out loud."

"That's how I feel too," I admit. "This person...he's everything I'm not. He's good-looking, he's clever, he's popular... then look at me. He'd not look twice at me even if he didn't have a girlfriend."

"You're too hard on yourself, you know that? Whenever I come in the café you're smiling and cheery. It's nice to get that in a world where everyone's always racing around from one place to the next."

I tut, but am secretly flattered. I assume everyone thinks I'm a chubby girl who doesn't have the brains to do anything more challenging than serve in a café. Being a smile to brighten up someone's day means a lot, I know how big a difference it can make. Those days when Luke was at his lowest ebb proved to me that the small things matter, that sometimes the littlest acts can raise your spirit. Maggie's thoughtful offerings, both of time and food, had been gratefully received, making my life easier at a difficult time, and the well-wishes of our regular customers had made all the difference. I'll never underestimate the power of kindness.

"Anyway," he continues. "It's his loss, that's how you've got to look at it. I'm a big believer in there being someone out there for everyone, it's just about being in the right place at the right time so your paths can cross. One of these days you'll be swept off your feet."

I smile. Even if I don't believe it, it's a nice thought.

"I'm not going to meet the love of my life here though, am I? All my time is spent either at the café or else I'm busy with family commitments."

I don't mention Luke and the brain tumour, and I certainly don't mention their aversion to Kelly and how she identifies. It's too much to have to explain and although Matt seems like a really kind person, and a good listener too, I don't want to dump my troubles on him.

"Love blossoms in the strangest places. I'm always surprised hearing the stories of how people get together. My mum and dad met at a cricket match, they were sat next to each other, and that morning they'd had no clue they were going to meet the person they'd end up spending the rest of their life with. So don't rule anything out. Maybe love could blossom in Fir Tree Park after all."

He clicks the lid on to his empty Tupperware container.

"I've got to get back," he says apologetically. "My next shift starts in five minutes. We should meet up for lunch again though. It's nicer than sitting alone." He looks mournfully across to the little hut, smaller than the shed in our back garden. I bet it can get boring being cooped up in there all day, like a soldier in a sentry box.

I had to agree, it had been good to talk to Matt. For a few blissful moments I'd almost forgotten about Josh and Candy and his optimism was surprisingly infectious.

"I'd like that."

"Great, let's do it. I'm off tomorrow, but see you here same time on Monday?"

I nod.

He turns back to give a friendly wave as he walks away.

After five peaceful minutes I reluctantly make a move myself. I can't be late getting back, Kelly's waiting for her break. I just hope Josh and Candy have finished their drinks and gone, so I don't have to see their beautiful faces, smug and loved-up. My heart would be so much safer if I gave it to someone who actually cared, but you can't choose who you love. The heart has a mind all of its own. The problem is, I think my heart's in need of therapy. It's clearly deluded.

Lacey

My stomach is flipping like a pancake on Shrove Tuesday. I'm an absolute bag of nerves. It didn't help that I'd hardly slept, tossing and turning as I'd played out every possible disaster that might happen. Injuries. Fainting from exhaustion. Not being physically able to finish the course. Then when I'd finally fallen asleep the dreams that had taken over were no better, twisted versions of my Sports Day nightmare. I'd been running the half marathon in a dressing gown, a pair of clogs and a flat-cap, as Mo Farah lapped me for the second time and laughed in my face. Which seemed a bit harsh even in my dream, and out of character for the smiley marathon man, but still...it hadn't done much to keep my anxieties at bay.

Now that I'm at the park, surrounded by serious runners clad in skin-tight shiny Lycra and all wearing high-tech sports watches, I'm worse still. I'm way out of my depth this time, and beginning to panic a bit about the time limit. After rereading the pack they'd sent when I'd salvaged my race number and four tiny safety pins to attach it to my vest, I'd noticed the course closed after three hours. That might sound like a long time, but 13.1 miles is a long way and speed isn't my forte. It'll be a close-run thing, pardon the pun.

"Stop looking so nervous," Warren instructs me. "You've done everything you can to prepare so just enjoy the day. Soak up the atmosphere and appreciate how amazing you are for doing this."

His words give me a warm, fuzzy glow. I'll probably be last one over the finish line – that's if I make it over the line – but three months ago I'd barely been able to run at all. It doesn't matter if I'm the slowest person in Fir Tree Park. What matters is that I'm doing this.

"It looks pretty special, doesn't it?" I say, casting an eye over the park.

Bunting has been strung between the trees, pale pink and cerise triangles fluttering in the light breeze (something I'm sure I'll be thankful for later). The local radio station has sent a DJ down to do an outside broadcast and he's stood behind his decks, which are precariously balanced on a decorating table. He's blasting out chart hits as the runners stretch out their hamstrings and loosen their shoulders. I half-heartedly join them in their warm-up, pulling my knees up towards my chest. My stomach is still churning and I wonder if I've got time to dash to one of the Portaloos but then the DJ, wearing an unflattering and unnecessary white puffy body-warmer is inviting all runners to make their way to the starting line.

"Enjoy yourself." Warren beams. "I'll be cheering you on. See you at the finish line."

He reaches out for my shoulder and gives it a little pat. I'm surprised at the effect it has on me, giving me a warm, pleasurable rush that runs right down my arm to the tips of my fingers. Gulping down my nerves, I look at my bright orange trainers and think of Auntie Marilyn as the serious athletes, toned and lithe, prepare to lead the surge of runners through the decorated park. I let out the breath I don't realise I've been holding. The sooner I start running, the sooner this will be finished.

Let's get this over with.

I'm coming to the end of my third lap. There's a searing pain shooting up my right calf muscle, which has been bothering me for the past mile or so and the thought of getting through another three miles with each step hurting as much as it does makes me want to weep.

"Come on, Lacey!" Warren's excitedly jumping up and down, cupping his hands into a self-made megaphone, which he doesn't need. His voice is surprisingly boomy and I can hear him above the slap-slap-slapping of feet pounding the pavement and the chatter of the supportive crowds.

I pass Uncle Carrick and Uncle Lenny waving their home-made banners, and there's Maggie from the café, holding out a tray of jelly babies to give the increasingly tired runners a burst of sugar to kick on for home. Even the gelatinous joy of the little orange man I grab for isn't enough to stop me wincing with every painful step. Each time my foot hits the floor the pain shoots up my leg.

"Hey, are you okay? What's happened?" There's a worried look on Warren's face, concern etched around his eyes, which have narrowed as he scrutinises my movement. His caring words are all it takes to push my fragile self over the edge. It's all too much, the exhaustion, the pain, Auntie Marilyn...I snuffle back my tears but the floodgates have opened, enormous hopeless tears streaming down my cheeks.

He's over the barrier that's designed to cordon off the racers from the spectators in one skilled leap, crouching down to look into my tear-filled eyes as I slow to a walk.

"I twisted my ankle," I explain through my sniffles. "Went over on it back near the boathouse and it didn't feel right. It's bloody painful."

"I can tell. Those faces you're pulling aren't the face of someone who's having the time of her life."

I take another tentative step, clutching on to Warren's arm for support, both physical and emotional. Having him there helps, but it doesn't make it any easier to move.

"I don't know if I can do it. There's another three miles to go. Not to mention the time limit." I look down at my watch, which is already showing I've been moving for over two hours.

"Stuff the time limit."

"They won't let me finish if I take longer than three hours, it said so in the pack. They've got to open up the park again to the general public."

I had no chance. I was going to have to tell everyone who'd sponsored me what an absolute failure I was. A total let-down to both myself and Auntie Marilyn's memory.

"They can't stop someone having a walk around the park," he said sensibly, linking his arm through mine. "I'm walking with you though, and if it gets too much then you'll have to stop. It's not worth injuring yourself just to prove a point."

We walk slowly, our arms still entwined, as even the slowest of runners pass us. There's a guy dressed as Elmo from Sesame Street, with an enormous fluffy red head that must be weighing him down perched on top of his furry body. Even he zooms past us. But I don't care, all I care about is getting over that finish line somehow, regardless of how long it takes. If I don't get there before the time limit then so be it. I'm doing my best and with Warren's fast-paced chatter lifting my spirits and working as a distraction tactic it's much easier than it had been motivating myself to keep going. It's me versus the pain and I'm not letting that get the better of me, no way.

We walk on, or rather I limp as I daren't put much weight on my right leg. There are plenty of people milling around but all I focus on are the finishers proudly displaying their medals, round golden discs on the end of a pink and white ribbon, as they guzzle on energy drinks in every colour of the rainbow.

There aren't many runners still working their way around the course, there's an older gentleman who's still jogging (albeit slowly) – he's got a red towelling headband strapped across his forehead that reminds me of the Karate Kid, although this guy has a fair few years on Ralph Macchio in the film. He's more on a par with Mr Miyagi. Then there are two girls together, probably in their late teens, and they're walking too, obviously beaten by the sheer distance of the half marathon. They're chatting as they go, arms at right angles as they power their way towards the twelve-mile marker.

"I don't think I can make it," I huff, still gripping Warren's freckled arm tightly. It's a bit clammy, probably a mixture of the warmth and being knotted up with my own sticky limb. "It's hard enough without an injury."

He stops still, stares me down. "Do you remember that day when your legs were burning? When you thought you couldn't carry on any more and were petrified about failing?"

"That could have been one of many days." I mumble it quietly enough that I hope he won't hear, but from the way he squeezes his lips together and shakes his head I know he has.

"You said nothing would stop you. Remember how you felt when you said that? How determined you were then? You need to get some of that drive and anger back, force yourself to push on. How will you feel tomorrow if you give up?"

The look he gives me is probably the sternest I've seen him give. It's enough to give me pause for thought. How *would* I feel if I had to tell everyone a twisted ankle had beaten me? I'd know it was the truth, but it'd sound like an excuse.

"I'd feel like I gave up too easily," I admit grudgingly.

"Exactly! I know it hurts, but either you grit your teeth and get that medal you've earned or you accept that you can't do it. That all those doubts were right all along."

I know he's doing it to rile me. He's trying to get a rise and get me fired up enough to walk this last mile. Normally a mile wouldn't seem that far; I walk a mile each way to work and back five times a week. But right now it feels like forever.

Once again it's like he reads my mind. "It's twenty minutes, even at your current pace. Twenty-five, max. Come on, let's get going." And he links his arm back through mine, and I start to walk alongside him and more than anything else, I start to believe. In inner strength, in mind over matter, in *me*.

By the time we reach the finish line the organisers are tidying up the tables. They've given up ticking finishers off against a list of names to make sure no one's lying injured in a ditch somewhere. Not that there are any ditches along the route, it pretty much followed the circular path I'd been training on for the last three months. The big electronic clock is still ticking though and I look at the luminous yellow numbers as Warren and I pass between the two pillars. Three hours, fourteen minutes and twenty-two seconds.

"Not my finest hour," I say as I fall in a heap on the floor. My ankle has been gradually swelling the whole time we've been walking and there's now a worryingly large lump around the size of a golf ball bulging beneath my running sock. "They probably won't even bother recording my time, seeing as I'm so far outside the recommended finish time."

Two fit males (fit in the healthy sense, not the Brad Pitt lookalike sense) are picking up large cardboard boxes filled with who knows what, glad to be going home. That's when Warren jogs over to them. I watch on curiously, wondering if they're people he knows. They don't look familiar to me, even though I've lived in this area all my life. But then I'd never seen Warren until recently either, even though we went to the same shops and the same pubs and his Nana Olwen had lived on the same street as my primary school best friend. Maybe we'd seen each other before but not remembered, or maybe we'd not been meant to meet until that day on the bench. Either way, it was possible that these fit runner-man types were people I'd crossed paths with but had totally forgotten.

They're too far away for me to be able to hear their conversation, but I can see one of them put down their box and start fumbling about in it. Warren turns to me and smiles, raising both his hands in a double-thumbs up. Even in my tired, achy and slightly delusional state I recognise the way my body responds, the way I catch my breath. I shouldn't allow my mind to even go there, but it does. Warren's cute. Proper cute, like puppies and kittens and that baby meerkat on the insurance advert. Now that the race is over, does it mean the end of us spending time together? I'm not ready to say goodbye to our heart-to-hearts, not yet.

I'm torn from my daydreams by Warren plopping himself down beside me, a large grin of delight on his face.

"I've got something for you," he chants teasingly in a sing-song voice and he pulls something out of his pocket. The pink and white stripes look like a stick of seaside rock, the circle of metal cheaper and tackier up close than it had seemed when I'd so coveted it before.

"Congratulations," he says with a smile, placing the ribbon over my head. "You're an official half-marathon finisher."

I blush, partly at the comment and partly at his touch. We'd been arm in arm for the past hour but this seems more intimate somehow, sat here in an emptying section of the park with his fingers skimming the wisps of hair that had fought free from my hair bobble.

"I am, aren't I?"

"You're a lot of things, Lacey. You just don't realise it." His words catch, his voice breaking as he continues. "I think you're pretty amazing, actually."

And then he leans forward, his lips meeting mine, and I don't care if I'm hot and sticky and my hair resembles a scarecrow's. Because Warren thinks I'm pretty amazing, actually. And that makes me feel like the happiest girl alive.

Fern

"Are you sure you want to go with me? There must be someone else you'd rather take."

Matt's giving me 'the look' – head cocked to one side, eyebrows furrowed – as though I'm being ridiculous. "Why would I offer you the ticket if I wanted to take someone else?"

He has a point.

"But what about your other friends? I'm sure they'd be better company. I don't do getting drunk," I add apologetically.

I don't know why I feel as though I need to warn people I hardly ever drink alcohol. I suppose it's because everyone expects people our age to be off their heads at every opportunity. It's not like I never touch a drop, because I do. I'll sometimes enjoy a glass of wine with a meal and I'll have champagne to make a toast at weddings. I don't like beer though, or cider, the cheap drinks that most people my age choose to get value for money. I don't like spirits either, not since I had a bad experience after drinking vodka and coke on my eighteenth birthday. One night on the lash had resulted in me throwing up on the shoe rack in the hall. My parents had gone ballistic and insisted I buy replacement shoes for the whole family with the money I'd been given by kind relatives. It had been a harsh lesson, but one I'd been grateful for many times on nights out. People around me would be going home with strangers who'd bought them a drink just to get into their pants or stumbling across the road like dazed bumblebees, but I'd be fresh, confident that I'd not be a YouTube sensation, because I'd kept a clear head.

"They've got tickets already," he says, which makes me wonder if I was an afterthought. Suddenly I don't feel quite so special. "We can meet them there, and so what if you don't drink? I won't have much myself. I've got to be here before ten tomorrow morning and I don't deal well with hangovers."

"Well, if you're sure..."

"I'm sure. Anyway, you can't pass up a chance like this. It's not every day a band like Psychedelic Lizard come to town."

I don't have the heart to confess I only know their most famous song, a guitar-heavy rock anthem with indecipherable lyrics that's been used in a car ad on telly. It's a generous offer anyway, to give me a ticket that he could easily have sold online for far more than face value.

"Sure," I find myself saying, immediately worrying about what I can wear that won't leave me too hot, sweaty or self-conscious. "Thanks for asking."

"Not a problem," Matt says, screwing the greaseproof paper his ham sandwich had been wrapped in into a ball before tossing it into his rucksack. "I'll see you later, around sevenish?"

He names a pub I know near the club, which was the surprisingly small venue for tonight's event, and I nod.

"Be ready to rock!" he says, sticking out his tongue and posing like Ozzy Osbourne.

"I'll be ready," I lie. Truth be told, I'm bloody petrified.

I arrive at the pub, bang on schedule, and am immediately overwhelmed by the cacophony of noise that greets me; well-lubricated vocal chords singing along to the songs playing on the jukebox. (What is it about alcohol that makes everyone think they can sing like Adele when the reality is they can't hold a tune? Yet another reason I avoid it. At least I know my singing is more like cats scrapping out on the cul-de-sac in the middle of the night.) It's also jam-packed, everyone squashed together like sardines as they clutch their drinks tightly, fearful of spilling one measly drop. I'll never be able to find Matt, it's just too busy.

It doesn't help that I really don't like crowds – nothing to do with being shy or low in confidence, although that probably doesn't help. Whenever a room's full to bursting like this I panic there won't be enough air to go round; my head starts fuzzing up as though it's filled with candyfloss and noises blur. The rational part of me knows there are laws about the amount of people they can let in to ensure it's safe, but there's still a niggle that I can't escape despite that. I don't think I can muster up the energy to fight my way through the hordes of people, not when I'm feeling like this.

I step back on to the street. The air's thick with cigarette fumes where the dirty smokers are loitering, puffing away as though their lives depend on it. I lower myself down, resting my feet on the road as I perch on the cold, hard curb. Down here I can breathe; the road's quiet so there's no car-related pollution filling my lungs and the curling wisps of white-grey smoke are drifting away from me as they reach towards the early evening clouds.

Burying my head between my knees, I regulate my breathing. I clasp my hands tightly around my ankles, clutching the pale bare skin where my jeans are too short and don't quite reach my trainers. I'm safe out here, away from the crowds. I'm invisible, plain, and I'm sure the smokers haven't even noticed me join their midst. They'll carry on, sucking furiously on the long, thin sticks until the end glows amber, only for a fraction of a second until it dulls again, dead and grey.

That's how I feel, as though I've had my moment. Matt asking me to join him had been a flattering high. People never ask me anywhere cool. The only people I've spent time with socially lately have been Kelly and Maggie, and that's been when I've been invited to join them on one of their girlie nights in. They're the sort of bonding sessions mothers and daughters have in films, where they paint each other's nails and giggle. I don't know why Kelly's so adamant that Josh is the blue-eyed boy, because although I know them so well, I'd still felt like an imposter, sat there wearing a banana and honey facemask as they quoted every line from *Pretty Woman* word for word.

I touch the pendant Maggie gave me for my birthday, dragging it along the chain, left to right to left to right. It's calming, somehow. A metronome swinging from side to side, a rhythm to keep me focussed on what's important.

I'm scared of going back into that pub, where everyone looks so much more comfortable in their own skin than I feel in mine. My ill-fitting jeans and plain pink t-shirt, which had seemed fine at home, look too casual now I'm out. The ten minutes I'd designated to applying make-up had turned out to be nowhere near long enough and my too-thick foundation feels heavy against my skin. Even my pores are struggling to breathe. I couldn't tame my hair either, despite using three different products that Kelly had thrust at me, insisting they were fool proof.

All I want to do is run, scuttle back home and hide in the safety of my bedroom. I could walk from here, or get the bus, it's only about a mile and a half. I could be in my pyjamas in half an hour, wiping the gloop off my face with relief.

But something stops me from doing it, from choosing flight over fight. I can't explain it – it's something either so deep within me that it's unrecognisable or an outside force pushing me into action – but with one deep breath I brush my sweaty hands over my jeans and walk back into the pub, forcibly jostling my way through the excitable huddle. I head to the bar, because that seems logical, squeezing awkwardly past the ultra-cool people.

It's a relief when I see him, my heart slowing at the familiarity of the spike of his bright blonde hair. I'm the moth and Matt's the flame. I only hope I'm not going to end up getting burned.

Maggie

"It was awful. I felt like such an idiot." Fern shakes her head from side to side, her ponytail bobbing behind her. "I need to do something about this...this *phobia* or whatever it is. I can't spend my whole life being afraid of walking into a room."

"Is it crowds in general? Or when everyone's in a small space?"

"It's when there are too many people in a room. I'm fine outside, or even inside if I've got a seat. I've been to concerts and football matches with far more people than there were at the gig last night and been fine. But everyone was pushing into me, surging towards the stage the minute Psychedelic Lizard came on. My feet came off the ground – I swear I thought I was going to get crushed. That's when it happened."

She looks so ashamed and I want to scoop her up into a huge hug, but I don't want to make her feel worse. Poor Fern, she's so low on confidence to start with that after last night she's worse than ever, adamant she's going to hide out in the kitchen all day to avoid having to face Matt. I'm glad Kelly's working too, at least then Fern can talk about her worries with someone closer to her own age.

"It's a good job you had Matt to look after you. You must have been petrified."

I've no experience of fainting myself, but I went through a phase of having giddy spells when I first started my periods. The loss of control had been frightening, so I can only imagine how nasty it must have been for Fern, blacking out in a sea of strangers.

"The worst bit was when I came round and saw him there. He looked so anxious." Fern bites down on her lip, her embarrassment evident as she relives the experience.

"I bet he was, having his date collapse."

"He missed the whole gig to stay with me and make sure I was all right," she says, looking sheepishly at the floor. "And Psychedelic Lizard are never likely to play here again, they're far too popular now. I made him miss it because of my stupid phobia."

Kelly butts in, firm but fair, with her two-pence worth. "Firstly, he chose to stay with you, which shows he's a decent guy. I bet there are some douchebags out there who'd have left their girlfriend to watch the band instead. Secondly, they might not come back, but if Matt's that bothered he could get the train to London or Birmingham. It's less than an hour to either and I'd put money on them announcing a date at the O2 before the end of the year. And thirdly, it's not a stupid phobia. The whole thing about fear is that it takes you by surprise, that's how it works."

"I'm not his girlfriend."

"What?" Kelly frowns.

"You said not many guys would stay with their girlfriend when they could be watching their favourite band." Her voice is feverish. "We're just friends, that's all. There's nothing romantic between us."

"At least you've stopped mooning over Josh," Kelly says. "When he came into the café yesterday demanding cake and milkshake you barely even blinked! Maybe Matt's cured you after all..."

Of course, I had my suspicions that Fern had a soft spot for Josh, but I'd never questioned her on it. It didn't feel like my place. Matt's a better match for her really. As much as I'd love a daughter-in-law like Fern, I know my son. He needs someone feisty who'll stand up to him, a no-nonsense woman. Someone like Candy. She's not the type to let anyone tell her what to do.

"I hope you're finally seeing my brother for what he is rather than staring at him dreamily through rose-tinted glasses," Kelly says. "Matt's a much better choice. Sweeter, kinder and better looking than my brother, and that's not me being biased – it's fact."

I look disapprovingly at my daughter. "That's a bit harsh, Kelly. Josh does have some redeeming features, you know."

"Not many," she retorts haughtily.

"Anyway, I think it's lovely that you and Matt are seeing each other, Fern. From what I've seen of him, he's lovely."

"I'm not seeing him!" Fern's voice is shrill. "It was just a gig that he had a spare ticket for, that's all."

"I think you're protesting a bit too much," I say teasingly. "Snap him up quick, the good ones don't hang around on the shelf forever."

That said, I'd been on the shelf for a long time until meeting Paolo. I was probably the equivalent of a short-dated packet of biscuits, sat sadly in the reduced goods section alongside a dented can of beans and a bottle of antibacterial spray with a faulty nozzle. I'd got used to being the damaged goods that no one wants. As soon as men hear my name the murmurs start, buzzing like an incessant and irritating fly. I almost changed back to my maiden name, Sykes, purely to escape the jibes and preconceptions, but I didn't want to have a different surname to Kelly and Josh.

"Don't be ridiculous," she says quietly. "As if Matt would be interested in me."

Kelly tuts, rolling her eyes skywards. "Duh. He asked you out. How many times do I have to tell you – he likes you. I know he does."

Fern's eyes brighten.

"Has he told you that?" Then she seems to remember herself and return to self-preservation mode. "Not that it matters," she adds, although it's plain to see that it does.

"Not in so many words, but it's obvious. The gig, the lunchtime meetings...heck, even the way he looks at you. There's some spark there, and I'm sure that if I can see it then you must feel it. Because if someone looked at me with that much adoration I think it'd feel like all the fireworks of Bonfire Night and New Year's Eve rolled into one exploding in my chest."

Fern looks thoughtful now, as though she might actually be listening to what Kelly's saying. I hope she is digesting it, understanding that she's worthy of being loved. School was miserable for her. Kelly told me how even the cruel kids in *her* year used to make digs at Fern about her weight, not remotely put out by the fact she was three years older than them. Hopefully the attention from Matt will give her a much-needed boost.

"I'd better get behind the counter," she says, changing the subject in the least subtle of ways. "And Maggie, are you making another coconut cake ready for the lunch time rush? That one from this morning has sold out already."

"What if Matt comes in?" Kelly jokes. "Shall I ask him outright if he wants to be your 'boyfriend'?" She punctuates the word with air quotes.

Poor Fern looks horrified at the thought.

"Don't you dare," she hisses, with the closest thing to a glare she's probably ever done in her life.

"I won't."

But although Kelly's reassuring her, I can see my daughter's fingers, tightly crossed by her side.

Pearl

Oh, it's a miserable day. The kind where the heavens open and huge, hot rain pelts down. It's almost monsoon weather. The humidity alone is enough to make my head whirl and the rain on top only makes it worse.

Mitzi hates it; she's a fussy little thing and gets twitchy at the first raindrop she sees. This, though, is on another level. It's coming down in sheets, the sky a wash of charcoal-greys and dull, dark purples. It wouldn't surprise me if there's a full-on storm brewing, the clouds are looming with the threat of thunder and lightning.

We're not far from home, but it's far enough. My fitted shirt is already clinging to my skin, the uncomfortable sensation reminding me of burnt skin peeling when I've spent too long in the sun.

"Come on, Mitz. Let's shelter in the bandstand."

She's looking at me with doleful eyes and showing no sign of moving, so I resignedly scoop up her body, her fine coat of fur sodden and slippy, and hurry as quickly as I can towards the landmark.

Other people have had the same idea. The weather's been so beautiful recently that we've been lulled into a false sense of security and now we're caught out, as though Mother Nature has played a trick on us all. There's a tired-looking mum with two young children. The eldest, a boy with long sandy hair, is kneeling on the floor and running a toy car along the bench. The younger girl, a toddler who is unsteady on her feet, is tottering around, garnering smiles from the elderly crowd who've sought refuge here.

I suppose people look at me and think I'm elderly too, although in my mind I'm still in my twenties. My legs aren't arthritic yet, and I only need glasses to read the small print in the papers. I'm retired, but not yet entitled to state pension. I still have my marbles, or at least, as many as I had to start with. I certainly don't feel old.

I peer across the park towards my back garden, wondering whether we should make a run for it. We could be back in under ten minutes, and Mitzi would be happier if I could dry her off. She's wriggling like mad in my arms. Fidget bum.

Puddles are forming on the well-walked pathways as the rain continues, and the grass is bound to be a boggy mess. More and more people are sheltering, scurrying to seek cover. The bandstand and the café are the logical places to go to keep dry. I bet Maggie's rushed off her feet.

"We'll give it a few minutes to see if it blows over," I whisper to Mitzi, who whimpers sadly. "Don't be like that," I say, like a parent reprimanding a child. "I don't very much like being wet either, but if we go out in this we'll need wringing out! Look at it."

Mitzi tilts her head, appraising me as though she knows I'm right. She does that sometimes, turns all thoughtful, which is out of character compared to her usual youthful exuberance, proving she does know how to listen to me, she just chooses not to.

There's not much room to move in the bandstand now, people are squished together like tinned sardines. It's claustrophobic and I'm glad we're on the outside edge, even though it means we're still getting caught by the rain when the wind changes direction. I wouldn't want to be in the middle of this crowd and Mitzi would be going bonkers. She's squirming like mad as it is.

There's a man in a sopping wet black cagoule trying to squeeze into the cramped space; hovering on the step, shoulders hunched forward in a bid to keep his face dry. The rain's relentless, and shows no sign of easing off. I shuffle back to make more room.

A young couple move, leaning back against a pillar. They're facing each other, glowing with love as they place delicate kisses on each other's lips and cheeks and noses. Their bodies meld so closely together that there's enough room for the man to fit in, and he laughs with relief as he pulls down the hood of his cagoule, revealing a mop of mussed-up blonde hair.

"It's a tight squeeze in here!" he quips, and people smile; finding it amusing and charming how he's stating something so blatantly obvious.

The rain pelts relentlessly against the roof of the bandstand, as though it'll never stop. It's bouncing off the paths, shimmering and slippy with their wetness, but I don't care; I know I have to get out of here, and fast. He's just a few feet away from me, his pointed jaw sharp and threatening, his white-blonde hair a few shades lighter than my own.

Pulling Mitzi tighter in to my chest I force my way out of the bandstand and into the elements, jostling with my elbows when necessary.

I can't breathe, it's as though there's a tennis ball lodged in my throat. I have to find Carrick. Or Maggie. Please don't let him get to Maggie without me warning her. I run, as fast as I can with the rain beating down on me and a sausage dog tucked under my arm, because I have to tell them. I have to let them know Clint is back.

By the time I reach the café, I'm soaked to the skin and feeling flustered. An enormous sense of relief rushes over me when I spot Carrick sat nursing a cuppa.

"I'm so pleased to see you!" I gush, throwing my arms

around him. He's the only person who could possibly understand what I'm feeling right now.

"What's the matter, Pearl?" He squints at me as I stand back, scrutinising me. "You're sopping wet and white as a sheet. You look like you've seen a ghost."

"I have," I say grimly. "He's here, lurking in the bandstand. Honestly Carrick, he looks just the same."

There's a puzzled expression on his face.

"Who? Alf?"

"Of course not bloody Alf! I didn't mean an actual ghost, it was a metaphor!" My voice is too loud, too excitable, and a few people turn to look at the commotion. I need to quieten down. Drawing attention to ourselves will only cause more problems. I make a conscious effort to talk in hushed tones. "Clint's here. Walking around, bold as brass as though he's never been away." My heart's racing again at the thought. "What shall we do? Do you think we ought to tell Maggie?"

I look across to where she's stood, leaning nonchalantly against the counter. She's chatting away to Paolo, her eyes alight with love, and every so often she reaches out to place her hand on his arm, as though it's impossible to be near him and not touch him. She looks so relaxed. So happy. I can't bear to think of that happiness being smashed to pieces by her scoundrel of an ex-husband.

"Clint?" Carrick looks pretty pale himself now. "Are you

sure? There are plenty of tall, blonde men around. It could just be someone who looks like him. He's probably on your mind because we've been talking about him."

"Of course I'm sure," I hiss. "I know it's been a long time, but I'm not going to forget what my own son looks like, am I?"

Carrick swallows, the lump of his Adam's apple bobbing. When he speaks his voice is so quiet I have to strain to hear his words. "I've never heard you call him that before."

"That's what he is though, isn't he? My son. *Our* son. And he's right over there in the bandstand."

"What do you think he wants?"

"I'd hazard a guess that he's here to stir up trouble, seeing as that seems to be what he does best. He'll probably want to see Kelly and Josh, and I can't imagine he'll be too happy to see this place packed to the rafters. Not to mention that Maggie's got a new man – Clint's always thought highly of himself. He won't be best pleased to find he's been replaced. I've got to warn Maggie that he's here. He could walk in at any minute."

Carrick sighs, placing his fingertips against his temple. "It's not our place to interfere, Pearl."

"They're our family."

"It's all right for you! At least you're 'Auntie Pearl'." The bitterness in his voice makes me wince. "As far as they know, I'm nothing more than the old man who tends the roses."

"But *I* know you're more than that. They will too, when the time is right."

All the emotions I felt when Clint was sent to prison surge through me. The hurt, the anguish, the guilt. Oh, the guilt. Guilt at getting pregnant out of wedlock, then guilt for giving him up. Was he like he was because of me, because of genetics, or had I, unbeknown to me at the time, damaged him by giving him up?

"He put Maggie through hell." I say it as much to remind myself as to remind Carrick. "No woman should feel worthless. No woman deserves to be cheated on time and time again, especially not someone as lovely as Maggie. She deserved better than Clint, and now she's finally got it. I can't stand back, Carrick. I've got to warn her."

He doesn't try to stop me, although I know he wants to. He just sits there quietly, clutching desperately at the handle of his mug.

I tentatively interrupt the two lovebirds by tapping gently on Maggie's shoulder.

"I'm sorry to barge in like this, but could I borrow you for a moment please, Maggie?"

I'm sure my eyes must be full of pleading desperation, and my voice certainly is. There's a definite wobble in my words. I don't know how I'm going to say what needs to be said. It's not like I've had time to prepare a speech and I'm a bag of nerves.

Maggie peels herself away from Paolo. "Whatever's the matter? Have you had some bad news?"

"Not exactly. Look, could we find somewhere quiet to talk? I'll keep it as brief as I possibly can, but this would be better said away from other people. The walls have ears, as they say."

I'm rambling. All I want is to get this over and done with as quickly as possible.

"We can go through the kitchen?" she suggests, before frowning as she catches sight of Mitzi in my arms. "I'm sorry though, Pearl, you can't have Mitzi in here and certainly not out the back. It's against hygiene regulations. I'd be strung up if the environmental health officer happened to drop in and I had a dog on the premises."

"I'm sorry. I do know that, of course I do. My head's not screwed on properly today. I'll see if Carrick would be good enough to drop Mitzi at home."

I can always give him a key to let himself in and he's a hardy man, used to being out in all weathers with his job. He might not delight in having to go out in the rain, but he's a kind soul and I'm sure he'll do it without a grudge.

"You go and hand over that little wriggler and I'll wait for you out the back, okay?"

She looks so innocent, so unaware of the bombshell I'm about to drop and for a moment I doubt myself. Is this the right thing to do? I'm suddenly unsure, but I silently nod, making my way towards Carrick.

I can't back out now. It's time to come clean about the past. All of it.

Maggie

"Are you sure you're all right, Pearl? I can get you a stool to perch on if you like?"

The older woman's hand is trembling, and although I've not got the faintest idea what she wants to talk to me about I know it must be something serious. There was an urgency in her voice and even now her face is etched in fine lines of anguish.

"I'll be fine here, thank you," she says, placing her hand against the stainless-steel work surface, "but we do need to talk. And you might benefit from sitting down."

There's no threat or malice in her tone, but it still leaves me uneasy. My stomach has dropped, like that moment on a rollercoaster where you're suddenly descending at speed after a long, tedious climb. It's an unpleasant, yet exhilarating fizz.

"That sounds serious."

"I'm going to get straight to the point here, Maggie. Clint

271

is back. I saw him sheltering in the bandstand about quarter of an hour ago."

Even though I had a hunch that he'd turn up sooner rather than later I'm unprepared for the emotions pulsing through me. Anger, mixed with a hint of fear. Nostalgia, laced with hurt. I'm a teenager again, flushed with love. A new mum, beaten by exhaustion. A woman scorned, thrown aside like an empty chocolate bar wrapper. My life's flashing before my eyes, a cinema reel playing out before me on fast forward. For one awful moment I wonder if I'm dying.

My vision blurs. My knees buckle. Then it all goes black.

Pearl

I rush to Maggie, who's fainted on to the hard kitchen floor. Thank heavens for small mercies, because the way she's landed with her arms beneath her head might just have protected her. Perhaps I should have gone with a softly-softly approach rather than being so direct, but I didn't know how to break it to her gently. It would have been a shock either way, so I thought it better to spit it out.

"Maggie? Maggie, can you hear me?" I shake her shoulder gently, and am relieved when she groans. "Thank heavens you're all right. You gave me an almighty fright passing out like that!"

"Owwww. That hurts."

Maggie slowly pushes herself to a sitting position, massaging her left shoulder as she does so.

"You did go down with a thump."

She has a dazed, faraway look on her face, her eyes glazed

as though she's fighting to keep her focus. I can't help but think she'd be better leaning against the cupboards, just in case she keels over again.

"Please don't fuss. Honestly, I'm fine. I think it was the shock of hearing Clint's name. After all this time pushing him to the back of my mind, it's hard to accept he's back. I knew he'd want to see Josh and Kelly and I don't blame him – they're as much his children as they are mine, after all." She sighs, dejected. "You won't understand what I mean when I say this, but I'd almost forgotten he was real. There were the moments he'd pop into my mind, but for the most part it was like the life I shared with him happened to someone else. I was a different person back then. Weak. A pushover." My face must show my disagreement because she continues, "I'm not one of those women who blames herself for her husband's philandering – that was all Clint's own doing. And as for the rest of his behaviour...I can't defend it. Clint Thornhill can waltz back in here making all the demands he wants and it won't make a blind bit of difference."

She sounds feisty, and aside from the fainting incident she appears, outwardly at least, to be handling this a good deal better than I am.

"You're a strong woman, Maggie. I admire that in you. That's why I had to tell you that he's back in town. Give you a chance to get your head around it all."

"And I really appreciate it, thank you. He's been out of prison for a month or so now, so perhaps the surprise is that he didn't turn up sooner. It doesn't make it easier though. Life's settled down for me, with the children so much more independent and the business going great guns. Not to mention Paolo."

She blushes with embarrassment. It's so endearing.

My throat's dry and I cough, preparing myself to say the words that will change my life. They're words I wasn't sure I'd ever be able to say aloud, words I wasn't sure I'd ever *want* to say aloud.

"There's something else. Something I should have told you years ago, but it got harder and harder to do the longer I put it off." She's watching me with interest and I squeeze my eyes closed to block out the intensity of her gaze. "When I told you that Carrick and I used to date, that wasn't the whole story. We were lovers, and for a while it was perfect. We were young and happy – you know how it is when you're in that first flush of love. It felt like we were unbeatable, for a while." Tears are welling up behind my closed eyelids and I wonder how long I'll be able to hold back the inevitable flow. "We'd been together for three months when my period was late." Maggie gasps. "I was on the pill and thought that meant we'd be safe. It was different back then, before we knew about HIV and AIDS. Unplanned pregnancy was all we had to worry about. Of course, I knew right away I'd been caught out. I had a feeling, some kind of mother's intuition maybe? And Carrick was so kind and sweet when I told him, even though the terror was there in his eyes." I open my own eyes and look at Maggie. She's thinking, I can tell. Wondering why I'm telling her this now and what it's got to do with her. "He asked me to marry him. Out of duty, more than anything else. He loved me, I know he did, and I loved him back, but we weren't ready, not for that kind of commitment and certainly not for parenthood. So I turned him down and went to live with my Auntie Gertie in Wolverhampton. I knew I couldn't keep the baby, you see, so I wanted to get away before I started to show."

Memories rush back of that awful time, my one and only pregnancy. It should have been awe-filled, full of wonder and delight. Instead I'd felt like a stupid little girl playing at being an adult.

"Things were different to how they are these days – there was still a stigma to being an unmarried mother, especially in a town like this, but I couldn't marry Carrick just because of the baby. I didn't want him to feel he had no choice. So we agreed the baby would be adopted."

I swallow down the tennis-ball lump in my throat but I can't swallow down the guilt.

"We thought that once the baby was born that it would all be over, we'd be able to get on with our lives, but it didn't work out like that. It sounds selfish and crass, I know, but both Carrick and I wanted to forget about our child, because thinking about him only made us feel this sense of pain and regret."

"Him," Maggie echoes quietly. "You had a son."

I nod.

"We did, and he was the most beautiful baby you ever did see. He had the brightest blue eyes, like chips of topaz, and a mass of flyaway fair hair. Carrick said he looked like me, the first time he saw him, but those eyes...they were the image of Carrick's. He visited us at the hospital. We chose a name for him too, even though we knew his new parents wouldn't keep it. Phillip, that's what we liked. He looked like a Phillip."

"Oh, Pearl. I had no idea! That must have been horrible, handing over your newborn. I can't imagine it. Not being able to see your own flesh and blood grow up...it must still hurt, even after all this time."

I close my eyes again, more tightly this time. There's no hiding now, this is the moment. It's time to say what has to be said.

"We did get to see him grow up. We saw him all the time, both of us." My lips are bone dry and my mouth feels hollow as I brace myself to say the words.

"My sister was the one who adopted him. It's Clint. Clint is my son."

Maggie

It takes all the strength I can muster not to collapse again. Surely I misheard, or maybe my head is still fuzzy from earlier. Clint – my Clint, or at least, the man who used to be my Clint – can't be adopted? Poor Vivienne. She'd been put through hell because of his antics and despite it all, she'd stood by him as best as she could because that's what mothers do. All the anguish, all the hurt...she never deserved it.

People had said such terrible things. They did terrible things too, like spray-painting obscenities on the outside wall of her house and leaving a heap of stinking manure on her doorstep. All this when Clint was already in prison, as though she were solely to blame for his actions. Never mind that he was a grown man with a mind of his own. Never mind that he'd left home years ago. It was the association. That was enough. Surely she would have said something if what Pearl is telling me is true?

"I'm sorry to break it to you like this, I know it must be a shock. It feels like we've been deceiving you for a very long time, but we couldn't come clean, not when Viv and Glenn were alive. They'd never wanted Clint to know; they felt it was easier to let him believe he was biologically theirs."

I feel as though I've been winded. Everything I thought I knew about my family, about my *children's* family, has been pulled out from under me. Pearl and Carrick, they're my in-laws, sort of. And they're Kelly and Josh's grandparents.

"I can't believe you never said anything." I sound desperate. "All this time I've known you and you never said a word."

"It wasn't my place. Biologically he may be my son but I gave up all rights to him when Vivienne and Glenn adopted him. I've carried it with me all these years, and I have thought about talking to you, honestly. You won't remember this, but when Kelly was born I saw you in the supermarket. She was crying and Josh was pulling at his reins, desperate to go and look at something or other that had caught his attention. I was behind you in the queue and offered to hold her whilst you sorted out paying. She looked exactly like Clint did as a baby, right down to the bright yet suspicious eyes. As though she was watching out for anyone trying to fool her. And I wanted to tell you then, but couldn't. When I gave up Phillip…Clint…I gave up Josh and Kelly too, even though I didn't know it at the time. I gave up the chance to have a wonderful, hard-working daughter-in-law. I gave it all up."

"I can't get my head around this."

"It's a lot to take in and I understand that. But I don't want to waste any more years missing out. I know he broke your heart, Maggie, and I'm truly sorry for any part I played in making Clint the person he turned out to be, but those beautiful, beautiful children of yours – I want them to know I'm their grandma. And I want to support you if Clint turns up. You have every right to tell me to take my bare-faced cheek and get out of your café, but all I want is the chance to be a part of your family, if you'll let me."

Pearl's eyes are pooled with tears, the crepe-paper skin around them damp and glistening. I don't want to hurt her, but I have the children to think about too. It's going to be an impossibly hard time if their father is swanning around wanting to see them after all these years where the only contact has been a letter at birthdays and Christmases. I don't think rocking the boat any more than it's already going to be rocking is ideal right now, and I tell Pearl that in no uncertain terms.

"I understand," she replies, full of magnanimity and grace despite her tears. She reminds me of a member of the royal family – not the Queen, or Princess Anne, but maybe one of the minor royals, like the one that goes to Wimbledon every year. I can't remember her name, but she's got that earthy yet regal aura. Pearl's like that. She carries herself well, with class. "You need to put Josh and Kelly first, they're your priority. You're a wonderful mum, you always have been. I'm not qualified to pass judgement, but anyone with eyes in their head can see they're your world, which is as it should be. Neither Carrick nor I would ever want to push you into anything you feel uncomfortable with. That said, obviously we hope that, with time, we'll be able to play some part in their lives, if you and they will allow us to. I'm not suggesting we have a roast dinner every Sunday or anything like that. We just hope that maybe, one day, we'll be able to be honest about it." Her eyes gleam. "I want to be one of those annoying, big-headed grandparents showing off photos of their family to the cashier when I do my weekly shop, or bragging about the fact they're so smart. I know that has nothing to do with me – that's all your input and dedication to bringing them up properly – but I don't have any other family, not since Alf died. Kelly and Josh, they're all I've got."

"And Clint."

"Pardon?"

"Clint. I'm assuming you'll be contacting him too to tell him the truth?"

"Well," Pearl answers with a sigh, "Carrick and I have

been discussing whether or not it's the right thing to do. We're under no illusions that it'll be difficult for Clint to come to terms with. After all, he has no idea that the people who brought him up weren't his biological parents."

"I can't believe Vivienne never told him." I remember my mother-in-law – ex-mother-in-law really – with her narrow eyes and thoughtful expression that left everyone feeling like they'd been dressed down. She'd been a strict, indomitable woman, and had an enormous presence despite her small stature. Her tongue was sharp and she'd liked to talk, or gossip, after she'd made her harsh assessments. "He was the absolute apple of her eye."

Pearl sighs. "I know. It broke her heart when he turned out like he did and I can't help but feel responsible. If nature plays any part in it, I take the blame."

"You can't think like that, Pearl. Clint's like he is because he made bad choice after bad choice. He's a grown man who acts like a child and he's paid the ultimate price for the decisions he's made over the years. Missing out on seeing his children growing up."

There's a sadness that seeps out, my own personal guilt. Did I do the right thing, shopping him in? It was my own personal revenge, my pay-back for the pain he'd caused with his never-ending run of affairs. I'd kidded myself by saying it was civilian duty that made me make that call when I saw the CCTV footage of the bank robbery on the local news, but really it was my ego, sick and tired of being crushed and beaten and mauled by Clint Thornhill and whichever brazen floozy he'd been sleeping with that week. I hadn't known then that Pearl had been the woman he'd been pointing the gun at. That she knew it was Clint, but hadn't turned him in through family loyalty. Mother's loyalty, I realise now. It was only in court that she stated, unequivocally, that it was him who'd demanded cash or he'd shoot.

"I know you're right. He brought it on himself. He's a bad apple, isn't he?" Her heartache is evident on her face. "But he's still my son, and he's back." Her eyes catch mine, harrowed and heavy. "Oh Maggie, what am I going to do?"

Fern

There are so many people in here that the windows are steaming up casting the illusion of a veil of fog hanging over the park. Everything outside is hazy, even the outline of the bandstand, which I can just make out through the misted flashes of lightning spiking across the sky.

At least we're busy, even though the bodies squashed together into such a small space reminds me of the night I collapsed at the gig. I don't feel as anxious as I did then though, here in the café. It's a safe place, where nothing bad can happen. Here it's cakes and smiles and friendship, nothing as dreadful as brain tumours or panic attacks or self-loathing. "Can I have another tea, please, petal?" asks Carrick, who's returned soaked to the skin and without the sausage dog. His seat was snapped up as soon as he vacated it, especially as more people chose to run to the café for a warming drink and some shelter. He's leaving a trail of water behind him and a puddle is forming around the soles of his dull mustard-coloured gardening boots. "I need warming up."

"It's not slowed down out there, has it?"

I fill a small pot with scalding hot water and pop in a teabag, ensuring I leave the tag and strings dangling over the edge. There's not much more frustrating than having to fish out a soggy label.

"Nothing like a British summer to keep us on our toes!" he quips with a broad smile.

There's a pause as he eyes the door to the kitchen and he emits a small cough. "Pearl still around?" he enquires.

"Still out the back talking to Maggie. They've been in there for ages."

The smile disappears, replaced by a borderline frown, deep grooves appearing around Carrick's eyes and lips. He opens his mouth as though to speak before pressing his lips together as though he thinks better of it, but then says, "Could you go and check they're all right? Or could I?"

I'm puzzled by the request. "Is something the matter? You can tell me it's none of my business, but you're worrying me now. Is it Pearl? Is she sick?"

I've noticed Carrick and Pearl getting ever closer recently, and although some people have been making comments about it being too soon after Alf's passing for Pearl to be rushing into a new relationship, I'm glad to

see them happy. Right now though he seems more flustered. Ruffled. Having seen first-hand how quickly illness
can take over and the complete devastation it can cause,
I'm silently praying that my gut instinct is wrong and that
Pearl is in good health.

"She's not sick, no." I exhale with relief. "But she needed
to talk to Maggie about something important. Can you
pop your head round and make sure they're both okay?"

He looks so desperate that I don't have the heart to say
no, even though there are already people queuing for
top-ups. They'll have to wait a bit longer, because Carrick
looks fraught.

I knock before I enter. Something about the situation
makes me feel uneasy and I don't want to interrupt a private
conversation. It's only when I hear Maggie call for me to
come in that I push the door open.

"It's getting pretty busy out the front," I begin, "and also
Carrick's back. He wanted to make sure you were both all
right." I don't mention that he's most likely wearing the
lino down with his pacing.

"We're done," Maggie says. "I'll be out in a moment, and
I'll bring some more cupcakes through. They've been selling
well today."

"Tell Carrick I'm fine," Pearl says, before adding, "and
tell him that it's done."

I don't have the foggiest idea what 'it' is, but judging by

the look on both women's faces, it's not good. The pair of them look as jittery as anything.

"Woah. It's a bit crazy in here today," says Matt.

He's manoeuvred his way through the throngs of people and is stood directly in front of the counter, looking more gorgeous than ever, if that's possible. I've never understood how good-looking men get even more attractive when they're wet when I end up looking, and feeling, like a drowned rat after being caught in a shower. Matt's hair looks different after being out in the rain – flatter, shinier and a shade or two darker - and the raindrops trailing tantalisingly down his cheeks and neck make him look like a male model. I'm aware that I'm staring, gawping almost, but I can't help myself. If seeing Josh used to make my heart beat faster, seeing Matt like this makes it leap right out of my chest and sing hallelujah. I can't quite believe that I ever doubted his physical appeal because right now he's very, *very* appealing.

"I bet it's busier than you've been," I laugh. "Doubt there's much call for pedalos and rowing boats in this weather."

"We've closed for the day. Drizzle's one thing but a full-on downpour is another. So I've got a bit of unexpected free time."

He raises his eyebrows, semi-suggestively.

"It's all right for some. We're rushed off our feet in here.

Not helped by the fact Maggie's been hiding out the back with Pearl for the past half an hour."

I'm still wondering what they could have been discussing that's so important. The café is always at the forefront of Maggie's mind, and the only thing that comes before that is her children. Could it be something to do with Kelly and her decisions about the future? Or maybe it's Josh – him and Candy might have got engaged and she wanted to tell family first. But it was Pearl who instigated the conversation and made the elusive 'it's done' comment, which makes me think it's her that needed to talk more than Maggie. I'm sure I'll find out soon enough. It's a small town and things don't stay secret around here for long, the amount of people asking after Luke is testament to that. It's both a blessing and a curse having everyone know your business.

"No chance of you getting off early then?" he asks with a mock pout. "I'd hoped we might be able to hang out for a bit."

"I don't think so," I sigh, although there's nothing I'd like more. "I'm supposed to be finishing at four though, unless Maggie needs me to stay on longer. With these crowds it's entirely possible."

He looks at his watch, then double checks. "It's half past three. I can wait."

"I might have to stay later. I'll ask Maggie, if she ever gets out here again."

I look towards the kitchen door, and as though on cue it swings open, an uptight-looking Pearl coming out and heading straight for Carrick who sweeps her up into his arms. I'm more confused than ever by this turn of events.

"Like I said, I can wait, if you can provide me with a cappuccino and a blueberry muffin. Although I may have to perch here and watch you work, seeing as there's nowhere else to sit."

He props his elbows on the edge of the counter as I serve him. I can feel his eyes following me and my heart races. Strangely though, it's a pleasant sensation, not the tightening that accompanies my anxiety attacks. This is more like anticipation. Hope.

"I'm sorry about the other night," I blurt, my back still to him. It's easier this way, not having to make eye contact. "I find it hard in big crowds sometimes, especially in unfamiliar places. And it was so hot..."

"Sssshhh." Although he's cut me off he's not being rude. "You don't have to explain or apologise. More than anything I'm relieved that you're all right. It was frightening to see you collapse like that."

"But you missed the show because of me." I place his coffee and muffin in front of him, an apologetic smile on my face.

"Because you're way more important than a gig."

He peels back the frilled wrapper from the muffin before

pulling the puffy top off and taking a bite out of the disc. The blueberries have bled into the spongy muffin, like ink spreading across a page.

"More important than Psychedelic Lizard? Are you sure?" I tilt my head as I speak, looking up at him through my eyelashes. Flirting, unashamedly and blatantly.

"Far more important," he says, fixing his eyes on mine. "I don't think you realise just how much I like you, Fern. Kelly told me you thought I'd asked you to the gig out of pity. That couldn't be further from the truth."

I swallow. "Really?"

"Yes, really. And if we're being totally honest, I didn't have a spare ticket." He blushes, pulling his lip ring into his mouth with his front teeth. "I bought it off a mate of mine because I wanted an excuse to ask you out. He charged me three times what it cost him, but I didn't care. You're worth it. You're more than worth it. You're special, Fern."

Whether it's the look on his face or the words that he's saying, I'm not sure. All I know is that, for once, I feel special too. Because the person I like likes me back, and that's something I've never experienced before.

Now the sun's broken through the clouds the sky's a bright cornflower blue. It makes it hard to believe that just one hour before the park had been enveloped in a gloomy darkness, but it shows how quickly things can change.

Candy and Josh walk in, arms linked, and although I notice their arrival it doesn't stir up the feelings inside me that it would have previously. All I can think about is the comment Matt made earlier and how he's stood waiting for my shift to finish, making his coffee last by taking the smallest sips known to man.

"Fernephant!" Josh grins as he speaks. I cringe at the use of the nickname that had been used to taunt me for so many years, hating how it makes me feel like a vulnerable twelve-year-old again. "Is Mum around?"

"Baking out the back," I mumble, mortified. I can't believe he called me Fernephant in front of Matt.

"Can you go and tell her we're here?" he simpers, and for some reason I do as he asks, and I'm irritated with myself for letting people trample over my feelings, again. Matt had made me feel extraordinary, like I was one in a million for all the right reasons, yet Josh had belittled me with just one word. Kelly had been right all along. Someone like that wasn't deserving of my affection.

"Josh and Candy are here," I say through gritted teeth.

Maggie is sat cross-legged on the kitchen floor, staring at the oven door as though it's a TV set. It's not an unfamiliar scene – she prefers to watch what she's baking like a hawk if she has the opportunity – but the blank look on her face is not her usual animated expression.

"Is everything all right?"

She sighs, dejected, before melodramatically adding, "I don't want to talk about it. Not yet, anyway."

"You know where I am when you do," I say with a smile. I haven't forgotten how wonderful Maggie's been about Luke and if I can repay her by being a willing sounding board for her troubles, then I will. "Do you want to come out to see Josh or should I send him back here?"

"I'll come out," she says quietly, turning the oven off. "These biscuits are done now anyway."

I sniff the air, trying to guess what she's been baking. Macaroons maybe?

"And it's the end of my shift too," I say apologetically. "You know I'm happy to stay longer if you need me to, but Matt's waiting for me..."

Maggie's eyes shine at my revelation. "I knew there was a spark between you two!"

"I don't know if I'd go that far..."

"Well, there's something. Go on, you get off. I'm sure I can rope Josh in to give me a hand if needs be."

And as I whip my apron over my head I can't keep the smile off my face.

The woodland area of the park has always been one of my favourite places. I've heard people say it's overcast compared to the green, which is drenched in sunshine on every long summer day, but the winding pathways and the natural tunnels created by the overhanging trees magic me away until I'm no longer in a park, I'm in a fairy-tale.

"It was Josh, wasn't it? He was the crush you had. The one who didn't like you back."

Matt's words surprise me, but it's his perception that surprises me more than anything. Over the past few weeks I'd barely thought of Josh and since the gig my mind has been running amok wondering if Matt liked me 'like that'. Perhaps he was the cure for my Josh addiction. It's a shame I hadn't met him years ago.

"Yes." My voice comes out quietly and I look at the ground. For some reason I feel ashamed. As though by admitting it I'm making a fool of myself all over again. "How did you know? Was it Kelly shooting her mouth off?" I know she'd not have said anything in malice, but she can't half chat. She probably let it slip without even thinking.

"No, actually. It was the look Josh gave us when we left the café together."

I frown. "What look?"

"A pissed-off look. As though he didn't like it."

"Don't be ridiculous," I laugh. "He couldn't care less who I hang around with. Anyway, he's with Candy."

My stomach flips at the thought that Josh noticed Matt and I together and I fleetingly wonder if he might be jealous. Not of me and Matt as such, but of the fact that my attention has finally shifted from him. I'd been a lovesick puppy hanging around him for so long that he probably found it hard to believe I could be interested in anyone else.

"He was firing daggers at us," Matt confirms.

"I don't think so."

"If looks could kill I'd be laid out on the ground. Are you sure there's never been anything between you? Because he looked like an ex-boyfriend who'd had his nose pushed out of joint."

"No!" The thought amuses me. As if. "You've seen Candy. She's the kind of girl he goes for."

"More fool him."

"She seems nice enough. I mean, I've only seen her when they've been in the café but Maggie approves of her and that's what's important. She's a DJ, you know."

"With multi-coloured lights and a playlist of novelty hits?" His voice is drenched in sarcasm.

I raise my eyebrows. "Not that kind of DJ. She works in a club."

"I'm not interested in Candy. Or Josh either, for that matter." There's an awkward pause as he looks at me and I shift uncomfortably. The sunlight is breaking through the trees, casting glitter ball sparkles on the shadowy tracks. "Sorry." I bite my lip apologetically. "Let's talk about something else." I wrack my brain for something to say. "Did you watch the first part of that new police drama last night? It had that woman from EastEnders in it. She was really good actually, I was surprised because I'd always found her a bit wooden before—"

Matt holds his hand up to stop me.

"Fern. I didn't watch anything last night. I messed about on the Internet for a few hours and then fell asleep on the settee. But I don't want to talk about that either."

"Oh, OK."

I start walking again. The speckles of light dance across the trail ahead of us.

"I wanted to spend time with you away from everyone else because I like you, Fern. I really like you. And I know I'm nothing like Josh, I'm not as clever and I don't have that whole young Hugh Grant look going on that women seem to love."

"I prefer Colin Firth. Mark Darcy melted my heart."

"Well, I don't have much in common with him either, except a couple of hideous Christmas jumpers hidden at the back of the wardrobe. But I'd like us to give it a real shot, if you think it's worth a go. I'd treat you right, Fern. Please, just give me the chance to show you how amazing I think you are."

I've stopped again, desperately trying to read his expression. He looks so earnest that I believe him, even though it's hard to believe he could be interested in me.

"Say something, then. If I've totally misread the situation, I'm sorry, but when you said yes to the gig I thought maybe you might like me too."

"I do like you."

"You do?"

"A lot. Especially since you looked after me when I fainted. That was really lovely."

"What can I say? I'm a nice guy."

I smile.

"You are. But not too nice, I hope?"

"What do you mean?"

"Do nice guys kiss on a first date?" I say, overcome with a new-found confidence.

He leans in towards me, until his mouth is close to mine. His lip ring is maybe an inch away from my face and I wonder what it would be like to feel it pressed against my lips. His breath skims my cheek and my heart pounds.

"I don't think they do," he replies.

My heart sinks.

"Oh."

"But I think they might on a second date, with the right person. And since we've already been out together, kind of..."

That's all the invitation I need. As I close my eyes, I savour the sensation. Matt's lip ring pressing against my mouth, and the warmth of his hand against the small of my back. The taste of coffee mixed with blueberry muffin, bittersweet perfection. And I feel happy. Happy, and loved.

Lacey

"Uncle Carrick!"

He's sat waiting for us at the corner table with Pearl, just like he said he would be, but although I raise my hand in a wave he doesn't seem to see me. Instead he's looking beyond me. They both are, and I turn to face the fair-haired man walking in through the door behind me that my uncle's gaze is fixed on.

I try again. "Uncle Carrick!"

"He's in his own little dream world," Warren laughs. "And to think I was really nervous about officially meeting him. He hasn't even noticed you, let alone me."

"Maybe he can't hear above all the noise," I mutter, although I don't quite believe it. It's busy in the café after the earlier storm, but it's not that loud.

I wrack my brains to try and think if I could've done something to upset him but come up with nothing. We'd talked on the phone just last night and he'd seemed fine. A bit distracted, but fine.

"We'll go and order first and see him in a minute, yeah?" I say.

"Sure. Anything I could bribe him with? I want to get into his good books, seeing as I know how much you two mean to each other."

"Ha-ha. Uncle Carrick will eat anything so long as it's sweet. But you can't go wrong with the lemon drizzle cake, or the Victoria sandwich. He prefers a proper slice of cake to a cupcake."

"Me too. You get more."

"Oh, blow it. I'll have a slice too. Maggie's cakes are too good to pass up."

The row of baked goods looks mouth-wateringly appealing and despite my best efforts I know I'll end up giving in anyway sooner or later. Might as well be sooner.

Maggie's behind the counter, and she smiles as she sees us. We've been in a few times now, partly because it's convenient and partly because the food is incredible. We're becoming regulars.

"What can I get for you two today?"

"Three slices of lemon drizzle cake, a cappuccino and…?" Warren turns to look at me.

"A lemonade for me, please."

"Coming right up," she says with a beam, getting straight to work on setting up a tray for our order. She has her back to us as she fiddles with the coffee machine, which is spluttering and gurgling away.

"Can I order a coffee?" says the man behind us.

It's the same one who'd followed us in, the one I thought Uncle Carrick had been looking at. He looks vaguely familiar, but I can't quite place him. Mind you, I still don't know everyone in this town. All those years away at boarding school meant I missed out on becoming a proper part of the community as a child. People that went to the local comprehensive all know each other.

Maggie freezes, still facing the back wall.

"No rush," says the man, his voice laced with menace. "No one's holding a gun to your head."

When Maggie turns, she's white as a sheet. Even her lips are a ghostly shade of lilac, as though every drop of blood has drained from her body.

"It's...it's you." Maggie's voice wavers.

"That's right, it is." The man's eyes flicker manically. "It's good to see you, Maggie. It's been a long, long time." His voice drawls. "Far too long."

"Not long enough."

"Now, now. No need to be like that, is there? I was everything to you, once upon a time, wasn't I? I was your whole world. You could be a bit more...welcoming." He smiles, but it's not a pleasant look. There's something about him that I don't like.

"But you're not welcome, Clint. In fact, I'd appreciate it if you'd leave my café immediately," says Maggie.

The man shows no sign of moving, instead standing his ground. As he places his elbow proprietorially on the counter, Maggie recoils.

"That's no way to treat your husband."

"Ex-husband," Maggie spits. "And I'd like you to go."

"So soon?" His voice is laden with sarcasm. "I haven't even seen the rest of the family yet."

"I'll tell Kelly and Josh you came by." Maggie practically throws a pen and a paper bag at Clint. "Leave a phone number. I'll let them know they can call if they want to see you."

He scrawls a number on the paper and thrusts it towards Maggie. It's like watching a scene from a soap opera.

"I want to see my children, naturally. There's not much else in this shithole to bring me back," he sneers. His voice booms, and people turn disapprovingly at both his volume and his language.

"You've said your piece, and you're upsetting my customers. Get out now, or I'm calling the police."

"Calm down, Maggie. I'll leave in a minute."

He turns his head to the corner, where Uncle Carrick and Pearl are watching on. They look anxious.

"Hi, *Mum,*" he calls, waving his hand.

Pearl's face loosens, and it's as though she ages ten years in a matter of seconds.

"What's going on?" Warren murmurs. "I've lived here for years and didn't know Pearl had a son."

"She doesn't," I reply, although a bad feeling washes over me. Something about this situation is making me decidedly uncomfortable.

"But he called her Mum?" Warren whispers.

I study the man, trying to place him. He's tall and thin and his clothes are ill-fitting. His face is angular, with a bone structure models would kill for – high cheekbones and a sharp, pointed chin, punctuated by thin lips and narrow eyes. But it's the colour of the eyes that makes my heart stop, a vivid and unusual forget-me-not blue. They're exactly the same shade as Uncle Carrick's.

"You don't have to lie to me anymore, *Auntie Pearl*. I know all about your dirty secret. Did you know that Mum sent me a letter before she died? Not that she's my real mum. Maybe I should refer to her as Auntie Vivienne instead."

He laughs. It sounds sinister.

"Oh yes, she told me everything," he continues, his voice booming for the whole café to hear. "I wouldn't have thought you had it in you. Maybe that's where I get my rebellious streak from. There's no hiding from genes."

"What you have is more than a rebellious streak, Clint." Pearl's voice trembles but there's a steely determination in her eyes. "The things you've done are unforgivable. Every night I pray to God that it's not my genes that made you turn out the way you did. You're rotten to the core and I wish you were still locked up."

"Well, you did your best on that front too, didn't you? That day in court when you gave your witness statement. That's what got me sent down."

"I told the truth," Pearl replies evenly. "I told them that I was working my shift when a man walked into the bank and told me to empty the safe or he'd shoot me. I told them I recognised the man as Clint Thornhill. I told the truth."

"It was your fault I was sent to prison! If it wasn't for you I'd still be happily married. I'd have been able to see my children grow up rather than missing out on everything."

"I think you'll find all that was your fault, not mine." Pearl's face is purple now, as though she may explode with rage. "You ruined your family with your continual philandering and you went to prison because you committed a crime. You brought this on yourself, Clint. Don't try to turn this onto me."

"You're an angel, are you?" he snarls. "Yeah, right. Whatever you say. Maybe it's my father that made me this way then. Was he a bad boy? Like a bit of rough back then, did you?" He laughs. "That's if you know who my father is. Mum said you never even told her who he was. I reckon you were a slut who slept around, weren't you? I bet you don't have a clue who my real dad is."

There's a visible fire raging in Pearl's eyes.

"You're a bastard, Clint."

"And don't you know it, *Mother*," he taunts.

"Don't you ever speak to her like that, you hear me?" Clint turns, as we all do, to face the voice that is so familiar to me. "If you know what's good for you you'll butt out of this. It's nothing to do with you."

"That's where you're wrong," Uncle Carrick replies. As he pulls himself taller, I'm filled with dread. I grab on to Warren's arm to steady myself, preparing myself for what I somehow know is about to happen. "I'm your father."

Uncle Carrick looks at me momentarily, an apologetic expression on his face, but I can't look at him. I can't bear to be in the same room as him. I love him so much, yet for all his talk of respect and honesty he'd lied to me my entire life.

"Come on," I say to Warren, tugging on his arm. "We're leaving."

And as I drag him out of the café, tears streaming down my cheeks, I run to the rose garden, where I vomit over one of Uncle Carrick's prized blooms.

Pearl

I'd imagined this moment in my mind so many times, yet never once had I thought it'd end up like this, with Carrick and Clint squaring up to each other in the middle of a crowded Lake House Café.

"You?" Clint prods Carrick's chest with a bony finger. "You aren't my father. You're just the weird gardener that talks to the plants. We always used to think you were a freak." He laughs cruelly. "All the kids thought you were dodgy. The way you spoke to us all like we cared about your stupid roses...you were like a paedo trying to groom us."

"Enough!" The voice is shrill and sharp, and at first I don't realise it's my own. "You're confused and you're angry, but that doesn't give you the right to say such slanderous things about Carrick. I'm your mother, and he's your father, whether you like it or not."

"Oh, I certainly don't like it. You've lied to me my whole life, and you would have carried on doing so if Mum, who by the way will always be my real mum, no matter what you say, hadn't told me that you'd been lying through your teeth the whole time." He turns back to Carrick, his lip curled in distaste. "No wonder Auntie Pearl gave me up. Probably couldn't bear to be associated with a freak like you. She must have been ashamed. Embarrassed."

Carrick's voice remains calm, quiet. I've no idea how. "Shame? Embarrassment? How dare you say that! After everything you've put her through – put all of us through – and you're twisting the past around to make out you're the one who's hard done by?" He's speaking through gritted teeth, his jaw hard, his eyes glassy. "Maybe we didn't do the right thing by keeping it from you. Maybe we should have told you the truth from the off, or at least when you were old enough to understand. But do you know something, Clint? When you did the things you did, the awful, deceitful, criminal things you did, I didn't want anything to do with you. You might be my flesh and blood, but I'll be damned if I've anything in common with a vile excuse of a human being like you."

All eyes are on us, the free entertainment show. I have no idea how my life is such a mess, how I've become the centre of this circus. All I know is that I need it to stop. My heart is leaping into my throat, and I'm floundering wildly. It's exactly how I felt on my wedding day when I knew I was keeping secrets from Alf.

"You're a loser," Clint says, his face only millimetres away from Carrick's, "and you mean nothing to me. Nothing. Do you hear me?"

"I hear you. The whole bloody town can hear you. When Pearl and I gave you up, my heart broke in two. I'd lie awake at night, convinced I could hear your cries from across the other side of town. I loved you with every breath in my body, and I thought watching you grow up from afar was the hardest thing I'd ever have to do. But in the end you made it easy for me. You turned into a spiteful, vindictive young man and you know what, Clint? I was glad no one knew you were mine. I was glad!"

Clint's on his toes, dancing like a boxer about to go twelve rounds. Carrick's hands are balled into tight, angry fists. He might have started off calm, but he's far from calm now. For one awful moment I truly believe they might come to blows.

It's only when Maggie steps between them, literally, that my fears are alleviated. This whole situation is horrific enough without fistfights and bloodshed. Carrick's heartache might have been over years ago, when he gave up on our son, but it's only now that I understand I've been carrying a quiet, distant hope inside me that maybe prison would have changed him for the better, that maybe our innocent baby son is still inside Clint somewhere, even if he was buried deep.

But as Maggie grabs Clint by the collar of his coat and throws him out of the door to the bemusement of the startled customers who have never seen her anything but joyous, I know. I might have given birth to him, but Clint Thornhill is not my son, and from now on, I won't even think of him as my nephew. He's nothing more than a villain who once threatened to shoot me dead.

And then my knees buckle and I fall into a web of arms as Carrick, Maggie and I hold each other tightly, trying desperately to stop the torrent of tears for the boy we all once loved.

Maggie

I never normally like locking-up time. The café is supposed to thrive, so shutting the door on the very people who bring it to life seems wrong, somehow. But not tonight. Tonight I can't wait for everyone to leave, so I can disinfect every crevice. I feel violated and dirty, as though Clint invaded my safe space and sullied it with his presence.

"Are you sure you're all right to be on your own?" Carrick asks kindly as he and Pearl stand to leave. His eyes are full of concern. "You've had a nasty shock."

"We've all had a shock," I correct, "but I'll be fine, thank you. Paolo and Kelly will be here soon, so I won't be alone for long."

I'd phoned Kelly and Josh as soon as Clint was out of sight, just in case he took it upon himself to go and find them. Telling them my version of events was important, because Clint has a habit of twisting everything to make himself the victim in any given situation. It seemed unlikely that he'd go to the house, but nothing Clint does surprises me anymore, so I'd been forced into two awkward conversations to fill them in on the surprising turn of events, where they'd asked questions I didn't have the answers to myself. Josh hadn't answered, probably getting ready for his date with Candy, but Kelly had, despite being in town with Luke. I felt bad for spoiling her day, especially when she said she was coming straight to the café on the next bus. Then I'd phoned Paolo, because what I wanted more than anything was to feel his arms wrapping me safely up, like I'm a china doll and he's the bubble wrap that'll ensure I don't break.

"If you're sure," Pearl says. "We can always stay until they arrive, if you like?"

It's a kind offer, but I can see how tired Pearl is. The exhaustion is obvious from her hunched shoulders and the way her arms are crossed protectively in front of her stomach, as though she's been winded. Clint has that effect on people, leaving them battered and bruised.

"I'll be fine."

I hold the door open for them, two people who I thought I knew well, when actually I never really knew them at all. They step on to the terrace, still slick from the rain. I close the door behind them, drop the latch and turn my back on the park. Leaning against the door, I slide my back down the glass until I'm on my haunches, and exhale, relieved to be alone with my thoughts. Then, and only then, do the tears flow.

By the time Kelly's face is pressed up to the glass, framed by an eerie summer mist, I've already disinfected every surface twice. It's done little to relieve the anger, the hurt, the hatred, but the café is the cleanest it's ever been, and that's saying something.

"I got here as quickly as I could," she says. Her cheeks are flushed, her loose hair tangled, and I wonder if, however unlikely and out of character it might be, she ran here. "I was worried about you."

My daughter examines my face, trying to read what's going on in my mind. Good luck to her with that, because right now I'm not sure I know what's going on in there myself. It's a pivotal moment, roles reversed. Her wanting to protect me from the evils of the world.

"I'm fine," I sigh. "Well, not fine. I'm far from fine, but I'm okay."

She glances around the café, taking in the sheen of the surfaces, inhaling the bleach-fuelled air.

"I can't believe Dad turned up out of the blue and then caused such a scene in front of the customers. And I can't believe he didn't want to see me and Josh."

The hurt is evident in her face, the downturn at the corner of her lips and the pain behind her eyes. She was such a

Daddy's girl when she was small. This latest rejection is just another way that he's letting her down, the most recent in a long string of empty words and broken promises.

"He left a phone number. So you can call if you want to."

I'd wanted to screw up the paper bag the digits were written on. I'd so very nearly done it too, but I couldn't bring myself to. If Kelly and Josh want to see Clint then they need to know how to contact him. However much I want to cut all ties, he is still their father. I will never be able to disentangle myself from him, not fully.

"I don't want to." Her voice sounds strangled, pained. "I don't think I want anything to do with him."

"Don't make any rash decisions, love. Not in the heat of the moment. It's a lot to take in."

Kelly shakes her head.

"It's not just about him not getting in touch sooner. It's not even about him not coming to find me and Josh. When you told me what he said to Carrick…that's just unforgivable." She sobs, her whole body shaking. "My dad's not a nice man, is he?"

Biting down on my lip, I shake my head.

"No, darling. He's not."

"Then why did you marry him? Why would you let him put you through everything he put you through if he's so awful?"

"I loved him." Oh, and how I'd loved him. Every cell in my body had been bursting with the emotion. "I really loved him, Kel. He wasn't an angel, and I knew that, but I wanted to be with him regardless. I was young, and naïve, and I thought maybe he'd change once we had children. That was my mistake, thinking he'd ever change. People like him never do."

"I'm sorry, Mum."

I look up, confused.

"What have you got to be sorry for?"

"I'm sorry he treated you the way he did. You deserved better."

The door opens, the golden bell happily jangling in response as Paolo hurries in, gushing with words of comfort.

"I did," I reply, gladly sinking into my boyfriend's arms. I breathe in his scent, taking my strength from him. "But I've got better now."

Fern

"Well, this is a bit posh."

I admire the chandeliers twinkling over my head, the pure white tablecloths spread over the tables and the floral decorations around the room. It looks more like a wedding reception than an Indian restaurant but is absolutely stunning.

"Nice, isn't it?" Matt replies. "I saw a review online and thought it sounded like the perfect place to take someone special on a night out."

I smile with embarrassment.

"Thank you. I just hope I'm dressed appropriately. I didn't realise it was going to be this fancy. I'd have made more effort if I'd have known."

I look at my plain black linen trousers and cream blouse. I'd taken time over my hair, twisting it into an elaborate up-do, and finished my look with just a touch of make up. I'd not even gone with the small diamond earrings I'd thought about wearing in the end either, and I regret it now.

"You look beautiful, just like you always do," he says, taking my hand in his. "Every guy in the place did a double take when you walked in. I'm the envy of them all."

"Don't be ridiculous," I splutter, hoping a waiter will come and seat us soon. I'm suddenly very self-conscious and will be happier once I've got a table to hide behind. My inexperience at dating is showing.

"I'm not being ridiculous," he insists. "I still can't believe you agreed to come."

"I can't believe you're dressed in a smart shirt," I say with a laugh. "Normally I only ever see you in your uniform. I've got to say I could get used to seeing you dressed like this."

He scrubs up well. The powder-blue short-sleeved shirt brings out the colour of his eyes and his shoes are polished to oblivion. His hair's still spiked and he's still fiddling with his lip ring with his tongue the way he does when he's uncomfortable. I've worked out that he does it when he's in new or unfamiliar situations. It's his stress release and I find it totally adorable. It's one of his little quirks that makes me love him all the more.

"Don't get too used to it," he says, fiddling with his collar. "I'm more at home in casual clothes. It's nice to make an effort once in a while though, and if it makes you happy maybe I'll do it more."

A waiter dressed in the stereotypical white shirt and black trousers welcomes us and guides us to a table in the far corner of the restaurant. We're next to a large window, which delights me. I love getting to people watch and this way I can see everyone coming in. I'll enjoy looking at their outfits, especially as some of the people in here have gone all out. The lady in the silver sequin sheath dress is captivating. Every time she moves she glistens. And her partner is dressed in a suit, which must be by one of the big-name designers. It screams expensive.

The waiter places the leather-bound menus in front of us, and bows – yes, bows – as he leaves us to choose our starters. We look at each other and laugh.

"I think this is a bit upmarket for us," I say. "Why would he bow?"

"He probably thought you were a princess," Matt says. "You've got that look about you tonight. I think it's the hair."

"Very funny."

"I wasn't joking. It must have taken you ages to do, whereas mine took all of two seconds." He gestures running his fingers through his hair and then gives a wide smile and a thumbs up. Seeing him touching his hair makes me want to do the same. It looks so soft. He must notice me watching as he looks confused. "What? Why are you looking at me like that?"

"Your hair looks so fluffy," I say, even though I know it sounds ridiculous. It was bad enough thinking it, let alone saying it out loud. For some reason, when it comes to Matt I am losing my inhibitions. I'm being braver all the time. "I was thinking about touching it, if you must know."

He smirks, obviously pleased that he could have that effect on me. It's flattering. "You can touch it if you want," he says.

I reach across the table, carefully avoiding the lit tea light in the centre of the table and slowly and deliberately run my fingers through the long fronds of hair at the front. Matt swallows as I do, and I can hear his lips part. I long to kiss him, right here in the restaurant, but although we're in the corner and it's likely no one would notice I daren't. Instead I sit back down with a smile.

"You drive me crazy, Fern." He shakes his head. "I've never met anyone like you before. No one's ever made me feel the way you do."

"Not even the woman you mentioned?"

I'm not fishing for compliments, I'm just curious, that's all. From what he'd revealed to me before it sounded as though she'd unknowingly broken his heart. I hoped I'd be the one to mend it.

He smiles and then studies the menu.

"That was different," he answers finally. "It was never going to go anywhere. With you I feel like this could be it."

"Could be what?"
He looks me straight in the eye.
"Love."

The food was as fantastic as everyone had predicted and I couldn't stop staring at Matt. He was as delicious as the food, every movement he made had my heart fluttering and my mind racing. We chatted about anything and everything. I could talk to him about Luke and the brain tumour, about my parents and their old-fashioned views, about how painful school had been because of the comments the other kids had made about my size and appearance. And he told me about how difficult it had been moving to the area, and how at first he'd struggled to adapt. It had been the perfect date, with the perfect person.

It's as we prepare to leave that it all goes downhill. I see them heading towards the restaurant through the windows, the bright lights of the restaurant like a spotlight on the two of them. It doesn't bother me that we'll have to walk past them on the way out. My evening had been so totally brilliant that nothing was going to bring it down or ruin it, not even seeing Josh and Candy.

"Have a lovely evening, madam," says the maître d' as he holds my coat open for me. "And we hope to see you again soon."

I don't think there'd be much chance of that. Although

Matt had done his utmost to hide it from me, I'd seen the bill – a three-figure sum that I'm sure is more than he could comfortably afford to pay. Despite my protests he'd been insistent he didn't want to go halves.

"I want to treat you, Fern. Don't spoil a lovely evening by arguing."

And I hadn't, because he was right, it had been a lovely evening and I didn't want to mar it so it became anything less than wonderful.

We're just heading out of the door when Josh and Candy pass us. At first I think they haven't seen us as neither of them say anything, but then I hear the call of "Fernephant!"

It only takes that one word for everything to crash down around me. I no longer feel beautiful, like a woman worthy of being treated. I feel as small and mousey as I did back in the corridors at school, when people shouted hurtful names after me as I pretended I couldn't hear them; when all the while they might as well have been stabbing me with a dagger for the hurt they were causing.

"What did you say?"

Matt's mouth is in a hard line, his eyes narrowed. He actually goes as far as to take a step forward, so he's right up in Josh's face.

"Leave it, Matt," I mumble, reaching for his arm to try and pull him back. "It's okay."

It's far from okay but I don't want to make a scene. Right

now all I want to do is get away from Josh as quickly as humanly possible.

He shrugs me off, his eyes not leaving Josh.

"Where the hell do you think you get off calling my girlfriend names? Is that how you get your kicks, by making someone feel inferior to you?"

Josh sneered. "I was talking to her, not you."

To give Candy her dues, she looks as uncomfortable as I do, although she remains silent, cuddling her clutch bag to her stomach as a child might do a teddy bear.

"You weren't talking, you were goading." I've never seen Matt look like this, so angry. "If you know what's good for you, you'll stay away from Fern and stay away from me." His voice remains even, but there's a menace to his tone. "And you never, and I repeat never, call her that name again. Not to her, not to your small-minded friends, not to anyone. Do you hear me?"

Josh tips his head back, his dark hair flipping out of his eyes. Once upon a time that would have made me melt, but not now. Now I see him for what he is. Selfish and cruel.

He casts his eyes dismissively over me.

"I wouldn't waste my breath, mate."

Matt shakes his head.

"I'm not your mate, and I wouldn't want to be. Now piss off and leave us alone." He puts his arm around my shoulder and I'm glad of it. I hadn't realised until then that I'd been shaking. My knees buckle and it's only because I have Matt's arm around me, holding me up, that I don't fall to the ground in a heap. "Come on," he says, bending down and placing a kiss on top of my head. It might be lost in my hair but I don't mind. It gives me back the self-belief I need.

I turn my head to watch through the window as Josh and Candy are seated, coincidentally, at the table we've just vacated. Something about seeing him there, laughing, riles me. A fire ignites in my belly. I'm not that teenage girl who lets people walk all over her. I'm worth more than that.

Matt sees me looking, mistaking my watchful gaze as one of sadness.

"Don't let him get to you," he says. "You've got me now, Fern. I promise I'll never hurt you like he has, and I won't let anyone else hurt you either. You're far too precious to me."

"Give me a minute," I say quietly. "There's something I need to do."

I pull open the door by the smooth brass handle and smile politely at the maître d'.

"I'm so sorry," I begin. "There's something I forgot at the table. I'll only be a moment."

Every step I take sounds loud to me as my heels strike against the exquisite parquet flooring. In my mind it echoes, reverberating around the room, bouncing off the high vaulted ceiling. It probably doesn't, but it seems like it to me. I feel as though I'm playing a part in a film. I'm Glenn Close in Fatal Attraction, even though in reality I'm Fern Hart. Either way, no one messes with me. Not today.

By the time I reach the table I'm brimming over with anger and confidence. It's a dangerous combination.

Josh looks up from his menu, his face falling as he sees me there. Candy looks confused, as does Matt, who's watching on through the window.

"What are you doing here?" Candy asks. "I thought you were leaving."

"I was." I smile sweetly. "But there was something I forgot to do."

"If it was the tip, you could have given it directly to the waiter rather than coming to the table," she says with a frown.

"It wasn't the tip."

I look at Josh. Seeing him now, he doesn't look like he did in my memory. He's not dreamy and angelic; he's hard-faced. And where I used to think he looked like Maggie, now I don't see her in him at all. He's become ugly to me.

My mouth is dry and my legs are quaking but I know I need to do what I came here for.

"Excuse me," I say, turning to the smartly dressed couple at the next table. They're enjoying their dessert, and although probably wondering why they've been interrupted the lady with the glitter ball dress smiles. "I hope what happens next doesn't ruin your evening."

I pick up the bottle of Burgundy from the table. It's three quarters full and heavy in my hand.

"For years now you've made me feel inferior because I'm not stick-thin. You've called me names. You've made me the butt of your jokes and for some reason I let you do it. But you know what, Josh?" I spit his name. "Not any more. You don't get to judge me. It's taken me far too long to realise this, but I couldn't give a monkey's what you think about me. You're a pathetic person who tries to make them-selves feel better by putting others down."

I tip the bottle, the rich red wine dripping down the side of his face so he looks like a Hallowe'en ghoul. It's even more satisfying than I'd imagined.

"Enjoy your night," I say, taking one last glance at the pair of them, both open-mouthed, before I take some notes from my pocket and place them on the table of the smart couple.

"This is to cover the wine."

"Bravo!" the lady cheers, clapping her hands together.

Matt is grinning like a loon as I skip back out into the warm, balmy evening, but right now even his approval doesn't matter. All that matters is me.

This is my moment of glory. I'm me, and I'm enough.

August 2017

Lacey

The decision Warren and I made to go ten pin bowling was rash. I've never been before – something he insists is a travesty at my age – and am awestruck by the shoes. "I don't understand why they're half red and half blue. Wouldn't it be easier if they were all one colour?"

"Ah, but then they wouldn't be the fashion statement they are," Warren replies in a mock solemn manner.

"Very funny. Seriously though. What are they thinking? And why don't they do other colours?"

"If you're missing your neon footwear you could always go for a run tomorrow. I'll come with you if you like?"

I'd not been running for weeks, not since the day I'd learnt Uncle Carrick's secret. I couldn't face bumping into him as I jogged round the park and running around the housing estates didn't have the same appeal. And as for a treadmill at the gym – I'd tried it once and been bored silly. I'd missed the tweeting of the birds and the summer scents floating on the air. There are some things even the best gym in the area doesn't offer.

"I don't think so."

"You can't avoid him forever, Lace."

I look at my shoes, examining the stitching. "No one said anything about forever. I'm not ready yet, that's all."

"It's never going to be the right time. It was a shock for you, and Carrick will understand that you've needed some space. But you're going to have to talk to him sooner or later."

I sigh. "I know. But I've no idea what to say. I can't say it's fine, because it's not, but I don't see the point in arguing with him about it. It's not going to change anything."

"It's not good to be brooding over it like this. You're exhausted. It's like you're a totally different person to the one you were when you were training for the half marathon. You've lost your pizzazz."

I glare.

"Do you blame me? The person I trusted more than anyone in the world betrayed me. So excuse me if I don't feel like dancing on tables right now."

My sarcasm sounds bitter and I hate myself for it. I'm hating everything at the moment.

"It's going to be hard. But it's not going to go away, and right now all it's doing is eating you up. Think about it this way – how would you feel if something happened to your uncle and you never got over this rift between you?"

I push myself up from the seat, not wanting to even contemplate how awful that would be. Losing Auntie Marilyn had been hard enough and every memory I had of her was full of smiles and laughter. Heaven forbid something happened to Uncle Carrick and I never got to make up with him.

"You're right," I admit. "I'd never forgive myself. He'll probably be angry that I've not been returning his calls." I'd pressed the 'divert to voicemail' button more times than I'd cared to remember to avoid having to face the difficult conversation.

"I bet you anything he'll be over the moon to hear from you. I've seen the pictures of you together. You mean the world to him."

I brighten. "You think so?"

Warren laces his arm around my waist and squeezes me. "I know so. He loves you, Lace. And I do, too."

It's the first time he's said it.

"You love me?" My voice cracks as I speak.

"I love you," he affirms. "But that doesn't mean I won't whip your butt at bowling," he adds with a smile.

"We'll see about that!" I laugh, my determined nature shining through. I reach for the orange bowling ball. It's heavier than I expected but there's no way I'm giving in. "And Warren?"

"Yeah?"

"I love you, too."

By the time we leave the bowling alley I feel three stone lighter. I'd rung Uncle Carrick, and although it hadn't been the easiest of conversations, it was the first step to getting our relationship back on track. I'd cried at the sound of his voice, relieved that he wasn't holding the last few weeks' silence against me. He explained how he'd loved Pearl, but they'd been young and scared and that neither of them were ready for parenthood. Unfortunately, the strain of the pregnancy had taken its toll on their relationship and although he'd always loved her, Pearl had gone on to marry Alf. He was obviously choked as he told me how broken hearted he'd been, and how the reason he'd never married was because in his eyes no woman had ever compared to Pearl. By the time the conversation ended I felt as though I knew him better than I ever had before, and loved him more too, despite his flaws.

"I told you I'd win," I say to Warren.

I can't help gloating. I'd done better than I'd expected to, including getting three strikes. Maybe I'm not quite as unathletic as I thought, I just hadn't found my sport before. If you can call ten pin bowling a sport...

"Beginner's luck," Warren replies, sticking his tongue out. "Next time I'll bring my A game."

"You brought your A game. It just wasn't up to the same standard as *my* A game."

"All right, Little Miss Cocky. You won fair and square. I'm beginning to think there's nothing you can't do."

"My talents are wide ranging," I say. "I'll have to demonstrate some of my other skills later."

He raises his eyebrows. "Promises, promises."

I jab him in the ribs with my elbow. "That wasn't innuendo! You've got a filthy mind, obviously." I shake my head.

"You can demonstrate any of your skills, kinky or otherwise," Warren says, rubbing his ribcage. "So long as I'm with you, then I'm happy. More than happy, in fact."

"And that makes me happy."

I lean in to kiss him, taking in the scent of his aftershave as I do. It's a fresh, heady scent, and the combination of that along with Warren's lips on mine drives me insane.

"I meant what I said earlier," he says when we finally pull apart.

"We said a lot of things earlier," I tease. "Any bit in particular?"

"You know which bit."

"I do, but I want to hear you say it again."

"I love you. I love your smile and your laugh. I love that you're stubborn and feisty and determined. I love how you're fussy about having the exact right amount of milk in your tea and you won't drink it if it's even a fraction of a shade too weak or too strong. I love that you said you love me too."

And although I could reel off a list just as long of the things I love about Warren, I don't.

Instead, I whisper in his ear. "Come home with me tonight. I want to show you my skills…"

From the look on his face, I don't think he'll need asking twice.

Maggie

The sun's shining, the barbecue's lit and I'm surrounded by people I love. Josh and Candy have come to visit for the weekend, Paolo and Pepe are kicking a ball around on the lawn and Kelly's looking happier than she's been for a long time. Luke's sat on a bench at the far end of the garden, munching away on a hot dog as he chats to Fern. Today the siblings had sat down with his parents and explained exactly how important Kelly is to him and that their relationship isn't just a flash in the pan. After some initial resistance they had started to come round.

"Fern said Luke was brilliant. He wasn't rude about it but he was firm – he told them that after everything he's been through this year he wants to make the most of every moment."

"And what did they say?"

"Well they agreed, obviously. So then he told them about us, about how we've been seeing each other and that it's getting serious." Kelly's cheeks colour. "He said that he hoped they'd be supportive of our relationship because I've been there for him the whole time he's been ill. He actually said that he didn't know how he'd have got through it without me."

I pull her in for a hug.

"You've always given me strength and I'm sure you do the same for Luke too. He's fortunate to have you."

"Well, I feel fortunate to have him. He makes me so happy, Mum. And I think I've made my decision. I want to stay here next year, even if my grades are good enough for Birmingham. It's not just because of Luke, although I'd be lying if I said it hadn't influenced me. But you were right when you said history wasn't my passion. It was my favourite subject at school, but that doesn't mean I want to spend my life becoming an expert in it."

"Okay," I say cautiously. "So what do you think you'll do instead? There are plenty of shifts at the café if that's what you want?"

Kelly nods.

"In the short term that'd be great. I thought about the travelling and it's something I definitely want to do. Luke does too, so we're planning on going together next summer. I'll need to work as much as possible to save enough."

"That sounds like a plan and I'm sure you'll love travelling. It'll be an adventure. But without wanting to come across as a fuddy duddy, have you thought about what you'll do after that?"

Kelly grins.

"I have, actually. All those times you've said to me that it's important to love what you do because you'll spend a lot of your life working got me thinking about it methodically. I made a list of the things I enjoy doing, the things I'm good at and what I'm interested in learning more about. And I've decided."

I'm in awe of her logical mind, but of course Kelly would have made a list. She probably used different coloured pens for the 'fors' and 'againsts'. Heaven knows she's got a big enough supply of stationery to assist her plans.

"And?"

"I'm going to train to be a make-up artist. Ever since I was tiny I've loved how cosmetics can make such a difference to someone's appearance. I can tell which colours suit which skin tones, I've watched enough YouTube videos to know how to contour perfectly. I really think I'd be good at it, and I'd enjoy it."

I smile. It really would be the perfect profession for her. I imagine her striding confidently with an immaculately made-up face and one of those rectangular cases full of eyeshadows and lipsticks swinging at her side. She was born for this.

"You'll be brilliant at that."

"There's a course at the college that I can apply for. The open day's coming up soon and I thought I'd go and speak to the admission staff there, see if there are any spaces left for this year. If I can do it in the evenings I'd still be able to work at the café in the day. It'd be the best of both worlds."

"You've really thought of everything, haven't you?"

Kelly smiles.

"I've tried to, and I know this is the right thing for me. University was right for Josh, but it's not right for me, not yet anyway. Who knows, maybe one day I'll change my mind and do that history degree after all."

"Or a degree in hair and make-up."

"Or a degree in hair and make-up," she agrees.

"I'm so proud of you, Kelly. More than ever."

"Thanks, Mum."

Luke gestures for Kelly to join him and Fern on the bench.

"You'd better go. Your boyfriend wants you."

She squeezes me tightly in a hug before running over and wrapping her arms around Luke. She looks blissfully happy. And for once in my life I think that maybe I wasn't a failure as a parent. Maybe my best *was* enough, after all.

"And it's a wonder goal from Lionel Messi! The little Argentinian does it again! That's surely won the world cup for the south American side!"

Pepe's running around with his arms aloft in celebration, his mouth open wide in delight as his dad cheers him on. Anyone would think it was the actual World Cup final, not a kick about in my back garden.

"Does Lionel Messi want anything else to eat?" I ask with a laugh, holding out a plate of ready prepared hot dogs to Pepe.

"Yes, please," he says, collapsing in a heap. "I'm starving."

"I could do with something to keep my energy up too." Paolo chuckles, grabbing a hot dog and taking a bite. "Mmm." He closes his eyes as he savours the taste. "I needed that."

"Have you been wearing your dad out again?" I ask Pepe.

"He says he's too old to play for such a long time."

"Pah!" I say. "He's not old. He's a spring chicken."

Pepe frowns as he chews on his sausage. "What does that mean?"

I laugh. "It means he's young."

"He's not that young," Pepe argues. "He's thirty-four."

"I know it seems old to you, because you're only six, but thirty-four is actually pretty young."

"I feel ancient," Paolo says, rubbing his knees. "My legs are killing me. It comes to something when your own son runs rings around you on the football pitch."

"Most people are married before they're thirty-four," Pepe continues bluntly. "All the children in my class have parents that are married. Even if their mum and dad have divorced they're married again to someone else so they have a new family."

"Step-parents," I say. "That's what you call it when your parents split up and then get remarried. So if your dad got married again, his wife would be your step-mum."

"So you might be my step-mum one day?"

I blush, hoping Paolo won't think I'm hinting. Things are going really well between us but it's still early days. And Clint coming back had made me think a lot about what I wanted from a relationship. I love having someone to share my time with, someone who laughs at the same things I do and who gives me a hug when I need a bit of reassurance that everything's going to be just fine. And the sex has been a very welcome addition to my life, and the fact that Paolo knows exactly what he's doing has been a bonus. After all the years in the wilderness my body's been reawakened and it's fantastic. But I'm enjoying things the way they are for now, having my own home and space to retreat to but still enjoying getting to know both Paolo and Pepe better.

"Don't put Maggie on the spot!" Paolo says, laughing and draping an arm around my waist. He's all sticky from running around but somehow that only makes him more attractive to me. "We're happy as we are."

Pepe pouts. "So there's not going to be a wedding? I wanted there to be a big cake with lots of icing."

"Ah, now we're getting to the crux of it," I tease. "You just want cake! Well, I'll let you into a secret – if you go and look in the fridge there's a chocolate fudge cake that I made especially for you."

His eyes light up. "With that chocolate icing? The really gooey one?"

I nod. "That's the one. Do you want to go and fetch it?"

Pepe runs excitedly to the kitchen, still full of beans.

"Sorry he asked that. He's all about the awkward questions at the moment."

"Have you got onto the 'how are babies made?' one yet? I remember Josh wanting all the details about it when he was younger. I didn't know what to say. I didn't want to lie and say babies were brought by the stork, and anyway, he knew that wasn't true because he remembered me being pregnant with Kelly. But I didn't want to have to go into all the gory detail."

"So what did you tell him?"

"I chickened out and made him ask Clint, who dealt with it pretty well actually. It was all fine until the day we were at the supermarket and Josh asked the rather large checkout lady if a man had given her a special hug and planted a seed in her tummy."

Paolo laughs. "I bet that was embarrassing."

"I've never packed my bags as quickly in my life. I don't think I even hung around for my change."

"Out of the mouths of babes."

"Indeed."

There's a whoop as the opening chords of the song Kelly's been blasting out all summer begins playing. She's immediately on her feet to dance, literally pulling at Luke to get up and join her. Candy and Josh are pushing their hands up to the sky in a 'raise the roof' motion and Fern and Matt are singing along. They're young and happy and full of life.

"Do you want any more children?" Paolo asks, following my gaze.

I shake my head. "I'm too old. I don't think I could go through the new born phase again at my age. Those sleepless nights were torture. Why, do you?"

He shrugs. "I don't know. I'm lucky with Pepe. He's a good kid. I don't think it'd be possible to get another one as amazing as him."

"All parents think that though. They don't think there's enough love in them to accommodate another child, but when that baby arrives arrive the love multiplies. It's as though your heart expands. I can honestly say that I love both Kelly and Josh exactly the same, although both of them insist the other is my favourite. Don't let that put you off having more children."

"I don't think that would be the deciding factor. But if you don't want any more, that might be."

I catch my breath. "What are you trying to say?"

"I know we've not been together for long, but I like you a lot, Maggie. And I know both of us are cautious because we don't want to rush things, but at the moment I can't imagine my life without you in it. You've brought the sunshine back into my life, and Pepe's too."

I smile. "What a lovely thing to say."

"I suppose what I'm saying is that if things go well, do you think you might be open to considering us being together. Marriage, blending our families...not yet, but in the future. Like Pepe said, 'one day'."

He looks so earnest, so full of love and I can't help but be touched by how considerate he's being.

"Last time I trusted in love I ended up getting my fingers burned. More than my fingers, my heart too. For a long time I didn't believe I'd be able to trust a man again. Clint made sure of that with his cheating and his lies. But with you it's different. Somehow I know you would never set out to hurt me."

"I promise you that, Maggie. Whatever happens in the future I would never do that."

"None of us know what the future holds, but if things keep going as well as they are, I definitely wouldn't rule out making a commitment to you, if it was right for all of us. And I mean, all of us. Our relationship isn't just about us, there's Josh, Kelly and Pepe to consider. They've had enough upheaval in their lives already."

"I agree."

"But if I was going to start again with anyone, it would be you."

I reach out and stroke his cheek. He's got the first prickles of stubble on his usually clean-shaven face. It suits him.

I see Pepe walking across the decking, clutching the cake plate tightly. I'm nervous as he approaches the steps down onto the grass, hoping he and the cake won't go flying, but he manages to descend them with ease. As he gets closer I spy the ring of chocolate ganache around his mouth, a sure-fire giveaway that he's been craftily getting his cake before anyone else gets a chance.

"So you might consider being Pepe's step-mum one day?" Paolo says quietly.

I nod.

"Maybe one day."

Fern

I'd only gone to get another burger. I wasn't prepared to be face to face with Josh, with just a decorating table covered in cheap paper tablecloths separating us. Since the showdown in the restaurant I'd been able to avoid him, partly because he'd been in Oxford for most of the summer with Candy, but also because I'd become adept at timing my breaks to coincide with his visits to the café. Now he's right here in front of me, adding a dollop of mayonnaise onto his own burger.

At first I avert my eyes, consciously looking at anything other than him, but a flip in my stomach causes me to look up. Not that same buzz of excitement I used to feel whenever he was near, this is different. This is pride, inner strength. He can't control me, no one can, and I refuse to let him crush my new-found confidence.

"I wanted to say sorry," he starts. "I've been a twat and I'm sorry I hurt you for so long."

It's funny, just a few months ago those words would have been sufficient. I didn't value myself enough to believe that I actually mattered. Not any more though. Now I want him to know exactly how he made me feel, and not because I'm nasty or malicious, but because I let his opinions affect me for far too long. He needs to know his comments, whether deliberately cruel or just downright thoughtless, have consequences.

"You did hurt me, Josh, and I don't think you've got a clue how much. I hated school because of you and your friends. Really hated it. I'd go home and cry because the comments you made – the names you called me – made me wish I was dead."

He looks at the ground, and I hope he does feel ashamed.

"You've no idea how little confidence I had to start with, and how bit by bit you managed to sap every last ounce of it out of me. There were days I couldn't even get out of bed. I told my parents I was ill, because I couldn't bear the pain of being laughed at. Then on the days when I was brave enough to go, I'd be a nervous wreck."

"I'm sorry," he mumbles.

"Every day was miserable, and then I was put on anti-depressants because I couldn't take any more."

He looks up, horror in his eyes.

"I didn't know, Fern."

"I needed them to function. I still do, because that feeling of being worth so little hasn't gone away. I start to think I'm getting better, but then the fear takes over, something I can't even put into words because it's so goddamn awful, and I'm right back where I started. And I appreciate that you're feeling guilty, but that doesn't take away the fact I've spent almost half my life feeling worthless, and that you contributed to it." I have to stop to catch my breath, because it's as though every thought I've ever had, every moment of rage where my love for Josh enabled me to feel useless, has caught up with me.

"I didn't realise things were that bad. I knew what I was saying upset you, but I didn't know it had made you ill."

"What I don't understand is why you'd keep saying something if you knew it was making me upset? Even if you didn't understand the extent of it, why would you do that? Are you really that heartless and cruel?"

"I'm not like that now, Fern. In the past I was, I admit it. But I've changed, honestly. And with the way things are going between Kelly and Luke, we're practically family. That's why I wanted to speak to you, to see if we could move forward."

"I want to. But why should I believe you've changed when you've been so horrible to me for so long?"

"They're not empty words, Fern." He places the lid of his burger bun on top of the meat, salad and sauces and presses down. Ketchup and mayonnaise ooze out of the sides, making a desperate bid for escape. "I don't want to be like my dad. When I was younger, I did. I know that sounds strange, because he was never a good choice of role model. But he was still my dad, you know? And everyone told me I was so like my mum, because of the curly hair and the facial features...I guess I wanted to take on any of his attributes I could, even the negative ones."

"That's crazy."

Crazy, but understandable. I'd never thought about how his dad going to prison had affected him. And he'd been so young at the time. He was probably as messed up as I was, deep down.

"I know. Crazy, but true. It's only since he came back that I've been able to see him for what he really is. I always glossed over the fact he treated Mum like something he'd trodden in. He left me his phone number. He's living in Bristol now. I thought he might want to see me, make up for lost time, you know?" His face crinkles like a scrunched-up ball of paper. "But when I rang he was only interested in borrowing money. He didn't want to know about how I was doing, only how much I'll be earning when I start the research job in London. He didn't even tell me he was proud of me."

My heart lurches for him. For all the differences my parents and I have had, I've never once doubted their love for me or their pride in my achievements, no matter how small. Heck, my mum had even framed my first width swimming certificate and hung it on the wall in the hallway.

"That sucks."

"It made me realise what a dick I've been, and I don't want to be that person any more. I don't expect you to forget, but do you think you might be able to forgive me? If not now, in the future?"

"Your words and actions damaged me. I'm trying to build myself up, but it's not easy, not when I'm fighting this devil on my shoulder."

His whole body crumples. "I'm sorry. Please believe me, Fern"

"I do believe you," I say, because his regret is evident from the expression on his face. "And I'll try to forgive you." It's all I can offer.

"Thank you," he says, picking up his flimsy paper plate.

I'm adding a generous tablespoonful of coleslaw to my burger when he adds, "And Fern?"

"Yeah?"

"Please don't tell my mum about my dad asking me for money. It'd only upset her."

"I won't say a word."

As he walks back to Candy, I see him for what he is. Not an angel, but not a monster either. Just a human being trying to cope with his life as best as he can, much the same as the rest of us are.

Pearl

The tears won't stop, years' worth of them spilling uncontrollably out. So much has been locked up inside me. Maybe if I'd been a bit braver in the past things wouldn't be as difficult in this moment. If I'd opened up to Alf when we first got together, let him know about Clint and Carrick and everything that happened before him, perhaps I wouldn't have been in such a state now. If I'd believed in myself a bit more, thought that I would be a competent parent, things would have been different then too. I might be Mrs Braithwaite, living with Carrick in his small ramshackle cottage across the road from the rose garden, where he can keep an eye on his prized blooms from his living room window.

Instead all I've done is inadvertently hurt everyone I care about – Carrick's family has been divided by the revelations, tension is running high between me and Maggie, my grandchildren are confused. Even Mitzi is wondering what's going on, especially since I've been taking her out for her walk after dark, to avoid as many of the gossip mongers as possible.

And Alf...poor, poor Alf. Would he have stayed with me if I'd had the guts to tell him the truth, or would that have been our relationship over? I'll never know. All I know, as ridiculous as it seems, is that by being here at his graveside I can ease my own conscience, never mind that it's many years too late.

"I'm sorry, Alf. I'm so very, very sorry that I didn't tell you about Clint. You loved him so much, as our one and only nephew, and I should have been honest. When you said he had the same pale skin colouring as me, the same white-blonde hair, I should have said 'that's because he's mine'. But I couldn't do it, because I was trying to protect you." The tears continue to fall, landing with a plop on the black marbled stone.

Alfred Armitage
13.2.1957 – 2.12.2015
Husband of Pearl, Friend of many

It wasn't much to show for a life – a name, two dates and one short epitaph. There had been so much more to him than that – his gentle nature, his patience, his silly sense of humour. He'd loved anything slapstick, the old black-

and-white silent films, the shows with video clips of people falling over. But most of all he'd loved me through everything, and in my heart of hearts I knew Alf would have loved me whatever I'd told him.

"I never wanted to lie to you," I say, as I fiddle with a pink chrysanthemum that doesn't want to sit in the right position in the vase. The other flowers are open, the darker pink outline of each petal standing out for all to see. This one is closed tightly. I wonder what secrets it's keeping, whether it could possibly be anything as monumental as I'd kept to myself.

"I almost told you so many times. Do you remember that day at the beach, when you and Clint were playing cricket with a tennis ball and racket? The pair of you were laughing, thick as thieves." I laugh wryly. "Poor choice of words, given the circumstances, perhaps. Anyway, I was licking my ice cream as you two giggled away. I spoke to Vivienne about telling you the truth, but she was having none of it. 'You made me a promise, Pearl. You said that he'd be ours, mine and Glenn's, and that you'd sit back and let us bring him up our way.' I told her it was different then, before I had you in my life. But she was adamant that no one was to know. 'Think about Clint,' she said. 'It'd confuse him.' So again, I kept quiet, the taste of vanilla souring in my mouth. I knew it was the wrong thing to do but I couldn't get out of it."

I brush a stray leaf from the headstone, ensuring that it looks spotlessly perfect. I owe Alf that much. He'd have expected it too, I'd always been house-proud. I'd been the perfect wife, except for the secret. Tea on the table every night at six, not so much as looking at another man throughout all our married life. I hadn't needed to. I'd had the best.

"And now he's gone again, and I don't know how I feel. He hates me, understandably, for standing against him in court, and he hates me even more for the lies. And although I've brought it all on myself, I can't help but feel sad, Alf. I feel as though I'm giving up on him all over again." My shoulders shake with a grief and remorse. "This is my legacy. And I've made a mess of everything."

The clouds pass over the sun, a cool darkness engulfing the crematorium. It matches my mood, and as I walk down the winding driveway to the car park near the entrance, I take a deep breath and wipe away the tears. There is no point dwelling on the past, I need to look forward now.

I know what I must do. As I climb into my car, strap the seatbelt across me and start the ignition there's only one place I need to go. Fir Tree Park, to make amends with what's left of my family.

The doorbell tinkles as I enter the empty café and it's then that I notice Maggie, not in her usual place out the back, mixing up the dry ingredients ready to whip up one of her specialities. She's at a table, her head in her hands and despite after all the drama she's been through I can't remember ever seeing her cry before. Whatever it is that's upsetting her, it must be bad.

"Hey," I say soothingly, placing my hand on her shoulder. "What's the matter?"

Maggie looks at me with red eyes and cheeks speckled with tears. "Oh, Pearl, it's you. I didn't hear you come in." Her voice is strangled and she frantically rubs at her eyes with the back of her hand. "I'd put the closed sign up. As you can see, I'm not really up to serving customers, and Fern's on her break."

"You should have phoned, I'd have gladly come and given you a hand. Now, take a deep breath and talk to me. What's upsetting you?" She looks so fraught, which is at odds with her usual unbreakable nature.

She bats her hand in front of her face. "Oh, it's nothing. You'll think I'm being silly."

"If it's upsetting you, it's not silly," I correct. "Come one, tell me what's up. Maybe I'll be able to help? Is it to do with Clint?"

I silently pray that it's not. Please don't let him be causing yet more upheaval for this poor woman.

She shakes her head sadly, the light-brown ringlets falling in front of her eyes.

"It's not Clint." She sighs. "It's Paolo"

"Paolo? I thought things were going really well with you two?"

"They are," she says, sniffling. "Or at least, they were. I've probably ruined everything by being overly cautious."

"Whatever's happened can't be as bad as all that, surely?"

"It's Antonia." The look I give her must be blank because she adds, "Pepe's mum. Paolo's ex. She's here."

"Ah. And you're jealous?" I guess.

"No!" she exclaims, before sheepishly adding, "I don't know. Maybe I am. It's a new situation for me, being in a relationship. I've been on my own for so long with just myself and the kids to think about, and now all of a sudden everything's changed. I never imagined myself with someone who had a child. I know that's a bit hypocritical, but it's the truth."

"It must be difficult, especially when Pepe adores you as much as he does. He already sees you as a mother figure."

"I know, and I think the world of him too. He's such a lovely boy. But now Antonia's here I don't know where I fit in. The three of them have gone to the safari park today and Pepe was high as a kite at the thought of it when they popped by to get some snacks to take with them." She shook her head. "They looked like the perfect family unit heading out on a day trip." She smiles sadly.

"But they're not," I remind her. "Paolo and Antonia gave it their best shot and it didn't work out. I don't know the ins and outs of their relationship or why it broke down – it's none of my business – but I know that man worships the ground you walk on. He loves you, not her."

"But she's so beautiful," Maggie moans. "You should have seen what she was wearing! Expensive cigarette-cut trousers and a fitted blazer with these kitten-heeled shoes. For a day at the safari park! If I'd been going I'd have rocked up in my jeans and t-shirt."

"Which would be perfectly sensible given the occasion."

"Not for Antonia." Maggie rolls her eyes. "She looks like she's going into a high-flying meeting. Why on earth was I fooling myself believing Paolo could have any interest in me? If that's the kind of woman he goes for then I might as well give up now."

I give her the look. "Come on now, you don't really think that."

"I suppose not," she says meekly.

"There's no suppose so about it," I reply sternly. "That man is crazy about you and love like that doesn't come around all that often." I think back to the excitement of new love, when it fizzes inside your stomach with the possibilities. I had it with Alf. Heck, I'd had it with Carrick too, in spades. "When it does you need to run with it, because it's the most exciting thing in the world."

"You don't think that after spending time together he'll think him and Antonia should give it another go?"

"Well, I can't speak for Paolo. But let's say I'd be very surprised. It's obvious to everyone how happy you two are, and the whole place is rooting for you. You've had a bumpy ride, Maggie. Don't go looking for problems that don't exist. Not every man is like Clint. There are some good ones out there, and for what it's worth I think you might have found one in Paolo."

She smiles.

"He's a good man, isn't he?"

I nod. "From what I know of him, yes, he is."

She puffs out a breath of air and fans her face. Her cheeks are still blotchy and tear-stained, but she looks calmer now. "Thanks for listening without judging, Pearl. And for everything else too. It must have been impossibly difficult for you, keeping so much hidden for so long."

I examine my fingernails, knowing that if I look her in the eye it'll be me crying next.

"And I never said it before, but when you stood up in court and told them that you knew, without a shadow of a doubt, that it was Clint who'd been pointing that gun at you, you changed my life for the better. I didn't know it at the time. Then I thought my world was ending, but it was the catalyst I needed to get my life headed where it needed to go. If Clint had never gone to prison, I dread to think what my life would have been like. He'd have gone on treating me like dirt, telling me lies about where he was getting his money from and why he wasn't home in time to tuck Kelly and Josh into bed. It was the best thing you could have done for me and the kids, in the long run."

Relief courses through me.

"I hadn't realised how much I needed to hear those words until now," I admit, swallowing down the lump in my throat. "I did it for you, for my grandchildren, and I always wondered if I made the right choice."

She reaches for my hand. "You did."

Maggie

"I don't know about you but I've come over all queasy."
I instinctively clamp my hand over my mouth as my
stomach churns, just as a precaution. Talk about nerves
getting the better of me.

"I'm surprisingly relaxed," Kelly says with a smile. "It's
a good job one of us is, because you're shaking like a leaf!"

"You worked so hard for those exams, that's all. I want
you to get the results you deserve."

"I did the best I could have done, so whatever the results
are I'll be proud of them." Kelly grins. "But I must admit
I'm glad not to have to worry about what grades I get too
much. Imagine if I'd still had my heart set on Birmingham?
Then I really would have been a nervous wreck."

Kelly had spoken to an admissions tutor at the college
about any vacancies on the make-up course for September
and she must have made a good impression because she
was offered a place there and then. She'd already bought

the necessary kit ready for the start of the course and Carrick, in his newly open role as her grandfather, had kindly paid for it. She'd insisted she needed a vast selection of palettes, despite only having one small face.

"Can you hurry up? I'm not good with stress."

"Really?" Kelly teases. "I'd never have guessed. Anyway, it's not me, it's the system. I think it must be overloaded with everyone trying to log on."

She presses F5 to refresh the page.

"Don't they know your A-level results are more important than theirs?" I'm only half joking.

"Ah, we're in," she says as the screen changes. "Let's see…"

I peer over her shoulder, trying to catch a glimpse of the results but can't see what I'm looking for. It's only as Kelly turns around and wraps herself around me that I can make out the grades. The same letter, three times over. Sociology, A. Art, A. History, A.

"I did it, Mum." Her voice crackles with well-earned pride. "I got the grades for Birmingham."

"You did, and I'm so very, very proud of you. No regrets about turning down the place?"

She shakes her head.

"None whatsoever. I'm looking forward to college too much. I can't believe it, Mum. Three As!"

I squeeze her tighter to me, stroking her long blonde hair. It's silky smooth and shines.

"You're not my baby girl any more," I say, my voice muffled in her hair. "You're my beautiful, clever young woman and I can't believe I had any part in creating you. Somewhere along the line I got lucky."

"I got lucky too," she said, and my heart bursts with love. "I got the best mum in the world."

She disentangles herself from me.

"I'd better start making those phone calls though – there are lots of people waiting to hear how I got on. I can't leave my public waiting," she jokes, as she reaches for her phone.

"Luke?" I ask.

She nods.

"His parents wanted to know too. Things are getting better, slowly, now they're getting to know me better."

"I should think so too. I know I'm biased, but they're not likely to find a better girlfriend for Luke than you if they search the whole of Britain."

She rolls her eyes at me as though she's embarrassed.

"Mum," she says. "Stop it."

"I'm allowed to be proud of you. You're one of my greatest achievements." I reach for my own phone. "Can I make some phone calls too, brag a little about my superstar daughter?"

"Who do you want to call?"

"I was thinking of your grandparents. They'll be so delighted for you."

"Which ones?" she asks.

It's a straightforward question, but one that knocks me off guard.

"I was thinking of Granny and Grandad Sykes," I say. "Although I know Pearl and Carrick will be delighted for you too."

I'm still getting used to the changes in our family tree. It's strange when everything you know to be true isn't actually right, and it's quite the adjustment thinking of Pearl as Clint's mum rather than his aunt, and especially of Carrick as anything other than the kind-hearted man who tends to the gardens at Fir Tree Park.

"You can ring Granny and Grandad Sykes," she confirms, "but can I ring Pearl and Carrick, please? It's the only time they'll get to hear one of their grandchildren tell them their results and they've already missed out on so much."

My heart swells once more. My girl, my lovely sweet girl.

"That'd be nice. They'll appreciate that."

She beams. "Thanks, Mum." She plants a kiss on my cheek before making her way out of the room and cheekily adding, "make sure you remind Granny and Grandad how they gave Josh money for university when he got his A-level results. The Europe fund could do with a boost."

Chuckling to myself, I pick up the phone. She'll go far, that one. Far in every sense of the word.

Fern

The radio's on full blast, Robbie Williams' latest upbeat release filling the café. Some of the older regulars are tutting – they'd probably prefer something a bit mellower, or at least Robbie in his *Angels* phase, but no one dares say anything to Maggie. She's bopping along as she waits on the table, telling anyone who'll listen how proud she is of Kelly's results. What with Luke and Maggie, I feel like I'm surrounded by the Kelly Thornhill fan club. Luke had bought her a ring to celebrate her fantastic results, a plain silver band set with a large teardrop onyx to remember the occasion, and he planned to give it to her tonight at the surprise party Maggie was throwing to celebrate.

"Is there anything else you need me to do for later?" I ask.

I'd already spent the morning decorating the café with 'Well done Kelly!' banners. I just hoped Maggie wasn't expecting me to blow up the pink and white balloons lying on the counter.

"Honest opinion," Maggie says, inviting me to sit down with her at an empty table. "Do you think there's enough choice of food? I've made sausage rolls and cheese and onion bites, and I'm going to throw together some tuna mayo sandwiches later, and maybe egg and cress for the vegetarians. There's a bag of dry-roasted peanuts, three different pizzas and I've just prepared a green salad for anyone trying to be healthy. I've got some crisps and dips too, because everyone likes a nibble, don't they?"

She's rambling, which suggests she's trying to stay on top of her mental list. Maggie doesn't know how to do things by halves, it's just not in her remit. If Kelly's having a party, it'll be a full-on bonanza.

"That sounds like plenty," I say. "I take it there'll be cake too?"

She looks at me as though it's the most ridiculous question in the world.

"Naturally! I've gone for something classic, a simple sponge with royal icing, and there's a batch of cupcakes that need to come out of the oven in..." she looks at her watch. "...two minutes. Oh, and there are mini trifles in the fridge too. I've done the jelly and custard layer but wanted to wait until later to add the cream and sprinkles. It tastes so much better when it's really fresh."

"It sounds like you're on top of it all to me."

"Thanks Fern, you're a gem," she says with a smile. "I'd

better go and check on those cupcakes. We don't want them burning."

As she almost runs to the kitchen I smile to myself. I was really looking forward to this evening. My friends, my family, my boyfriend, they'd all be there. It was going to be a memorable night, I just knew it.

The look on Kelly's face is a picture and I wish I'd thought to have my phone ready to capture her expression. Despite Maggie's fears that someone was bound to blab and spoil the surprise, her look is one of total surprise.

"No way!" she squeals. "This is all for me?"

Maggie nods with delight.

"We're all thrilled for you and wanted to help you celebrate. It's not every day a child of mine gets all As."

Josh interjects. "We didn't have a party when I got my A-level results."

"That's because you went out to the pub with your friends instead," Maggie reminds him. "You wouldn't have appreciated something like this."

"True," he agrees.

He looks in my direction and I nod graciously, as he smiles warmly back. I might not be able to fully forgive him just yet, but I understand him better now than I ever did before.

"Look at the cake!" Kelly exclaims with a giggle. Maggie's

idea of 'keeping it simple' didn't quite fit in with everyone else's. The cake did have the layer of white royal icing covering the airy vanilla sponge, but she hadn't been able to resist going to town with the decorations. She's added make-up brushes made of fondant and a tube of lipstick so it looks as if the 'Congratulations Kelly' is written in the glossy red lip stain. "Thanks Mum, this is amazing."

"It was a team effort," Maggie concedes. "Everyone did their bit. I think they worked up a hunger doing it though."

My stomach gurgles in agreement. I press my hand on it to try and quieten it down, especially with Matt stood right beside me. It's not very ladylike making those kind of noises.

"So I think it's time you do the honours," Maggie says as she hands Kelly a pair of glistening silver scissors and points out the wide pink ribbon that's strung out in front of the buffet table. "It's your party, you need to declare the buffet officially open."

Kelly looks reluctant at first, but as she snips through the ribbon she whoops and holds the scissors high above her head declaring, "Let's eat!"

A Blondie classic starts up on the radio which gets everyone shaking their shoulders in time to the beat. Carrick, Pearl, Lacey and her boyfriend are dancing in one corner of the room and Luke sidles up to Kelly and wraps his arms around her waist from behind. She turns to kiss him and I automatically glance over to my parents, and am pleased to see they're smiling. They are learning to become more accepting, albeit slowly.

There are other people I recognise here, Josh and Candy, and a few of Kelly and Luke's friends from school who know that if there's one of Maggie's cakes to be had then it's a party worth being at even if it's quieter than the pubs will be. Mind you, Maggie's filled the fridge with beers and prosecco, so it's not like anyone will be going without a tipple. Her and Paolo are already making headway with the fizz, champagne flutes in hand as they canoodle in the corner.

"Are we going to be the first to break the last taboo?" Matt asks.

"What's that?"

"Starting the queue for the buffet."

"That sounds like a taboo worth breaking," I joke, reaching for a plate and a napkin. "I'm starving."

"Me too."

We pile our plates high, not caring that we've gone all out on savoury and would probably be groaning by the time we got to dessert. We'll find a way to squeeze it in somehow.

"Fern."

My mum beckons us over to her table.

"I'm sorry," I whisper to Matt as we weave through the

revellers. "We'd better go and eat with them. They'll only make a fuss otherwise."

My dad appraises Matt as he sits down. It's the first time they've met, and I can see from the way his nostrils are flaring that he's doing his best not to mention Matt's piercing. That's something else my parents are funny about, that and tattoos. It had taken years of pestering to get them to agree to let me get my ears pierced. They finally gave in when I was fourteen, by which point everyone else at school had moved onto cartilage, nose and eyebrow piercings.

"So, you must be Matt."

My dad's voice is clipped and serious. He doesn't do relaxed.

"That's right, Mr Hart," Matt replies, offering his hand. "It's a pleasure to meet you. Fern's told me so much about you both."

The grin he gives my mum is so infectious that I'm not sure even she would be able to resist his charms.

"It's good to meet you too," my dad replies affably. "Fern tells us you work at the boathouse."

"That's right, but it's only a holiday job. I won't be able to work hours like this when university starts up again. I'm in the final year of my masters, so I know I'll be hitting the books harder than ever."

My dad looks more interested now. "A masters?"

"Business Studies," Matt clarifies. "I'm especially interested in sales."

"Why, that's a coincidence," Dad replies, warming up. "I expect Fern told you, but that's my field too."

He continues rambling on about something or other I don't understand and I daren't interrupt, instead focussing on savouring the coleslaw. It's rich and creamy with the perfect amount of ground black pepper to set off the flavour. I'm happily munching when a woman sidles up to the table. It takes me a moment to place her without her easel and paints, but her flowing clothes give her away – it's the artist who paints the watercolours of the lake.

"Matt," she coos, brushing her long hair over her shoulder. "I thought it was you."

Matt shifts in his seat.

"Erm, hi Georgie." He looks awkward. "What are you doing here?"

"I'm Kelly's college tutor," the woman explains. "I wouldn't normally come to anything like this, but I know Kelly's grandmother so when I got invited I thought why not."

She smiles, perfect white teeth gleaming.

Matt smiles back, it looks forced.

"Well, it's nice to see you," he says.

"You too," she simpers. "How's university going?"

"Fine. The work load's been hard to manage, but I'm getting better at being more organised."

He smiles at her, then looks down at his plate, and it's

then that I know who she really is. It's obvious from his awkwardness, from the way he seems so on edge. She's not just an artist and teacher, she's the woman he had a crush on. She's beautiful and elegant, her floor-length dress only making her appear taller and more slender. She's undeniably attractive. The two of them talk for a moment about people I don't know, who I assume are former classmates of Matt's, until I hear my name.

"Sorry?" I realise I'd been staring at her and lost track of the conversation.

"I wanted to introduce you two. Georgie was my tutor at college." He bites down on his lip which only confirms my suspicions. I nod. "Georgie, this is my girlfriend, Fern."

"Lovely to meet you Fern," she says, giving me a winning smile. "I love your hair. It's so thick!"

She moves forward, and for a moment I think she's going to touch it, but she doesn't, thankfully.

"Thank you."

She looks around the room, waving when she sees a tall man with a shaven head and thick black-rimmed glasses.

"I'd better go," she says apologetically. "My partner's waiting for me. He doesn't know anyone here so he'll be cursing me for leaving him on his own. Good to see you, Matt," she says. "And nice to meet you, Fern."

She floats off towards the man and I watch, mesmerised as her dress swishes around her legs. No wonder Matt had fallen for her. I don't find women attractive, but there's something mesmerising about Georgie.

I raise my eyebrows at Matt as I bite into a tuna mayo sandwich. "Small world," I say, after I've finished chewing.

"It is," he agrees, swallowing down his food. "Which is just as well. Because if it was bigger, maybe I would never have found you."

The party is in full swing when Matt suggests we take a walk around the lake. As lovely as the evening's been, I'm glad to escape the hubbub.

"Have you had a good night?"

His hand is in mine, our arms swinging between us like a pendulum as we stroll.

"It's been good, yeah. It was nice to meet your parents at last, and you know, they're not as bad as you made them out to be."

I laugh. "They've become a lot more chilled recently. Believe me, if you'd met them this time last year you'd have a whole different opinion of them."

"Your dad said he might be able to put in a good word for me with his company when I finish my masters," he says proudly. "When you said he was high up in business, I didn't realise you meant he was on the management team at Blackman Stubbs."

I shrug.

"He's worked his way up through the firm. Sometimes I forget how he's practically running the place now."

"And have you had a nice evening?"

I think about it, about how lovely it's been to see Kelly and Luke be so open about their relationship, and how the café can be transformed into such a magical place with a bit of effort. Of Matt introducing me to Georgie as his girlfriend.

"I have." I smile. "And it was interesting to meet Georgie."

He places his hand on his forehead. "I had no idea she'd be there. I didn't know she was still teaching at the college so seeing her was the last thing I expected. I'm sorry if it made you feel uncomfortable."

I swallow down a lump in my throat.

"How did it feel talking to her again after all this time?"

"Weird," he replies quickly. "Really weird. For such a long time I'd built her up in my mind to be this goddess-like woman, and seeing her today I realised she's just a normal person. Yeah, she's nice and everything, but why had I put her on a pedestal for so long? I suppose it's like you and Josh. It's like they become part of your identity somehow."

"She's beautiful. Being beautiful helps."

"You're beautiful," he says, wrapping his arms around my waist and pulling me close to him. "And you don't even know it. I'm going to have to keep telling you over and over until it sinks in."

"Thank you," I whisper, moving my lips closer to his.

"You..." He kisses me softly. "Are..." A second kiss, more desperate than the first. "Beautiful."

The dusky sky envelops us as I willingly lose myself in the third kiss. I couldn't be happier than I am right now. And slowly but surely, I'm beginning to believe I'm beautiful. And it's not because Matt's telling me I am that I believe it. It's because I feel it inside. I'm a woman growing in courage, strength and self-confidence and that's radiating out of me. That's what Matt sees and what makes me beautiful to him. And it's the very same things that are making me beautiful to myself, too.

September 2017

Lacey

"I love the summer extravaganza," Warren says as he lays out the checked picnic blanket on the grass. "Some of my happiest memories are of sitting here at the end of the summer, dancing to whatever local band were on."

"Will you be sharing your unique moves with us tonight?" I tease. Warren's dancing was definitely unique. I'd been clubbing with him, and some the shapes he'd been throwing...well, they were all his own.

"Only if you're lucky," he replies with a cheeky wink.

Even though we're early there are hordes of people here, everyone keen to make sure the best spots aren't already taken. There are groups who've set up for the duration, wicker picnic hampers full to the brim with enough food to feed a small country and a cool box of drinks to boot.

We've gone for the more low-key approach, stopping off at the supermarket on the way in and raiding the chiller cabinet and deli counter for cold cuts of meat and ready-prepared salads. I'm quietly hoping that when the rest of the family join us our spread will rival some of the more extravagant buffets, especially if Maggie brings the leftovers from the café. I'd put money on our cake selection being the best in the park.

"Do you think we should have brought another rug?" Warren asks.

"Nah, it'll be all right. If we spread out a bit then we'll be fine. Pearl said she was going to bring a blanket too, and I don't think it'll be long until they arrive. They were leaving Devon straight after lunch."

"Have you heard from them?"

I shake my head. "Not since Monday, when they rang to say they'd arrived safely and that their room had a sea view. Uncle Carrick was most excited about that," I say with a smile. He hadn't been on holiday in years, and it had taken a bit of cajoling from Pearl to encourage him to leave his beloved rose garden behind for almost a week.

"I hope they've had a good time. They deserve it."

"They do," I agree. When they first told me they were going to start dating I'd been surprised, but after talking it through with Uncle Carrick he explained how they weren't going to be rushing anything. He'd told me that although he'd always loved Pearl, ever since they were teenagers, it finally seemed as though this was their time. They'd been to the cinema together to watch a rerun of *Casablanca* and for a posh afternoon tea at one of the hotels in town. Pearl had praised the atmosphere and the décor, but insisted the cakes were not a patch on Maggie's.

"What time are the others coming?"

I tick the people off on my fingers. "Kelly and Luke are coming with Candy and Josh, and I think Paolo and Pepe will arrive with Maggie when she's closed the café. She had wanted to stay open, but we managed to persuade her to have the night off instead so she can join in the fun. She said she'd bringing paper plates and cutlery too. She'd better remember or we'll be raiding the café."

"Or eating with our fingers."

"Savoury rice with your fingers? That sounds messy."

"Needs must. Desperate times call for desperate measures." I smile. "Anyway, she won't forget."

"She is always organised," Warren agrees with a laugh. "She's the opposite of me. Have you noticed that little notebook on the café counter where she writes down all the stuff she needs to get done? Most people have a to-do list, but she's got a to-do book."

"I need to get one of those for work. It's crazily busy at the moment. Everyone's started planning for their Christmas dos already."

Warren frowns. "In September?"

I nod. "Yep. Some of them have been at it since spring, especially the clients who splash the cash. If you want ice sculptures near Christmas, you have to get booked in early."

Warren looks genuinely confused as to why anyone would start planning for Christmas before the clocks go back. I suppose it does seem early, but if you have a venue in mind you need to get it snapped up. Christmas dos and summer weddings – they're the two events that need booking well in advance.

"I'd be happy with a night out at the pub. A few beers and a bag of chips on the way home."

"You're easy to please, that's why. You're so laid back you're horizontal."

He shrugs.

"It's a good thing," I quickly add. "Better than being the type of person who gets all het up about nothing."

He snuggles in close to me, the blanket crinkling beneath us. I lean over and plant a kiss on his lips, unable to resist. It's still a novelty, and I can't imagine it's one that'll wear thin any time soon.

"You're getting me het up now," he mutters, his voice gruff and guttural as I run my hand down his back. He shivers with pleasure. "Save it for later?" he begs. "Because if you keep on kissing me and touching me like that I think we'll get complaints from some of the families having a fun day out." He lowers his voice. "Not to mention your uncle's due to turn up any minute. You don't realise the effect you have on me."

I glance down at his shorts, where there's a hint of a tent-shape appearing.

"I can see the effect," I tease, looking up at him through my eyelashes. "Good to know you're not immune to my powers."

"Never," he says, rolling so he's lying on his stomach, presumably to hide his semi. "You do things to me, Lacey Braithwaite."

"Good," I say with a grin, as a brass band dressed in scarlet uniforms with gold braided trim stride towards the bandstand. "That's the plan."

Maggie

By the time the headliners take to the stage, a folk act with a scruffy looking lead singer sporting a surprisingly good voice, we're all feeling podged. We've eaten until we're on the verge of popping, groaning as our bloated stomachs swell with the delicious food we were unable to resist.

"That cake pushed me over the edge," Kelly moans, rubbing her stomach. "Stick a fork in me, I'm done."

"Me too," laughed Luke, wrapping his arm around her shoulder. "You should have stopped me going back for seconds."

They make a cute couple, and it's lovely to see how relaxed they are in each other's company. The advantage of being friends for such a long time before becoming a couple I suppose, much like Pearl and Carrick second time around. They're looking very cosy too, and although it's strange to see them together, they look so outrageously happy. Carrick keeps smiling over at Pearl as she taps her foot to the music, humming along to the shrill tune of the harmonica. They're a reminder that it's never too late.

"I feel a bit sick," Lacey whines. "I've eaten way too much."

"Don't blame me for your stomach aches," I say, holding up my hands in innocence. "Blame the customers who didn't buy the cake in the first place."

"Come on, Mum," Josh said drily. "I know you made it especially for tonight."

I grin, rumbled, but say, "Maybe, maybe not. You'll never know."

"Well, it was delicious," says Paolo, leaning over and planting a kiss on my cheek. "And Pepe is still managing to find room for another slice," he adds, nodding at his son who's cramming the Victoria Sponge into his mouth as quickly as possible. He probably thinks he's going to be told to stop eating any minute now so is shovelling it in as fast as he can.

"He's got hollow legs," I say, laughing. "Although it's nice to know the cake's not going to waste."

"When are you going back to Oxford?" Kelly asks Josh. "Tomorrow?"

He shakes his head. "Tonight. Candy's doing the last set of the night so we're driving straight there after the fire-works."

"I wonder if they'll be as underwhelming as usual," Luke interjects. "It always seems a bit sad."

It's a harsh assessment of the finale of the extravaganza, but a fair one. A few rockets being set off doesn't seem enough to mark the end of the summer, but it's all we get. It's a tradition.

"You'd be complaining if they suddenly came out with a firework display to rival the banks of the Thames on New Year's Eve," Pearl says with a smile. "The extravaganza has ended with a small and simple firework display for the past twenty years."

"It was Alf's idea, wasn't it?" Carrick adds fondly. "He loved being involved with the Friends of Fir Tree Park committee."

"He did," Pearl agrees. "Being part of this community meant the world to him."

"We're lucky to have the park," I ponder out loud. "The news is full of negativity, but even when bad things happen here, as they do everywhere, the way we pull together makes this a special place to be. I can't imagine I'll ever move away. I wouldn't want to be anywhere else."

"Not even for a holiday?" asks Paolo, winking in Kelly's direction.

She grins back, as Pepe brushes the crumbs hurriedly away from his lips.

"Is it time?" he asks excitedly. "Can we tell her now?"

Everyone is acting very strangely all of a sudden. I can't help but be a bit suspicious.

"Tell me what?" I ask warily.

"Daddy booked a holiday for us," Pepe says, bouncing up and down on the spot. "For all of us!"

"All of us? What do you mean all of us?"

"Everyone!" Pepe exclaims, joy on his face. "It was a surprise for you."

"What's going on?" I laugh nervously. "Why do I get the feeling you've all been in on something?"

"We planned it together," Kelly explains. "All of us. Paolo came up with the idea. He thought we could all do with a holiday and that it'd give us a chance to get to know each other better. Help us become a proper extended family. We're all going, everyone here."

I don't know what to say, and I open and close my mouth like a fish as it sinks in.

"It's a lovely idea," I manage finally. "I'm just a bit gobsmacked, that's all. Where are we going? And when?"

Paolo smiles. "Italy, the last week in October. That way it doesn't affect school for Pepe, and Kelly isn't at college that week as it's half term. I've rented a villa near the coast, through a family friend so it was a bargain. And then Pepe's going to stay with Antonia for a few days so me and you can have a few nights alone."

"We don't want to hear about your dirty weekend," says

Kelly, placing her hands over her ears and making 'la la la' sounds.

"Cultured weekend," he corrects.

"Cultured?" I ask, barely daring to believe what I thought he was hinting at.

"After the family beach holiday you and me are heading to Rome," Paolo says with a smile. "A little bird told me you've always wanted to go so I thought it would be a nice way to celebrate your birthday."

"Sssh." I giggle. "Don't tell everyone! You're making me feel ancient!"

"We know how old you are, Mum," Josh says with a roll of his eyes, as Candy jabs him in the ribs, presumably in a bid to stop him digging himself any deeper in a hole.

"I can't believe it. You did all this for me?"

"All for you," Paolo agrees. "Because we think you're worth it."

"It's been quite the year," Pearl says. "So much has changed."

And it really has. The secrets of the past have shown themselves, blooming openly and proudly. The seeds of love have been sown, ready to grow with a bit of careful nurturing.

"The park doesn't change much though, does it?" says Warren.

"No," says Pearl cheerfully. "We can always rely on that to stay the same as ever."

Seasons change and so do we. Sometimes the path we take in life isn't the one we planned to, and the people we end up with aren't the ones we thought we would. But as the rockets explode over the bandstand, a riot of colour against the midnight sky, I'm so incredibly grateful. Life might not always be easy, but right here, right now, the world is good. I wouldn't change a thing about this moment. And as I look at my family gazing up at the flashes of light, I'm sure that neither would they.

Acknowledgements

I started work on *The Café in Fir Tree Park* back in February 2016. I write these acknowledgements in March 2017 with the novel finished and ready to go into production, but there have been many times over the past year when I genuinely didn't believe I'd complete a second book. I'm blessed to be surrounded by amazing people who repeatedly told me I *could*, and so heart-felt thanks go out to –

Mary Jayne Baker, Emily Royal and Katy Wheatley, for the wordraces, the cheerleading, the beta reading and the friendship.

Everyone at HarperCollins/HarperImpulse, especially Charlotte Ledger and Kim Young for the unending support and advice. I'm so fortunate to work with you both.

Helen Williams, editor extraordinaire, for giving such constructive advice and feedback.

Books Covered, for creating the most beautiful cover I've ever laid eyes on.

Philippa Ashley, Brigid Coady, Miranda Dickinson, Kat French, Lynsey James, Erin Lawless, Rebecca Pugh, Chris Russell, Keris Stainton, all the Wordcount Warriors and Beta Buddies, and my fellow HarperImpulse authors. Writing would be a far lonelier profession without friends like you.

NaNoWriMo, for being the push I needed to reach my two favourite words in the English language – 'The End'.

Sam Clarke, who should have got a thank you in the acknowledgements for *The Singalong Society for Singletons*. Better late than never, as they say.

Grace Latter, for answering my questions about 'misbehaving brains'. What an incredibly inspirational woman you are.

All the bloggers, readers, and reviewers, who have contacted me to share supportive tweets, messages and blog posts.

Thank you for being so passionate about not only my books, but reading in general. I hope you've loved getting to know Maggie, Pearl, Fern and Lacey.

And last, but by no means least, my friends and family, who might not understand this weird writerly world I'm part of, but humour me regardless.

Katey Lovell, Sheffield, March 2017

Chapter One

Friday 9th September
Frozen – My choice*

'I've been waiting for this *all day*.' Issy sighs with audible relief as the ruby-red Merlot sloshes into the glass. 'Honestly, I can't tell you how ready I am. In fact, I'm more than ready. I'm a woman in need,' she adds dramatically.

'Only all day?' I reply with a laugh. 'Then you're a stronger woman than I am, Isadora Jackson. I've been waiting all *week*.'

My blonde curls bounce wildly. People say they look like a halo, but although I'm a good girl, I'm certainly no angel.

'Seriously,' I continue, 'the only thing that's got me through the madness that is reception class during the first week in September is the thought of wine o' clock. We've had so many children crying when their parents leave, the noise in that classroom is phenomenal.

Phenomenal! Thank your lucky stars that the kids you teach are past that.'

Issy gulps her wine, raising her eyebrows in a challenge of disagreement. I know that look. It's the one that says whenever anyone plays the 'I work in the most difficult age group' card, Issy's going to take that card and trump it.

'Teaching Year 6 isn't a bundle of laughs, you know. All those raging hormones and that snarky pre-teen attitude...' She visibly shudders. 'Can you believe I had Ellie Watts in tears this lunchtime because Noah Cornall dumped her? They're only ten! And the bitching and backbiting that goes on – I've not seen anything like it. It's the *Big Brother* house, but worse. How many weeks to go until half term?'

'Another seven.' I pull a face, unable to believe I'm already counting down to the holidays. The six-week summer break had worked its usual miracle of helping me forget how exhausting it is working in a primary school and although I'd not exactly been jumping out of bed with delight when the alarm went off at 6.15 on Monday morning, I'd felt a quiet positivity about the year ahead. There's something special about getting to know a new set of kids, and there had even been rumours of new furniture for the reception classroom. Heaven knows, the tables need replacing. Years of felt-tip pens being carelessly smudged over their surface meant their glory days were well in the past. But just one week in – four days, actually, if you discount the staff training day – and I'm already totally drained of energy, as I always am during term time. People at work say I'm bubbly and bouncy and full of beans, but that's because I raise my game. How anyone who works with children finds the time for a social life, I'll never know. When Friday finally rolls around, all I want to do is climb into my onesie and sleep for a week.

'My class need to be the small fishes again,' Issy says with a sage nod. 'It's always the same with the oldest in the school. They get ahead of themselves. Too big for their 'let's-get-one-size-larger-so-you-can-grow-into-them' Doc Martens'.' Issy looks so serious, which naturally makes me want to giggle. 'They'll be the ones in tears when they start at secondary school next year, just like your little angels in reception have been this time. It'll knock them down a peg or two.'

'It'll get easier, it always does.'

I know Issy thinks I'm being over-optimistic, but I can't help it. What can I say? I'm one of those people who naturally looks on the bright side of life, except when it comes to Justin. But that's no surprise, given that he'd gone from 'we can make long distance work' in December to 'perhaps we should take a break – not split up, but accept long distance doesn't work for us' in January. I think I've every right to feel bitter. I'm living in this weird love-life limbo.

'You'll be fine when they get to trust you,' I assure her. 'You said exactly the same about your last lot. Remember Billy Rush? You were convinced he'd turn you grey, and look, your hair's exactly the same murky shade it's always been,' I say with nothing but innocence.

'Hey, watch it you! My hair's not murky. It's salted caramel,' Issy replies, defensively stroking the thick, straight locks that tumble down past her shoulders. How she manages to look glamorous, even in her mint-green fleecy Primark pyjamas, I'll never know. She's one of those naturally well-groomed people whose skin always looks fresh and eyes bright, even when she's tired or has a stinking hangover. It's infuriating.

'Yeah, right. Whatever you say. 'Salted caramel.' Is that what they call it at the hairdressers?'

I poke my tongue out at her, but she knows it's all in jest. That's the great thing about our friendship. We tease each other mercilessly, but we can switch to drying each other's tears in a matter of seconds if needs be. And Issy, bless her, has done her fair share of being the shoulder to cry on this year, so it's important to remember to laugh about things as much as possible.

'They refer to it by number. But it's the darkest blonde they do,' Issy replies haughtily, running her hand over her locks once more. 'You'd see for yourself if we were in the right light. This house has terrible natural light, and you know it. It's the price we pay for living on the shady side of the street.'

She's right about that. Even in the height of summer there's a distinct chill in the lounge of the mid-terraced red-brick house we share. I swear we must've been the only people pulling down furry throws from the back of the sofa to keep warm during the one red-hot week that had passed as the British summer. Even long sunny days had done nothing to rid our lounge of its chilly gloom. And now, on an early-September evening, where it's still light outside, both of us are in pyjamas, dressing gowns and super-thick socks, a necessity if we're going to meet our annual challenge of making it to the half-term break without caving and putting the heating on.

'So, are you going to pour me a glass or that Merlot or what? I'm dying of thirst over here.'

'You're not exactly encouraging me to share when you're slagging off my hair and saying my job's easy. Maybe I'll keep the whole bottle to myself instead.'

There's a cheeky glint in Issy's eyes as she pulls the bottle to her mouth as though to swig from it. I know she's only messing around, but it's still enough to make me worry. It's Friday night. I need that wine.

'I never said it was easy,' I correct quickly. 'Just that

you've not got the screamers and the over-anxious parents and the snotty noses and the pooey pants to deal with.' When the negative aspects of the job were all strung out like that, working as a teaching assistant in a reception class sounded *bad*. Like a cacophony of noise and hassle and bodily fluids.

Issy shoots me a look. 'You knew what you were getting into, you've got a degree in child development. It's not exactly a state secret that four-year-olds have accidents and don't know how to use a Kleenex.'

'I know, I know.'

And I can't imagine doing anything else. My oldest friend Connie's stuck in a hell-hole of an office all day and she hates every miserable minute of it. She's crying out to do something more worthwhile than filing and answering phones. School might be exhausting, but there are plenty of rewards too – some of the things the kids come out with are hilarious and it's great watching them grow and progress day by day.

'I do love the kids,' I add, 'especially the little ones. They're continually evolving and that moment when they grasp how to do something new – there's nothing like it. The pride in their faces...'

I place my hand over my heart, recalling the happiness on one child's face today as he counted to ten by rote. It had been a touching moment, and one that reminded me how much I love my job.

'You're going to set me off crying at this rate.'

Issy rolls her eyes, but the grin that accompanies it is the real giveaway – it shows she understands. I might be more of a people person than Issy, but she cares about the kids much more than she outwardly shows. She just does a good job of hiding her love and loyalty. Issy plays her cards very close to her chest.

'It's great being with the little ones. I wish they'd have a bit more independence sometimes, though.'

'Like you said to me, it'll get easier. You'll have them whipped into shape by the summer. They're used to being mollycoddled at home, that's all. Come on, you'll feel better after a glass of wine,' she chivvies. 'And at least there's no alarm going off at some ungodly hour in the morning, so let's put a film on and forget about work. I've got a Toblerone in the cupboard, too, if you fancy a few little triangular pieces of heaven?'

'Mmmmm.' My mouth waters at the thought. Toblerone. My favourite. 'That sounds amazing. What do you want to watch?'

It's a ridiculous, pointless question. We've watched the same film every Friday night for the past three months.

'Ooh, let me think,' Issy replies sarcastically, putting the tip of her index finger to the corner of her lips, as though there's actually a decision to be made here. Her nails are coated in black polish and there's not a single chip to be seen. Typical: Immaculate Issy. After a brief, yet dramatic, pause, she announces '*Frozen*!'

I pull the shiny rectangular DVD case from the boxy Ikea bookcase as Issy snuggles into the corner of the settee, pulling the chocolate-brown throw over her knees in an attempt to get cosy, because when it comes to frostiness, 24 Cardigan Close can easily rival an icy Arendelle. Brr!

*

By the time Hans and Anna are capturing the brilliant white moon in their hands as they dance beneath the waterfall, Issy and I are both decidedly more relaxed. A second bottle of red wine's been opened and all that remains of the chocolate is the iconic triangular prism box and a screwed-up ball of silver foil strewn on the table. The cares of the week are slowly slipping away; the weekend has truly arrived.

Until the doorbell rings, rudely interrupting the peace.

Issy groans. 'Can't we leave it?' I know there's no way on earth she'll get up from that settee; she's set up camp for the night. Begrudgingly, I inch myself into a standing posi-

tion while she chunters on. 'Who calls unannounced on a
Friday night anyway?'

'Exactly,' I say. 'It must be important.'

'Or one of those door-to-door charity collectors.'

A ferocious banging follows, five loud knocks that it
would be impossible to ignore.

'That'd have to be one desperate charity collector.'

I pull my dressing gown more tightly around my waist
as I reach for my key from the small hook on the back of
the door. The knocking continues, louder and more frantic
than before, followed by a voice.

'Mon! Mon! It's me!'

The desperation in the high-pitched cries urge me into
action. The voice is instantly identifiable. I fling the door
open and my sister stumbles over the threshold, a bulging
black sports bag slung over her shoulder and a wheelie
suitcase by her side. Her face is deathly pale in stark contrast
to her chocolate-brown hair, and her cheeks are stained
with the snail-trail tracks of tears.

'Hope! What's going on?'

I'm shocked at the state of her. Actually, I'm beyond
shocked. I'm not used to seeing my older sister like this.
Hope's always been the stronger of the two of us, the one
with the 'don't mess with me' attitude and a permanent
look of disdain waiting in the wings to throw at anything

or anyone she considers beneath her. But right now she looks fragile and vulnerable, like a frightened kitten in a thunderstorm.

'I didn't know where else to go,' Hope sobs. Her long, dark hair falls in front of her face as she hunches forwards, a protective veil to hide behind. I know the trick; I've used it myself.

'Start at the beginning.' I try to keep my voice calm, although inside I'm flailing. Placing my hand on my sister's back, I gently guide her into the living room. Hans and Anna are no longer singing about love being an open door. Issy's pressed the pause button at an inopportune moment; the close-up shot of the princess showing her eyes closed and her face contorted. 'What's going on?'

'It's Amara,' Hope says finally, before looking up and locking her bleary, bloodshot eyes with mine. 'She's thrown me out. She said she's had enough of me pressurising her into telling her parents the truth.' She pauses for breath, gulping the air. 'I've been patient, haven't I, Mon? It's been four years now, but she still won't admit to her parents that we're a couple. Four years! I'm sick of moving my stuff into the spare room every time they come over, pretending we're just best friends sharing a flat.' Her shoulders judder as the tears start to fall. 'All I want is for her to be honest. I don't want to have to hide any more.'

'What exactly did she say?' Issy interjects, moving to the

edge of her seat. 'Do you think she means it? Or is she just angry at the situation and taking it out on you?'

'Oh, she means it alright,' Hope answers with a bitter laugh. 'She's ashamed to be with me. Her parents are coming up from London tomorrow and when I told her I thought it was time to come clean, she said that'd be 'impossible'.' Hope raises her hands, wiggling her fingers to indicate quotation marks. It's a move full of pain-drenched sarcasm. 'When I said I was sick of her pulling all the strings in our relationship, fed up of it being fine to hold her hand when we're clubbing on a Saturday night or walking around Endcliffe Park on a Sunday morning but having to outright *lie* when it comes to her family...she said she couldn't lie any longer either. She handed me my bag, told me it was over and ordered I pack and leave.'

Issy raises a perfectly shaped eyebrow and when she speaks her tone is disbelieving. 'And you did it without a fuss? I'm sorry, Hope, but that doesn't sound like the feisty girl I know. *She* wouldn't give up and walk out on the love of her life.'

'Can't you see? It's *because* I love her! That's why I've gone. If Amara can't tell her family that we've been in a relationship, then what's the point in being together anyway? I know I'm lucky. Mum was fine with me being gay, once she got her head around it. Amara's parents aren't like that. They're always on at her to find a nice young man and provide them with grandchildren. If she tells them she's gay, they'll probably disown her.'

'But even if she's not with you, she's still going to be gay,' I reason. I hand her my glass, thinking a sip of alcohol might calm her down. 'She's not going to suddenly start lusting over Daniel Craig just because you've moved out. So she'll still be lying to them either way.'

Hope winces as she sips the Merlot and it's only then I remember she's never been a fan of red wine, much preferring a crisp glass of refreshing Pinot Grigio. Ah well, beggars can't be choosers.

'I know,' Hope answers resignedly. 'But it's easier for her to call an end to it than tell them the truth. If she's on her own, she can make up excuses and fob off the questions. She'll say she's not found the right person yet or that she wants to travel or concentrate on her career. That'll be more acceptable to her family than the reality.'

'Concentrating on a career,' I snort. 'I've heard that one before.'

I grind my teeth, determined not to make this about me, but it's touched a nerve. I feel brittle, fragile. It comes over me like this every so often, and it makes me mad. These involuntary reactions are all little reminders that however much I profess to have moved on, I still catch my breath at the thought of Justin Crowson. He upped and left and broke my heart, but in just over three months he'll be back in Sheffield. The 'break' will be over; we can get back on track. I'm clutching tightly to that thought. It's been painfully hard having so little contact with Justin since Christmas, and I hate this feeling of being so distant. Going from inseparable to short, sharp emails and five-minute phone conversations has been like losing a limb.

'It's time's like this I'm actually *glad* to be eternally single,' Issy replies. 'You Brown girls sure know how to get shat on from a great height.'

Issy hasn't had so much as a one-night fling in the last eighteen months, let alone anything more. Drunken snogs are her speciality, but nothing ever goes further. She's adamant she's holding out for Mr Right, the man she'll marry and ride off into the sunset with.

'Well,' I say, cutting Issy off before she says anything that starts Hope off blubbering again, 'you can stay here for as long as you need to. The futon in the spare room's not all that comfy, but you're very welcome to crash on it. And right now I'm going to get you a glass of your own. Have some more wine and watch the end of *Frozen* with us. That'll make everything seem a bit brighter.'

That set Hope off crying again. She's never been an especially girly girl and in her current state, the thought of princessy Disney films was probably enough to push her over the edge.

'I'll need more than one glass of wine to get through *Frozen,* no matter how big it is,' Hope says.

'You make it sound like an endurance test rather than an animated film.' Issy laughs, but not unkindly, as I move into the kitchen to fetch a glass. 'It's hardly scaling Everest!'

'It might as well be. You two are bloody obsessed with that film. Even the kids at school have had enough of it now.'

Hope works with Issy and me at Clarke Road Primary, teaching the Year 4s. She never planned to go into teaching – falling into it out of necessity rather than a vocational calling – but jobs related to her degree in visual arts are few and far between. At least this way she's able to use her imagination in the classroom now and again, even if there isn't as much freedom as she'd like. Creativity's not exactly a priority in the curriculum these days but Hope's eye-catching display boards are always spectacular, a talking point with staff and pupils alike.

I peep around the doorframe, mock horror on my face at Hope rejecting my favourite film of all time. '*Frozen*'s not a fad, it's a way of life! It's a story of sisterhood and love for all ages. And it's one of the best films to sing along to. There's nothing like belting out 'Let It Go' at the top of your lungs to make everything better.'

'Excuse me if I've not quite got your level of optimism,' Hope mutters, just loud enough for me to hear.

I can see her shivering from here, and I've a sneaky suspicion that it's not just her body responding to the chilly temperature in the house. Maybe the realisation that she no longer lives with her gorgeous girlfriend in a modern, city-centre apartment but is crashing out with her baby sister in what is little better than student digs is hitting home.

'Anyway, I'm not sure the neighbours will thank us,' Hope says wryly. 'We're hardly Little Mix, are we?'

'Ah,' I reply with a smile, 'but that's the best thing about living near the university. Everyone else on the street is a student. Most of them aren't even back until the end of the month, and the ones that are will either be out in town or having a party involving something far more raucous than the three of us pretending to be Elsa.'

'I think you secretly love it,' Issy says breezily, attempting to stop Hope snuffling. She wafts a box of pastel-coloured tissues in Hope's direction. 'Even you've got to admit that despite being the bad guy, Hans is a hottie.'

Hope pulls a lemon-yellow tissue from the box, a rose-coloured fan appearing as if by magic to take its place.

'I'm a lesbian,' she states, in case anyone's forgotten. 'And even if I wasn't, I don't think I'd be resorting to animated characters.'

She blows her nose noisily into the tissue. It sounds like a steam train heading into a tunnel.

'I've always had a thing for Flynn Rider,' I admit, handing my sister the full-to-the-brim glass of wine I'd poured her. 'I think it's his chiselled jaw. Maybe if I grew my hair a bit longer and threw it out of my bedroom window I'd get someone like that to climb up it. Mind you, it'd take years to grow. It's the one major downside of curly hair, every centimetre in visible growth is actually three.' I finger a strand of hair ruefully.

'I don't think there are any Flynn Rider lookalikes wandering around South Yorkshire looking for plaits to climb up, so the slow growth of your hair is the least of your worries. Anyway, you're not looking for a man, are you?'

'I'm most certainly not,' I reply brusquely.

Issy's mentioned on more than one occasion that she thinks getting 'under a man to get over a man' might be a step forward, but it hasn't occurred to me. I've not so much as looked at another male that way. I don't want to, because no one else can possibly compare to Justin. How could they? We've got ten years of shared history. He's my first love. My first everything, in fact. Anyway, we're on a break, we're not broken.

'After what happened with you-know-who, I'm not putting myself out there,' I say. I'm not sure of my status anyway, there's no noun to describe someone who's on a break. 'I'm not ready to lay my soul bare to any man, not if all they want to do is trample over it.'

I've said these lines so many times that it's a well-rehearsed speech, but the doubtful looks on both Issy and Hope's faces make me wonder how convincing I actually am. Maybe I should say them with a bit more oomph.

'Come on, let's get this film back rolling,' says Issy. 'And is this wine mine?' she asks, gesturing to the full glass sitting on the mantelpiece. 'Because I can feel myself sobering up by the second, and tonight I plan to get very, very drunk.'

*

We're all glued to the television screen as the tinkly piano starts up and Elsa sadly climbs the snow-covered mountain, her purple cape trailing through the snow behind her. Even Hope's transfixed, although she'd never admit it.

'I love this song,' Issy says, pulling a cushion closer to her stomach. 'Even though I must have heard it a million times, it still gets me right here.' She points to the centre of her chest, pulling an over-exaggerated sad face.

'That's why Elsa's so popular,' I say. 'She gives up everything to be true to herself and doesn't give a damn what everyone else thinks. She's a much better role model than the sappy princesses of old. She's spunky.'

'Did you seriously just use the word spunky?' Hope shakes her head in disbelief. Her eyes already look hazy;

the crying and the wine a lethal combination. 'That's cringe-worthy, no one uses that word any more. Plus, it's one of those icky words that makes my skin crawl. That and 'moist'.' She grimaces.

'But Elsa *is* spunky. It's the perfect word to describe her.'

'Whatever.'

The misfit princess runs through the snow-covered land singing about her new-found freedom and how she can finally be the person she truly is rather than who everyone else expects her to be, and before long all three of us feel every ounce of the ice queen's angst as we sing along to 'Let It Go'. Elsa removes her glove and conjures magical wisps of ice from her hands and we shout the rousing chorus at the top of our lungs, well past caring what the neighbours think. We're out of tune and Hope isn't entirely sure of the words, but we don't give a damn. It's fun.

'It feels good to sing, doesn't it?' Hope says out of the blue. Her cheeks are flushed now, the pinkish hue making her appear much less frail than she'd looked when she arrived. 'To let rip and shout. Kids do it all the time, but as adults we're expected to have found other ways to express ourselves. But the truth is, nothing compares to getting everything out of your system by having a good old yell.'

'Letting go,' says Issy solemnly, before realising what she's said and dissolving in a fit of drunken giggles.

'I read something somewhere about singing being good

for the soul,' I recall. 'Didn't it say people who sing live longer? Or were happier? I can't remember, but it was all positive.' Funnily enough, I'm feeling better for singing too and my words are spilling out at an incredible pace. 'We've all had a tough year. I've been low since Justin went to America, even though the sensible part of me knows that taking a break was the only option. That doesn't make it any easier though, I'm still wondering if he's on a date with some American beauty or out on the pull. And Hope, who knows? Maybe Amara *will* come round and realise you need to be together in time, but right now you need to put yourself first. Don't look at me like that! I know you think I'm fussing, but I want my only sister to be happy.'

I reach over and squeeze Hope's hand, one small pulse that carries an infinite amount of love.

'And Is, I know you're happy being single, but I saw your face when your sister told you about her latest scan.'

Issy swallows, and part of me wishes I'd kept quiet. This is a sensitive subject. But it's too late now, it's already out there, so I carry on regardless. 'You're going to be the most amazing mummy one of these days, when the time is right. The best.' Issy's lips form an O, and I think she might cry, so I quickly move on. 'But for now, all three of us need to pick ourselves up and take control of our own happiness. It's like Elsa says, we're free! Who knows where we'll be in a month, let alone a year. We need to increase our happiness, channel the good emotions.' I'm on a roll, fire in my belly and well-lubricated by the wine. There's no stopping me now.

'And how do you suggest we do that, oh wise one?' asks Hope, her voice acerbic.

'A club, an informal choir. Make Friday nights a musical spectacular and sing ourselves silly! Think how good it feels to shout and laugh and forget about all the crappy stuff.' I beam, convinced it's a winning idea. 'We should make it a weekly event, a celebration of the weekend and being happy on our own rather than out in the meat market that doubles as town on a Friday night. It's got to be better than having your bum pinched by some drunken chancer out on the pull, and if it raises our spirits too then it's a bonus, surely? What do you reckon? Isn't it the best idea ever?'

I wait for their response, fully expecting them to throw back a string of reasons why it's a terrible idea. The pause is excruciating.

'Oh, go on then,' says Issy finally, knocking back the last of her wine. 'But no more people. The last thing I want is a house full of strangers on a Friday night.'

'And no more *Frozen*,' Hope adds emphatically.

'Okay,' I agree, knowing this is as much enthusiasm as my sister's likely to muster. 'But can I ask Connie if she fancies it too? Four people isn't too many and she could do with a boost. She's hating her job and she's fed up with being hit on by sleazeballs every time she goes out. This could be exactly what she needs.'

I grin and a small squeak of excitement slips out despite myself. I'm so looking forward to this. I haven't been part of a club since I left the Brownies.

'The Singalong Society for Singletons,' I say wistfully. 'To moving on and letting go!'

Printed by RR Donnelley at Glasgow, UK